HOMECOMING IN MOSSY CREEK

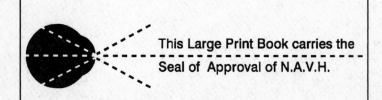

HOMECOMING IN MOSSY CREEK

A collective novel featuring the voices of
DEBRA DIXON, SANDRA CHASTAIN,
MARTHA CROCKETT
AND NANCY KNIGHT
with
BRENNA CROWDER,
DARCY CROWDER, SUSAN GOGGINS,
MAUREEN HARDEGREE,
CAROLYN MCSPARREN
AND BERTA PLATAS

THORNDIKE PRESS
A part of Gale, Cengage Learning

GALE
CENGAGE Learning®

Detroit • New York • San Francisco • New Haven, Conn • Waterville, Maine • London

GALE
CENGAGE Learning®

LIBRARY OF CONGRESS CATALOGING-IN-PUBLICATION DATA

Homecoming in Mossy Creek / by Debra Dixon ... [et al.]. — Large print ed.
   p. cm. — (Thorndike Press large print clean reads)
   ISBN-13: 978-1-4104-4669-5 (hardcover)
   ISBN-10: 1-4104-4669-7 (hardcover)
   1. City and town life—Fiction. 2. Georgia—Fiction. 3. Large type books. I. Dixon, Debra.
PS3600.A1H6 2012
813'.6—dc23
                              2011051280

Published in 2012 by arrangement with BelleBooks, Inc.

Printed in the United States of America
1 2 3 4 5 6 7 16 15 14 13 12

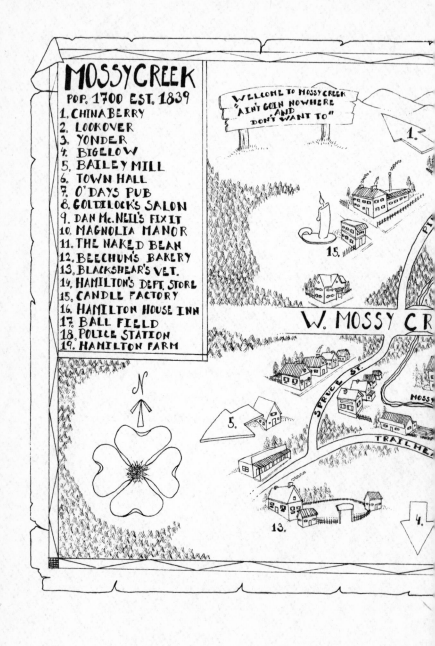

MOSSY CREEK

POP. 1700 EST. 1839

1. CHINABERRY
2. LOOKOVER
3. YONDER
4. BIGELOW
5. BAILEY MILL
6. TOWN HALL
7. O'DAYS PUB
8. GOLDILOCK'S SALON
9. DAN Mc. NEIL'S FIX IT
10. MAGNOLIA MANOR
11. THE NAKED BEAN
12. BEECHUM'S BAKERY
13. BLACKSHEAR'S VET.
14. HAMILTON'S DEPT. STORE
15. CANDLE FACTORY
16. HAMILTON HOUSE INN
17. BALL FIELD
18. POLICE STATION
19. HAMILTON FARM

WELCOME TO MOSSY CREEK
"AIN'T GOIN NOWHERE
AND
DON'T WANT TO"

W. MOSSY CR

SPRUCE ST.

TRAILHE

MOSSY

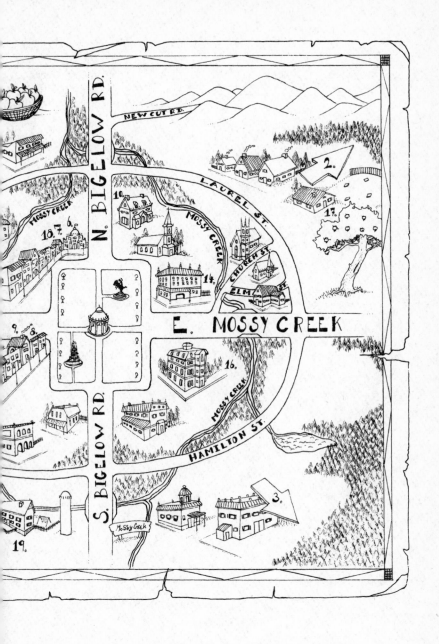

DEDICATIONS

For all the Creekites: Those who live in Mossy Creek and those who want to. If you don't know the way, just close your eyes and click your heels.
— *With love, Sandra Chastain*

To my best friend, Davy Crockett.
— *Martha Crockett*

For the friendship in my mama's arms, the wisdom in my daddy's heart and the love of Jesus in Sylvia's smile. You can always come home again.
— *Brenna Crowder*

To Brenna and Wil for always believing. How blessed I am to travel this road with you. And to John, for making me the lucky one.
— *Darcy Crowder*

This one is for all the readers who've loved Amos and Ida as much as I have.
— *Debra Dixon*

To the best mom and dad ever, Martha Kate and Howard Goggins, with love.
— *Susan Goggins*

For all the special people who make my life so rewarding: My ninety-one year old mother who is amazing; my son Mike and his family, Karol, Kristi and Michael; For Joyce, Ron and Trey; For Sandra who has been my best friend for thirty years; For Doug who's always there for me, and for Mikey (and his wonderful family) who brought back laughter and love.
— *Nancy Knight*

To Martha Crockett who pushed me until I got published, and to Debi Dixon, the world greatest (and toughest) editor. Also to my wonderful critique group who puts up with me week after week.
— *Carolyn McSparren*

To all the great friends who let me play with them in Mossy Creek!
— *Berta Platas*

Mossy Creek Gazette
106 Main Street • Mossy Creek, GA 30000

From the desk of Katie Bell

Lady Victoria Salter Stanhope
The Clifts
Seaward Road
St. Ives, Cornwall, TR3 7PJ
United Kingdom

Hey, Vick!
I've been telling you that Homecoming was on its way to Mossy Creek, and it's finally arrived. Festivities officially start on Thursday, with a Bake Sale and a play, but Creekites will spend all week getting ready.

Excitement is wafting through the air. This is the first Homecoming at Mossy Creek High School in 20 years. Imagine the fun everyone is going to have, getting together for all the festivities. I've heard

from over 40 expatriot Creekites who are wending their way
home for the weekend. Hamilton House has been booked for
months, as has the Best West-
ern and Days Inn down in Bigelow.

Town Square has been festooned
with green and gold. Gold mums
are planted in every flowerpot
in town. Creekites are digging deep into their fall
wardrobes for any and all
green and/or gold sweaters.

Tom Anglin bought a stuffed
Ram online and it's sitting
outside the Mossy Creek Hard-
ware store. Kids have been
getting their pictures made
riding on it, and the Booster
Club has taken to a night
vigil so it's not heisted by
some Bigelow vigilantes.

Gotta go for now. Albert
Bailey just came in saying
he's certain he's been smell-
ing moonshine brewing up

around Bailey Mill. Since you might not know the term, moonshine is homemade liquor and it's illegal as all get-out. Gotta go check it out!

Talk at ya later —

Katie

PART ONE:
THE GREAT
TIME CAPSULE CAPER

Things that were hard to bear are sweet
to remember.

— Seneca

Louise & Peggy, Thursday afternoon
"Just because Peggy and I are on the Home-coming committee does not mean we are capable of sorting out this mess." I folded my arms across my chest and stared hard at the three Mossy Creek town leaders: Mayor Ida Walker, Chief of Police Amos Royden and Town Council President Win Allen.

"Oh, come on, Louise," Peggy Caldwell said. "Where's your sense of mystery? The game's afoot, Sherlock. It's up to us to save the day."

"I always hated Sherlock Holmes," I said, ignoring Peggy's snort of disgust. "How hard is it for the so-called great detective to pick up on those clues when Conan Doyle is the one who set them up for him?" I

15

dropped my voice a couple of octaves. "I perceive, Watson, that the criminal is a left-handed tax accountant with buck teeth, a lisp and six toes on his right foot."

"Bite your tongue, Louise Sawyer! Sherlock Holmes is a genius." My friend Peggy is a retired college professor who is an omnivorous reader of detective stories. She named her four cats Dashiell (as in Hammett), Sherlock, Watson and Marple (after Agatha Christie's busy-body detective Miss Marple). That does not mean she can detect her way out of a paper bag in the real world.

Which this was.

"If y'all would please consider —" Win Allen, newly elected President of the Town Council, began.

But Mayor Ida Hamilton Walker gave an impatient snort. "Louise, Peggy, if you are through bickering, let's sit down and hash this thing out."

"What do we do if — and it's a big if — we locate the time capsule?" I asked.

"Call me immediately," Amos said. "Hold onto it until I can come get it. Don't talk to Mutt or Sandy whatever you do."

"We absolutely must have our hands on that box by mid-afternoon Saturday," Ida said at her most authoritarian. Believe me,

16

Julius Caesar was a wimp compared to Ida.

"We'll have to open it secretly and debug the darned thing before the Homecoming Dance," Win added in more placating tones. "Otherwise we could embarrass half of Mossy Creek," He was much newer at politics than either Ida or Amos.

But he was right. Small town secrets may seem trifling to big city folks, but here they can lead to feuds and hurt feelings that last generations.

I'd stopped thinking of that stupid box as a time capsule and started considering it a time bomb all set to go off at the Homecoming dance to spatter half of Mossy Creek with mud.

An innocent time capsule. How scary can that be? How many graduating classes and churches and school dedicators have buried cultural icons from their own day to be dug up at some specified time in the future? How can a bottle of New Coke or a Dacron blouse or an eight-track tape of The Beatles create guerilla warfare?

I'll tell you how. Leave the box unguarded on the table in the hall outside the gym beside the nametags at the Homecoming dance the night the school and the athletic field burn down, hide inside it a collection of secrets that nobody wants revealed, add a

17

big dollop of spite, close, dig a hole, bury said box and promptly lose track of it in the ensuing chaos.

"Wait a minute," I said. "The fire started before the dance. The last thing on anyone's mind must have been that stupid box. Maybe it burned up?"

"If only," Amos said. "A couple of the football players tossed it into the back of somebody's pickup truck, came back after the fire and buried it on the field."

"So they should know where to find it, right?" I asked.

Amos shook his head. "We were exhausted, still half-drunk and mad as a bunch of alligators."

Win, who was not a native Creekite, raised a brow at Amos's admission of youthful foibles. The Police Chief was so hard on teenage misbehavior, it was easy to forget he'd ever been one.

Amos continued, "Except for what little leftover light there was from the flames, it was still dark. Somehow burying that capsule despite the fire became a symbol that Mossy Creek High School would come back. We just didn't expect it to take twenty years." He shrugged. "Now look at it. After twenty years of reverting to forest, it's being razed again for the new stadium. There's no way we could point to a spot and say, 'Dig here.' "

Without a high school or a football stadium, no one had given the capsule a thought until the high school reopened and the town fathers and mothers decided to rebuild the football field. In my opinion, it would have been better if everyone who remembered the capsule had been knocked over the head and given selective amnesia.

The football stadium had over twenty years to revert to nature. Trees grow fast in the Appalachian Mountains. So do vines like poison ivy, oak and sumac. Instead of a rectangle of pristine grass and neat limestone lines, it became a haven for rabbits, possums, raccoons and, Heaven help us, copperheads and pygmy rattlesnakes. Before the fire, the stadium was a neat assemblage of bleachers and concrete block dressing rooms and restrooms. After the fire, the place sank into a jumble of split and charred concrete blocks, twisted metal rebar and rampant greenery. Even the goal posts resembled Henri Moore statuary run amok in an arboretum.

I doubt if the crew who built the stadium in the first place would have been able to figure out what went where after all this time. The location of a buried time capsule would have been the least of their worries. Plus the footprint of the new stadium didn't quite match that of the old stadium.

So we couldn't simply point to the place where the capsule was supposed to have been buried. Even if one single person who took part in burying it had a clue as to what they'd done with it, everything was now catawampus.

Our current problem began with a letter sent to Amos by a lawyer in California. One would think a letter marked 'private and confidential' would stay that way. This, however, was Mossy Creek.

Sandy, the police dispatcher, believed she had a right and duty to know everything about everything that happened in Mossy Creek, preferably before anyone else knows. She did not feel that 'private and confidential' refers to Amos alone, but to the entire police department. Therefore, she read the letter before it reached Amos's desk.

And, of course, she told Mutt, her brother and police cohort. She swore him to secrecy. *As if.*

Next Amos read the letter over the phone to Ida Walker, Amos's mayor and erstwhile light of love. Who knew who'd been listening in on the extensions?

Ida insisted that Win, as head of the Town Council, be apprised of the situation.

All that is the logical reason why the whole letter became 'secret' knowledge by suppertime. Mossy Creek, however, leapfrogs over logic. We don't actually use jungle drums to communicate, but whether news is transmitted via the honeysuckle vines or the clematis, we *do* have our own bush telegraph. A breath of possible scandal turns it into our own wireless network.

So why not simply leave the stupid box lost, you ask?

Because everybody who had a hand in creating the thing expected it to be opened with great fanfare at the first Homecoming dance in the new school. The time capsule was supposed to anchor the entire theme of the Homecoming weekend. That had been the plan before the letter. Now . . .

"As much as I'd like to, we can't tell everyone we lost it," Ida said. "You know what a furor that would create?"

"Not nearly so much as actually opening it and discovering a boxful of nasty little secrets," Peggy said. "If the box was going to be part of the Homecoming festivities, how come you've waited this long to look for it?"

"Everybody thought they knew exactly

where it was," Amos said. "But until we decided to make a big deal of this year's Homecoming, nobody figured we'd ever dig it up, so the actual location really didn't matter."

"And until they actually started clearing the land to rebuild the football stadium, nobody wanted to hunt for it," Win added. "We asked for volunteers at the last Town Council meeting. No takers."

"But you expect me and Louise to?" Peggy asked. "No way."

Ida gave an exasperated snort. "The field is being denuded as we speak, so the snakes are probably long gone. All you have to do is ask a few discreet questions. Somebody who was there must have been sober enough to remember where they put it. You don't actually have to dig."

"Discreet? In Mossy Creek?" I asked. "How come you got this letter now? Out of the blue?"

"Not precisely out of the blue," Amos said. "It was supposed to be sent to me a week before the box was originally scheduled to be opened."

"With a dull thud," Peggy said.

"Remember," Ida said, "This is a not simply a Homecoming for the last class before the arson, it's scheduled as a Homecoming for everyone who ever went to Mossy Creek High, whether they ever attended a football game or not. It's a huge deal."

For everybody, that is, except the unhappy girl who added all the personal nasties to the innocuous cultural icons before the box was buried.

"So the secrets will be revealed not only to the graduating class who buried it, but to the entire town of Mossy Creek," Amos said.

"What on earth makes you think Peggy and I can find it in two days without tipping our hand any farther than it's been tipped?" I asked.

"If anyone can, you can. Who'd suspect you two?" Amos said with a broad smile.

Win nodded his agreement.

Ida believes in delegation. "And you can be trusted not to gossip. We need you."

Now all Peggy and I were supposed to do was to find the thing so Amos could remove anything incriminating.

Why us? For that matter, why was either of us on the Homecoming Committee in the first place?

First of all — like Win Allen — Peggy was not a born-and-bred Creekite. She retired here with her husband. As a retired college professor, she was capable of sidetracking any opposition from faculty or administration we might encounter. She says academic bureaucrats make the three hundred Spartans at that bridge look like newborn kittens.

So Ida had appointed her to the Homecoming committee as our non-Creekite arbiter of disagreements. Of which there have been many.

I am on the committee because I *am* a native Creekite, I went to the high school before it burned, and I am old enough not to have had a hand in creating the time capsule in the first place. I can also go upside the heads of those who do not play well with others even after arbitration.

I was there now because I knew the girl who stuffed the box and wrote the letter.

None of that helped us to find the thing. Win and Amos, I could handle, but when Ida wants you to do something, you don't question the command, you salute and say, "Yes, ma'am."

Ida slid the letter across Amos's desk to me. "You remember her?"

"Oh, yes," I whispered. "That was one of the years I was working part time as cafeteria monitor. I remember poor Janey Stalcross."

"I certainly don't. Nor her family either.

Who was she?"

"She enrolled halfway through her junior year after school started. Her family had moved to town so her father could do some kind of construction. All the cliques had long since formed, of course. Amos, most of you had been together since grammar school."

"Tell me we didn't bully her," Amos said.

"You ignored her, basically. You were all caught up in college entrance exams and graduation and romance. She called herself 'the invisible girl.' She was overweight, had no idea how to dress or look after herself and no money to do it, anyway."

"I checked in the annual. Didn't find her picture," Amos said. "She's not listed in the Bigelow annual either from when we had to transfer over there after the fire."

"Her father moved the family on before graduation."

"But after the fire took place?" Peggy said.

I nodded. "So it would seem. Otherwise she couldn't have added what she says she did."

"I hate to wish anyone ill," Peggy said, "But I didn't know her. Thank God her lawyer forwarded it to you when he was supposed to."

"His cover letter says he was supposed to

send it to me exactly one week before the time capsule was scheduled to be opened."

"So why are you dumping this on Peggy and me on Thursday? Why didn't you give it to us on Monday?"

"The United States Post Office in its infinite wisdom didn't deliver the letter until yesterday afternoon," Amos said. "If we had the box, that wouldn't matter. She can't have known we'd lost it."

"Poor child," I said and felt tears sting my eyes. "To die so young."

"I knew she was a fragile diabetic back then," I said. "But I don't suppose she told any of you. You were all so young and beautiful, Amos. It must have seemed to her as though nothing bad could ever touch you." Guilt washed over me the way it always does when I fail folks. Janey used to come sit with me in the afternoons while I straightened up the lunchroom. I should have tried to keep up with her after she left, but I didn't. "I never realized she was so angry," I said. "Surely the secrets can't have been that dreadful."

"The scale of the secrets is not the problem," Ida said. She was getting impatient. Ida tends to lose patience whenever the rest of us don't cut to the chase fast enough to suit her. "It really doesn't matter if she put evidence of axe murder in the box . . ."

"Yeah, it does," Amos said.

Ida shook him off. "Oh, you know what I mean. It's probably stupid teenaged stuff."

"Like who was sneaking around on whom," I said.

"Or cheating on tests or drinking and driving," Peggy said. "Or smoking controlled substances behind the gym. Embarrassing but not life changing."

"Unless you got into Harvard on faked test scores or had an accident while DUI and never reported it," Amos said.

"Unless you killed somebody, the statute of limitations has long since run out," I said.

"We cannot count on that," Ida said.

"I refuse to believe Janey would use that sort of thing even if she had a way of knowing. I do remember she always carried a small camera around. She was forever taking pictures."

"One of those self-developing dudes?" Amos asked. "They'll have faded out after this time."

"No such luck. And not digital — they didn't exist." I answered.

Ida interrupted. She had reached the end of her patience — never a long trip. "The point is, we have to find the box and sanitize it before Homecoming."

27

"In the meantime, half the population of Mossy Creek is going to be wracking their collective brains trying to remember who Janey Stalcross was and what she had on them," Peggy said.

Ida ran her hands over her hair. "And don't tell me they don't know about the letter. Trust me, they know. I do not need this."

"We're on it. Come on, Sherlock." Peggy grabbed my sleeve and pulled me out the door of Amos's office. "The game really is afoot."

Mossy Creek Gazette

Volume VIII, No. One   Mossy Creek, Georgia

ADDLED YEARLING FORETELLS MOSSY CREEK WIN?
by Katie Bell

Homecoming got off to a wild start early Saturday morning when a young buck with a plastic Halloween jack-o'-lantern stuck on its head ran amok through town.

Havoc ensued, as did a wild chase by Mossy Creek Police officer Mutt Bottoms and half the football team, who were out for an early morning run with Assistant Coach Tag Garner.

"It swung by the Police Station at approximately eight hundred hours," Officer Bottoms reported. "I was the only one on duty, and didn't have time to even grab my keys. I hared off after it."

According to Officer Bottoms, the young buck took off across the square. It ran past Mt. Gilead Methodist Church, jumped the east branch of Mossy Creek, then past Mossy Creek

First Baptist Church. It narrowly avoided colliding with the football players who were running down Laurel Street. The team took off after the yearling and surrounded it on the softball field.

"The bucket was stuck on the animal's snout, hanging like a feed bag," Mossy Creek Quarterback Willie Bigelow said. "Looked like it probably was preventing the deer from eating or drinking. It had appeared to be snagged on the buck's ears or horn buds. We thought we had him pinned in, but quicker than Jack Lightning, it sailed over Tater's head and was gone. Disappeared out toward Lookover."

Later that day, two children in Lookover found a dented, hairlined plastic pumpkin in their yard, and other neighbors saw a young, thin deer running free. It rained on Saturday, which Veterinarian Hank Blackshear thinks helped the young deer wriggle free.

"I think this deer will be just fine," Blackshear said.

"Of course it means we're going to win," Coach Tag said when asked if this might be an omen for the game on Friday night. "Harrington's colors are orange and black, same as that trick-or-treat bucket. Even though it grabbed hold of him, that young buck defeated it. So will we."

Who can argue with that?

'Shine On, Harvest Moon

When it comes to anything that's social,
whether it's your family, your school, your
community, your business or your country,
winning is a team sport.
— Bill Clinton

Hayden Carlisle, Saturday
When life hands you lemons, you make
lemonade — or in Tiny's case — apple butter. Leastwise, that's how my wife, Clementine Carlisle (*CC* to Mossy Creek, *Tiny* to
me) looks at life.

Despite her citrusy name, which, personally, I think was her mother's way of thumb-
ing her nose at her husband's well-to-do
relatives, Tiny's roots run deep in the fertile
soil of Bailey Mill. Cousin to Hope Bailey,
Tiny grew up on the outskirts of the Sweet
Hope Apple Orchard.

So you might say, apple is her middle
name.

Now, I don't know exactly when my wife developed her great need to win the Jellies, Jams and Spreads Competition at the annual Bigelow County Fair, but I suspect it has a lot to do with her hankering to join the Mossy Creek Social Society. Though I can't see the appeal of wantin' to be a part of as uppity a group of ladies as I've ever seen. If that Adele Clearwater held her nose up any higher in the air she'd drown in a good hard rain.

'Course there might be just a smidge of friendly cousin rivalry involved, though I think Hope Bailey has more important things on her plate these days with running Sweet Hope Orchards and all. But don't tell Tiny I said that.

Then there's the fact Tiny is the Home Economics teacher at Mossy Creek High and feels a certain responsibility to excel at her, um, art. She transferred from Bigelow High along with all her home-grown students. Only her recipes don't always turn out like she planned. For that matter, her sewing isn't all it's cracked up to be either. She knitted me a sweater one time with one sleeve longer than the other and a collar so tight it like to cut off the blood flow to my head.

But her heart's always in the right place.

The kids at Mossy Creek High are lucky to have her. A few of them even know it.

So every year, without fail, I help her drag her old family copper kettle into the back yard so she can slave over yet another new and improved apple butter recipe. Trouble is she never wins. Losing breaks her heart a little bit more each time, and I have to pick up the pieces.

Now anyone will tell ya, I'm not an openly affectionate man. In fact, I'd just as soon barrel over you than step aside. Can't say why, always have been, but it served me well on the playing field back in the day, as Hayden "HayDay" Carlisle, Mossy Creek High football star.

My one soft spot is Tiny. I started calling her Tiny back in high school because she was just a little bit of a thing compared to my oversized football frame. Still is.

Seems like we've always been in each other's back pocket. We were about ten years old when she broke her shepherd's staff in the Mossy Creek Elementary Christmas program. When she looked up at me as those baby blues filled with tears, I gave her mine. And my heart right along with it.

I've loved her every day since.

Which makes it hard to explain why I spiked her apple butter.

■ ■ ■ ■

Now, the thing you need to know about Tiny and me, she's never won anything in her life. Nothing. Now, she's been known to say she won me, but I'm not ashamed to admit I'm not much of a prize.

On the other hand, I've always had good luck, seemed to win anything I set my mind to. When I stepped out on that football field, I owned it. I was on my way to winning a full-ride scholarship to UGA. Then all hell broke loose when Mossy Creek High caught fire and I ended up with a busted knee. Just like that, no scholarship, no professional career.

That was my first taste of losing — and I didn't like it.

Oh, I went on to get my degree in agriculture. Next to football, farming was the only other thing I knew. Right after Tiny and I married, my granddaddy passed on and left us his farm smack dab between Mossy Creek and Bailey Mill, in the shadow of Colchik Mountain. Over the years Tiny and I bought up more land and now run a right successful farming business. Tiny even has her own little apple orchard.

But I guess I never got over that sting

of losing.

It's the only explanation.

It was the Saturday before Homecoming. Mossy Creek was gonna play Harrington Academy, some fancy pants prep school down in Bigelow. We'd won every game in the season, except the last, so the tension was tighter than Adele Clearwater's girdle after lunch at Mama's Café. (Did I mention I don't much like that woman?)

But that wasn't the real cause of all the commotion.

The real reason every last Mossy Creekite was full to boilin' over with school spirit was because this was the first Mossy Creek Homecoming in over twenty years, the first since the high school burned down. All season we'd been playing our home games down in Bigelow, because even though Mossy Creek High had been rebuilt, we still didn't have a stadium. Groundbreaking was part of the celebration this weekend.

All this focus on the new Mossy Creek football team and their streak of success should have been my first clue.

The Booster Club was working overtime sponsoring all kinds of activities to raise money for the stadium — including one humdinger of a bake sale where all manner of famous Mossy Creek delectables could be had for a price. Which is why I found myself haulin' Tiny's copper apple-butter-makin' pot into the backyard at the crack of dawn for the second time this fall.

Wolfman Washington took a deep exaggerated breath and patted his beefy hands against his thick middle as he smiled at Nail Delgado and me across the pot. "Nothing like the smell of apple cider on a crisp, sunny day."

It was Saturday on the weekend before Homecoming. An unseasonably cold wind had peeled back the clouds hovering over Colchik Mountain, taking the warmth with it and leaving us exposed to a wide open blue sky and the first bite of autumn.

Nail just hunkered deeper into his jacket and shot me a look that said exactly what I was thinking. Wolfman was entirely too happy for a man who was gonna find himself standing on his feet all day, stirring until his arms were like to fall off. Wolfman let out a hearty laugh and grinned back at us like a cat living on a mouse farm.

That should have been my second clue.

The three of us stood as close to the pot and roaring fire as we dared and warmed our hands over the apple cider that was beginning to boil.

Wolfman, who lived over in Yonder, and Nail had been the first menfolk to show up. They'd helped me haul and stack enough firewood to keep the kettle boiling all day. I'd hired Nail a time or two for odd jobs around the farm, and over the last year he'd become a good friend.

But Wolfman and I go way back to the days his daddy and mine were friends. No one was better behind the wheel of a dozer than Wolfman. And when your life is all about playing in the dirt, a friend like Wolfman comes in handy.

Most days.

But we'll get to that.

The screened door to the kitchen slammed shut and we turned toward the old white clapboard farmhouse Tiny thought of as cozy. I'm not sure cozy is the right word for a place that's drafty all winter long and would cook you alive under that tin roof if we hadn't installed air conditioning, but it suits us just fine. Tiny's always reminding me that owning an old home is a labor of love.

And I'm always reminding her that life on a farm was all about keeping one step ahead of the weather and playing catch-up with everything else.

Tiny and her mom, Momma Harper,

came across the yard in an awkward waddle, the first bushel of naked apples held between them. Sweet Hope and Macintosh. Tiny said the Macintosh gave just enough tart to balance the sweet in Sweet Hope.

She and her momma had been in the kitchen since before sun-up trying to get a head start on peeling and quartering the twelve bushels of apples needed to fill the forty gallon pot. I'll do the math for you. That's 320 pints of apple butter.

And Tiny had her heart set on selling every last one at the Bake Sale on Thursday.

She looked like a college kid dressed in her jeans, T-shirt and favorite pink hooded jacket. When the wind caught her dark hair, she brushed it back from her face and smiled up at me like a little girl on Christmas mornin'. Tiny loved being with friends and family, loved the chill of autumn and the smell of apples and cinnamon in the air.

And I loved her. Yep, after nineteen years of marriage, that sparkle in her blue eyes still had the power to warm me from the inside out.

Just then I caught sight of Wolfman grinning at me like a fool. I shot him my best scowl and shoved the spoon ladle into his hands. It's one thing for folks to know you love your wife, but quite another to be caught gawking at her like some love-sick school boy.

As I rushed forward to grab the bushel and dump the apples into the boiling cider, Wolfman and Nail made their way into the kitchen for more. Just about then, Del Jackson, who lives over on the old Bransen farm just outside Bailey Mill, and his ex-wife, Sheila, showed up to help.

That's the thing about apple butter makin'. It takes a lot of friendly helping hands — some to peel, some to chop, but most to stir.

Hours and hours of stirring.

In no time we had all the apples in the pot and the girls had settled into the kitchen for a day of bread and pie makin'. The boys and I got to passing the time by passing the spoon-bill stirrer back and around and tossing wood on the fire.

For a bunch of guys mostly used to working alone, meaning not having to talk much, we did all right. The morning started off kinda quiet, with the occasional comment punctuated by assenting grunts, and grew to lively "remember back in the day" stories by early afternoon. Eventually the talk turned to the Homecoming game just a few days away.

Wolfman discovered his chatty side and

started reminiscing about all our best football plays from back in the day when he played defensive tackle and I played corner-back for Mossy Creek High. The more he talked, the more I felt like those apples in the pot — all hot and bothered with no-where to run. When he started in about that last Homecoming game the night of the fire, my insides turned to mush.

That should have been my third clue.

But I guess I wasn't on top of my game.

"Wolfman, I don't think we need to hear anymore about the night the school burned down. We've all heard the story one too many times as it is." I pushed a little harder on the spoon than I guess was necessary, and Nail had to jump back to keep from being splattered by sizzling hot apple butter that sloshed over the edge.

"Yeah. Yeah, but hold on a minute. I bet the guys have never heard how you inter-cepted the ball that night at the 20 yard line in true "HayDay" style." He leaned in. "Hayden drove the ball back down the field for a touchdown at the bottom of the second quarter, putting us ahead of Big-elow just as half-time started. The crowd was really worked up until all the lights went out. I mean, pitch black. Then someone yelled 'Fire!' "

He paused dramatically as Del and Nail turned to stare at me, then back at him.

"The crowd rushed across the field toward the school like an ocean wave, plowing down everything in its way. Some cameraman from the Bigelow TV station tripped over a cheerleader and went airborne. I'd never seen anything like it. Knocked Hayden clean off his feet in a picture-perfect tackle." His smile faded as he bulldozed his way to the end of the story. "Except the cameraman landed on his camera *after* the camera landed on Hayden's leg."

Everyone got silent for a minute.

Fists pushed deep into his overalls, Wolfman stared into the pot with a look of chagrin, like he'd finally realized his mouth moved faster than his brain.

"I knew you played, but I didn't realize you were in the game that night," Del said.

"Yeah, well. That was a long time ago." I glared over the pot at Wolfman. "And some things don't need to be rehashed."

Wolfman raised apologetic eyes to mine. "Sorry Hayden. I guess I forgot how that story ended."

Now, as I mentioned, Wolfman is one of my best friends, so I just grunted my agreement to the obvious as I shoved my feelings deep into my belly. Made no sense to stir things up more than they already were.

Wished I could'a held on to that thought longer than a minute.

Wolfman's face brightened. "I know! I got just the thing to make it up to you." He passed the ladle on over to Del and took off for his truck. We watched and stirred as he poked around inside the cab for a bit, then came back cradling something tucked into his jacket. He sidled back up to the fire, and then glanced over his shoulder at the house to be sure the girls weren't watching from the window.

"Come on, man, what's the big secret?" Nail asked.

Grinning, Wolfman pulled out a quart mason jar filled with a clear liquid. I didn't need to be told.

Moonshine.

"I came across my daddy's old still while cleaning out the back o' the barn a while back and thought I'd see if the old girl had any life in her." He raised the jar to his lips and took a swig. His eyes watered as he wheezed and coughed. Then he wiped his sleeve across the back of his mouth and laughed. "Turns out she does."

He handed the jar off to Nail who took a sip, then shoved it into Del's hands as he tried to catch some air back into his lungs.

Del raised an eyebrow and stared down into the jar like he was trying to decide how much he liked having a healthy liver. But being ex-military, he wasn't about to be outdone by a couple of country bumpkins. I could see it in the way he pulled himself upright like he was about to salute, and took a bold drink. Wordlessly, he handed the jar off to me, sweat breaking out across his forehead.

I stared Wolfman down. "Okay, one taste. Then you go put this back in the truck. I don't want Tiny lookin' out here at the bunch of us getting sloshed when we're supposed to be helping her make apple butter. Besides, you know she doesn't approve of drinkin'."

There was nothing tiny about Tiny's temper. And I didn't want to be on the backside of it.

"Gotcha buddy." He held his hand out as I tipped the jar to my lips. To say liquid fire streamed down my throat doesn't do the word moonshine justice. Let's just say that one sip was more than any of us needed to appreciate what it meant to breathe.

Now what happened next will long be open for debate. I held the jar out to Wolfman, and whether it was his large clumsy fingers or the dark spots blocking my vision, I'll probably never know, but we managed to fumble the ball. I mean bottle.

Pure, white hot moonshine sloshed into Tiny's batch of apple butter.

I managed to snatch the jar from the air before it fell into the pot then glared at Wolfman. "What did you do? Wake up this mornin' and decide 'I think I'll ruin Hayden's day?' "

Wolfman mumbled something about tryin' to be nice and that's when it happened. All this talk of football, all this Mossy Creek excitement over another Homecoming, all this fuss over a stupid stadium boiled up inside me and before I knew what came over me, I'd turned up the jar and poured all the moonshine into the pot.

That's right. Not just a taste, the whole darned thing.

Every last drop.

"I'm guessing that's not in the recipe." Del's words cleared the fog in my brain.

What had I done? My daddy's words came to me. *Son, don't ever let your temper get the best of you — there's hell to pay to get it back.* Well, I don't know if it was temper or not, but I reckon it felt a lot like spite. Either way, if Tiny found out, I was a goner.

We all stared down into the swirling apple butter — amazingly, we'd managed to keep the spoon ladle moving — and mourned the loss, of the apple butter that is. Leastwise I did. I was sure I'd ruined a day's worth of hard work and Tiny's chance of impressing the Mossy Creek Booster Club and the Social Society. That taste of moonshine felt like it was starting to burn a hole in my belly.

Wolfman jogged over to his truck and back, disposing of the incriminating empty jar.

Nail offered up a spark of hope. "Won't all the alcohol just burn off if we keep stirring?"

"I don't know. That moonshine is pretty powerful stuff." Wolfman poked out his lips. Guess he was mournin' the loss of all his hard work as well.

"It's worth a try." I grabbed another log intending to stoke up the fire.

"Hayden! What are you doing?"

Remember now, I'm not a small man, or timid by nature, but a chill ran up my spine right then at the sound of Tiny's voice. Sure enough, I'd been caught. I turned to find the women marching across the yard toward us and dread filled my heart as I braced for the look of disappointment in Tiny's eyes.

She placed her delicate hand on my arm and I realized I was still holding the piece of firewood. "Hayden, honey, it's been almost eight hours. It's time to put out the fire." She smiled and handed me the basket I hadn't noticed she was carrying. "But first, I need to be sure the apple butter's done."

She rifled around in the basket, while I held it for her, struck dumb. She hadn't seen us after all. I looked over the top of her head at the guys. Wolfman and Nail turned to stare off into the distance, Del winked at me. They had my back. Suddenly I felt like a silent member of the Foo Club — but that's another story.

Tiny pulled out one of her grandmama's china saucers, plopped a spoonful of apple butter onto the center of it and held it upside down. I held my breath, not knowing how the moonshine was going to rear its ugly head. The apple butter held firm for several seconds and Tiny declared it done.

Real quick we took up shovels and began moving the hot coals out from under the copper pot. All the while my guilty conscience kept thoughts churning over and over in my mind. Thoughts like, *she's gonna know as soon as she tastes it,* or *somebody's gonna smell liquor on our breath and we'll be found out.* I should stop and 'fess up before she wasted anymore time on this ruined batch.

But coward that I am, I held my tongue.

Once all the hot coals were moved away the apple butter stopped bubbling, and Tiny began pulling spices from her basket. Soon the scent of cinnamon and cloves, and I don't know what all else, filled the air. It actually smelled pretty good. Maybe the apple butter wasn't ruined after all and she'd be a huge success.

That's when the light dawned. Tiny's apple butter was never a huge success. So what if it tasted kinda funny? Most folks didn't expect much different. My good luck was holding after all. I was off the hook.

My sense of relief was short-lived though, when I realized I'd be consoling another broken heart in a couple of days.

The ladies busied themselves setting up an assembly line of sorts. Del and I worked from opposite sides at one end of the picnic table, dipping out the hot apple butter with small saucepans and pouring it through funnels into sterilized jars. The girls placed the canning lids and rings, and wiped the pints clean, while Nail and Wolfman boxed them up. In no time we had all 320 pints ready for the Booster Club bake sale.

I did have quite a scare when some apple butter dripped onto the back of Tiny's hand and she paused to lick it off. All activity came to a halt as me and the guys waited for her reaction. I was preparing to duck and run when she looked up.

"It's got a little bite to it this time." She shrugged it off. "I'm sure all the flavor will come through when it's had time to cool."

Homecoming and autumn had a firm grip on Mossy Creek. Fall colors mixed with Mossy Creek High green and gold all over town. Someone had even decked out a nearby scarecrow in green trousers and a gold sweater, a pitchfork in one hand and a school pennant in the other. Pumpkins, hay bales and bushels of gold mums were scattered among the tents and booths.

Mouth-watering aromas of roasting hot dogs, buttered popcorn, hot apple cider and the like floated past on a cool breeze. Running, laughing children dodged around the older folk ambling down the street. Seemed like everyone had turned out for the Booster Club festivities. Excited, smiling faces were everywhere.

I was miserable.

I'd spent the last four days going back and forth trying to decide how to tell Tiny about the moonshine. You see, we don't keep secrets from each other, 'least none that I know. But every time I started to say somethin' I looked into those excited, hopeful blue eyes and knew I couldn't steal her joy. It would be bad enough when things went as usual at the bake sale. Why spoil it for her now?

I know. I'm a coward. We've already established that.

So come Thursday afternoon, there I stood smack dab in the middle of Town Square, piling pints of apple butter onto the tables covered with bright checkered cloths. Nearby tables were already loaded down with pies, cakes, preserves and every other dessert known to man. I'd rather be anywhere else, doin' anything else, but I guess I figured helpin' out was a form of penance to ease my guilty soul.

Eventually passersby started picking up a pint of Tiny's apple butter here and there. I think they didn't want to hurt her feelings, as most of the other preserves and what-not appeared to be more popular. But my Tiny is a trooper and she opened a pint and started offering tastes to anyone willing.

Then a funny thing happened. People who'd already been by came back for another taste. Then they'd buy not one, but two pints, sometimes more. Before long we had to open more cases and restock the table.

Tiny was just about giddy over the experience.

At one point Mayor Ida Hamilton Walker and Sheriff Amos Royden dropped by. Of course, they managed to make it look like it was just happenstance that they were there together. Mayor Walker bought a pint without even tastin' it. But Sheriff Royden reached for a spoon. A funny look came over his face as he rolled the apple butter around in his mouth before he swallowed. Then he stared at me — hard.

I held my breath.

"Hayden." He tipped his head at me and I thought I caught the hint of a smile in those steely nothin'-gets-past-me eyes. But he wasn't askin', so I wasn't sayin'.

And wouldn't you know that old snooty Adele Clearwater, leader of Mossy Creek Social Society and Eustene Oscar eventually wandered on over to see what all the fuss was about.

"Hello Miz Adele." I nodded. "Miz Eustene." I could be sociable for Tiny's sake. I offered them the plate with little spoons of apple butter. "Care for a taste?"

"Why thank you, Hayden. Don't mind if I do." Eustene didn't hesitate to try a spoonful then raised her eyes heavenward. "Oh, Adele. You really must have some. It's so smooth, with just the right bite. There's something different, but I can't put my finger on it."

Hesitantly, she reached for another taste as I pushed the selection closer. "Shall I ring up a pint?"

Eustene pulled out her wallet. "Oh, my. Yes."

Out of the corner of my eye, I watched Adele reach for a spoon as I bagged Eustene's order. Her eyebrows shot up and what I guess could pass for a smile crossed her face. I turned back to them as she picked up a pint in each hand.

"I'll take two," Adele said.

Tiny practically danced over after Adele and Eustene left. "Thanks, Hayden. I was too busy packing up an entire box for Jayne. Imagine that, she's going to serve my apple butter in her coffee shop." She tipped back and forth on her toes. "I can't wait for the Bigelow County Fair next year."

Now you could say all this was good news. And under normal circumstances, it would be. But there was nothin' normal about it. Now I had a new problem doggin' my heels. I was goin' to have to spike Tiny's apple butter every dang year. How was I gonna manage that and not be found out? I reckon my good luck had finally deserted me.

By late afternoon things started to slow down as everyone closed up shop and made their way home to get ready for tonight's play put on by the Mossy Creek High Drama Club.

I'd had enough of Homecoming, so Tiny agreed to skip the play. But flush with success, she wanted to help cheer on the boys over in the practice field at the school on our way home. I guess this was my week for acting strange because over the years I'd managed to avoid many a high school game but before I knew what I was sayin', I'd agreed to go along.

Funny how one little decision can have such a big impact.

Coach Mabry and Tag Garner, his assistant coach, were really putting the boys through their paces. Turns out the same scout that was courtin' me all those years ago, also recruited Tag. He'd quarterbacked for the Atlanta Falcons before he retired and moved to Mossy Creek.

I managed to sit through a few plays before I started to get antsy, so I leaned over to Tiny. "I'm gonna walk around a bit, okay?"

Her blue eyes studied me for a minute, but she just nodded her understandin' without sayin' a word. She was good at things like that.

I caught sight of Wolfman near the fence and started to make my way over so we could discuss my moonshine predicament. On the field, Harvey Angus's boy, playing wide receiver, made a pretty good catch and tried to run the ball but defense nailed him good at the 40-yard line.

Not that I was paying all that much attention.

I glanced over to see some of the men from Mossy Creek had gathered near Wolfman to watch the practice and offer commentary on which player had the best arm, who had the best speed. I almost turned back to join Tiny up in the stands.

Don't ask me why, but I didn't.

All thoughts of apples and moonshine disappeared from my mind as instead, I stepped closer to the playin' field than I'd been in twenty years.

Had a knot in my gut the next half-hour or so, tryin' not to think about the last Homecoming game I took part in. But then I got caught up in the enthusiasm and team spirit of the Mossy Creekites standing around me and the hard-playin' kids on the field.

Some of these boys were gonna go places. I had no doubt I'd see their names on the back of pro jerseys one day. Their lives were gonna change in a big way. And that got me to thinkin'. I wasn't jealous, like I'd half expected to be. I was excited for them.

I'd had my glory days. Now it was their turn.

I waved up at Tiny sitting on folding lawn chairs with her friends, and she blew me a kiss. I liked my life just the way it was. If I'd a gotten that full ride to UGA, who knows, maybe Tiny and I wouldn't be together. It wasn't until after my accident that I'd worked up the nerve to tell her how I felt about her.

Maybe gettin' hurt on the field that night wasn't losin' after all.

After practice ended, I hung back to let the small crowd clear and watched as the boys packed up their gear and headed home. Tiny found me on the field and took my hand. "You okay?"

I pulled her against my side. "Yep." Sometimes you just don't need to say more.

She leaned up on tip toe and whispered in my ear. "Do you think Wolfman would be willing to give us more moonshine?"

I pulled her around in front of me and stared down into her smiling face. "You knew about that?"

"Of course, silly. Do you really think I

didn't see you pour that whole jar into the pot?" Her smile broadened. "Great idea, by the way. Wish I'd thought of it."

I threw back my head and laughed. Then I picked her up and swung her around.

"Hayden Carlisle!" She laughed. "Put me down this instant. What will people say?"

I pulled her close and kissed her, right there on the 20-yard line. "They'll say I'm a lucky man. A very lucky man."

PART TWO:
THE GREAT
TIME CAPSULE CAPER

Louise & Peggy, Thursday afternoon
As we climbed into my SUV in the parking lot behind the police station, I asked Peggy, "Aren't you the least bit interested in what kind of dirt Janey put in the box?"

In the back seat, my two Bouviers woke from their naps and crooned at us.

"I probably don't know half the people whose secrets are in the box," Peggy said.

"Well, I do. I feel like I raised most of them. My daughter's younger than Amos, but she dated some of those boys. Lord, there could be something about her! Bud would have a conniption if there was scandal about Margaret in that box." I took a deep breath. "Not to mention Charlie. Fathers never like to admit their daughters are grown women, even after they have children of their own."

"What about you?" Peggy said. "Aren't you worried?"

I waved a hand at her. "I knew she was a hellion, sneaking out to parties and dating the wrong boys. Things she'd kill her boys for, but to the best of my knowledge, she never did drugs or got pregnant or had a police record." I handed her the copy of the letter Amos had run off for us. "Read the relevant parts out loud."

Peggy sighed, but took the letter.

You took the time to be nice to me when you realized I was around, but most of the senior class had their noses so high they wouldn't have noticed me if they stepped on me. Well, I noticed them, and I always had my little camera and notebook, so I wouldn't forget. If people leave stuff lying around, they can't complain if somebody else finds it, now can they? When you open your precious time capsule, you'll find a few 'additions' I snuck into the box before it was sealed. Do you have the guts to wash everybody's dirty linen in public when the box is opened? Or will you chicken out and clean it out to spare everybody's tender feelings? Nobody spared mine, but I guess it doesn't matter now.

Janey Stalcross

"She put the whole burden on Amos whether to clean it out or not."

"She dumped it on him because he was nice to her," Peggy said. "Makes me glad I'm a curmudgeon."

She's not, of course, but she likes to act like she is. "Okay, so where do we start looking?" I asked.

She folded the copy and slid it into my handbag on the seat between us. "I cannot believe anyone would give a tinker's dam what's in the box after all these years. It's a tempest in a teapot."

"How long have you lived in Mossy Creek?"

"Long enough."

"Obviously not, if you think no one will care. You *do* realize we have less than two days to locate it in time for Amos and Ida to sanitize it and deliver it to the dance Saturday night? I don't know where to start."

"How about with where it was supposed to be? The original stadium plans have to be filed somewhere. The city assessor's office, maybe?"

"Do schools pay taxes?"

"No, but they pay utilities, and have plumbing and electricity inspections."

"Shoot. I just thought of something," I

said. "The bake sale. Town Square is going to be a zoo."

"I'll bet you anything the assessor's office is already shut down today so Felicia can go," she said, and I knew it was true.

"Pick up where we left off tomorrow?" I asked.

Peggy nodded. "Bright and early."

Mossy Creek Gazette

Volume VIII, No. Two   Mossy Creek, Georgia

MUM'S THE WORD!
by Katie Bell

I know a lot of you Creekites out there are too young to remember, but Homecoming Mums are a Southern tradition that began in the 1920s. Fresh Chrysanthemums were originally used with just a few ribbons trailing out beneath.

Enter the super-sized age! Since the 1960s, Homecoming Mums have been made from silk flowers with additional items added to signify different activities the students are involved in. They're Homecoming Corsages with stories!

The newly formed Football Moms Booster Club has been working hard to bring the tradition back for this year's Homecoming. They've been meeting every Saturday morning in the Fellowship Hall at the Mossy Creek Presbyterian Church to create floral, beribboned and trinketed works of art.

One finished custom corsage seen by

this reporter had a yellowish-gold silk bloom the size of a grapefruit that was nestled on a background of dark green leaves. The letters MCHS were prominent in dark green pipe cleaners and peering out from the middle of the mum was a small Ram's head. Two pounds of trinkets hung from gold and green ribbons that were about 3 feet long. The trinkets included a "Ram" bell to use as a noise maker during the game. This custom mum (I cannot divulge who it will be given to!) included the lucky recipient's name, the school name and her graduation year. There were also various trinkets describing the extra curricular activities she and her date are involved in.

Many trinkets are available for decorating the mums including charms for band, cheerleading, drama club, various sports, drill team, glee club, and many more.

The Football Moms Mums will have a booth at the bake sale on Thursdays. Prices will vary according to how many flowers, ribbons and trinkets are attached.

If you'd like to order a custom mum to be picked up at the booth, please call one of the Football Moms and place your order. Trinkets will be available at the booth, so you can also decorate your own there.

PAS DE GRIDIRON

Football is not a contact sport. It's a collision sport. Dancing is a good example of a contact sport.
— Duffy Daugherty

Argie Rodriguez, Monday
If my fellow dancers at the New York City Ballet could only see me now, up to my rubberized, pink polka-dotted Target rainbooted ankles in cow doo, they'd think their former lead ballerina had vanished to another planet.

"It's manure. Great for the soil. You'll see, Argie, you'll have the prettiest flowers come spring." Valerie wielded a trident with relish, turning over rich red clods of Georgia clay and smashing them so that the manure could be worked into it. "I'll come back to stick some ornamental cabbages and chrysanthemums in the dirt for you." She parked a gloved hand on her hip. "I'll bet the Mossy

Creek Garden Club will take you on as a special project."

My heart sank at the thought that I was a special project. I know she meant well, but the distressed yard around my ballet studio and the piles of manure seemed to be a rustic analogy of my life.

When I'd asked my Pilates class for gardening help I'd been bombarded with advice, but today Valerie the Valkyrie had shown up with a pickup truck full of manure, tools, some leafy twigs sticking out of wet burlap balls and a plan.

"The ballet studio is too little for wide flower beds," I said. I didn't want to discourage her too much, but it was the truth. The former gas station would look like a little gnome hut sprouting from the middle of a huge garden.

"Improved soil never hurt anyone. I figure we can put in a couple of forsythia shrubs — they bloom yellow in the spring, some azaleas, and then we can figure out what else you want. I can stick in a few chrysanthemums here and there for fall color."

"Okay, I know what chrysanthemums are, but I'm not familiar with forsythia and azaleas." I made an effort to smile at her. "I really appreciate your help, Valerie. You can tell how helpless I am here." I checked my watch and carefully stepped out of the smelly black clumps, still fragrant of cow. "Gotta go inside now. My afterschool beginning ballet class will be here soon."

"Aw, they're so cute in their little tutus and slippers," Valerie said. "You go on in."

I noticed Valerie didn't disagree with my gardening skill assessment, so I didn't tell her that the cute little ballerinas would actually be the Mossy Creek High football team. After a string of injuries, Coach Fred Mabry decided that the boys had to work on balance and flexibility. Since it was the Monday before the Homecoming game against Harrington, I made sure he knew there wouldn't be *a lot* of improvement by Friday. He assured me that he knew it was an on-going process and that he wanted the lessons to last through football season.

I was excited to get the business, but the boys weren't thrilled at the idea of ballet class. I hoped that Valerie wouldn't do or say anything that would encourage them to head back to their cars.

Before entering my little sanctuary, I ran my hand over the raised letters on the small metal sign that hung on the wall next to the doorbell.

Wisteria Cottage Dance Studio. Argelia Rodriguez, Owner

I'd ordered it made from cast-iron for permanence. I'd needed permanence and roots in my life when I moved here. My ballet studio was small, but it boasted a gorgeous and expensive floor, beautiful mirrored walls, smooth hardwood barres, a state-of-the-art sound system, and a cozy apartment home on the other side of the mirrored wall.

Every penny of my savings, as well as a small inheritance, had gone into renovating the old frame building when I'd moved here from New York City. Now all my classes were almost full, but I still wasn't convinced that I was a success, and adding the football team to my client list was like a vote of confidence for my ballet school. After years of living like a gypsy, of devoting every aspect of my life to dance, it seemed strange to be rooted in one small town. Sometimes it felt totally alien.

The phone rang, and I gingerly toed off my stinky rubber boots. I put them back outside by the stacked stone stairs, then crossed the unblemished wooden floor. The silky feel of the honey-smooth hardwood soothed my battered feet. Car doors slammed outside as I answered the phone.

"Argie, it's Fred Mabry. Got a minute?" His gravelly voice was unmistakable.

"Of course, Coach. Your players are just coming in."

"There's one more who won't be there today. Jeff Taylor got hurt. Do you have some exercises that he can do so he doesn't lose time?"

"What kind of injury?"

"Turf toe."

"Oh." Turf toe is a ghastly name for a painful mid-foot sprain. Ballet dancers get turf toe all the time, and apparently football players twist their feet jumping and landing badly, just like ballet dancers do. Except they don't fall off their toe shoes, of course. "There are lots of exercises that he can do to strengthen his core without putting weight on his foot. My Pilates class will be perfect."

I smiled as the door knob turned and the first of the boys lumbered in, looking around uncomfortably. He was tall enough to reach the ceiling tiles with his knuckles. He noticed my smile, but pretended to be interested in the window.

"Ms. Argie?" Coach's voice brought me back. "When should Jeff be there?"

I decided to use the coach to get the kid's attention. "Tell him class starts at three. Hold on, Coach. One of your guys just arrived."

At the mention of the word "coach" the boy stood straighter, emphasizing his broad shoulders. His hips were narrow, covered in droopy sweats that seemed about to fall off.

"Great. It'll give one of the guys time to drive Jeff there after school. Call me later and fill me in on how the first class goes."

"Maybe you should know that the Pilates class is mostly women over thirty."

He chuckled. "Love it. I'll let you go. Good luck, Ms. Argie."

I stared at the receiver a second. Had I noted a little apprehension in his voice? I put the phone down and walked towards the muscular young man hovering by the door.

"Hi, I'm Argie Rodriguez. Welcome to the studio." I carefully didn't say the words dance or ballet, in case they made the kid race out the door and down the street.

He nodded, shifting from foot to foot and moving his head around like a steer in a slaughterhouse chute.

As the simile occurred to me, I rolled my eyes. I must still be affected by the manure.

"And your name is . . . ?"

He stopped moving, probably because all the blood in his limbs was now in his face, but he still wouldn't meet my eyes. "The guys call me Tater. Tater Townsend."

Tater. I'd been on the wrong side of the farm. "Why don't you take your shoes off and stretch your legs a bit? Your teammates are on their way."

The other boys straggled in reluctantly — including Willie Bigelow, the quarterback — and Tater seemed relieved to have company. I greeted them and asked them to take off their shoes to save my floor. I turned the music on, softly. I'd crank up the volume and the beat when we were ready to get to work.

Five minutes later, we were missing only one boy, presumably Jeff. The rest were sitting — some on the long, cushioned bench usually occupied by waiting moms, some on the floor. They were uncomfortably quiet, eyes darting about the studio as if looking for the closest avenue of escape.

I clapped my hands to pull their eyes to me. "Gentlemen, I'm your instructor, Argie Rodriguez. How many of you have taken a dance class?"

Eyes swiveled back and forth, but there were no answers. I hadn't expected any. "Okay, we're going to change that this week. As Coach Mabry no doubt told you, football players have used stretching and ballet exercises for decades to strengthen their core muscles to increase timing and prevent injuries."

Time to show off. I figured a picture would show them that I wasn't all talk. I pointed the toes of my right foot and lifted my leg slowly until I held it straight to the side and horizontal to the floor, then held it there.

"Even if you don't dance ballet, the exercises will help your balance and core strength. Dance is not just about fancy leaps and jumps, or standing on your toes," I continued, keeping my leg extended and moving it toward the front.

Some of the boys were staring, obviously expecting it to start shaking or drop suddenly. That was not going to happen.

"It's about having the power to maintain a position using your muscles and balance." I lowered my leg slowly, widening my smile to keep from grimacing because it was starting to hurt. "If you don't think that's tough, then I invite you to stand at the barre." I gestured towards the smooth wooden pole bolted to the wall. "Gentlemen?"

The boys stood reluctantly, then shuffled to the barre. I walked to the doorway as they jostled each other. They made my studio look tiny.

"Please face me and put your right hand on the barre. Don't look at the mirror beside you. It's too close. You'll be able to see yourselves in the mirror across the room, but try not to stare at yourselves. Instead, concentrate on what your body is doing, your muscles, and use your reflection only as a reference to make sure that you are doing the exercises correctly."

As expected, the boys dragged their feet, but eventually they all stood by the barre. I sighed. At least none of them had refused to do the exercise.

I led them through the foot positions and demi-pliés, then the grande pliés, watching and encouraging as the boys sank to the floor in a deep squat, then rose, maintaining their position on tiptoe. Some wobbled, but no one was even breathing hard.

I braced myself for the inevitable. The exercise squeezed intestines, and there was always some passing of gas. Usually the little girls giggled and blushed until the last little fart had passed. Sure enough, the first blat sounded, and the room exploded with laughter.

Oh, brother.

"Keep going, gentlemen. This is perfectly natural. It won't be the last one."

Sure enough, it wasn't. More laughter and a few jeers this time. That was a good sign. Laughter helps ease tension.

"Let's do ten more grande pliés, and then we'll move to center work."

The raggedy, overgrown ballerinas' torsos headed south, then up again.

Snorts of laughter drew my attention and I stepped back to the center of the floor so that I could see all of my students. Three of the guys were still grinning.

"Remember to tuck your backsides in, tummies in, heads straight."

I turned away, giving them the opportunity to repeat whatever they'd done, keeping the mirror in my peripheral vision. I have terrific peripheral vision.

Sure enough. A foot swung out and jammed itself into the posterior of the boy in front, who jumped and turned with a wheelhouse kick worthy of a Jackie Chan movie. The intended target ducked, and the stockinged foot smashed into the barre right by one of the brackets that held it up.

The studio echoed with a loud crack, the splintering of glass, and a giant crash. My chest hurt as the boys leaped away from the wall, where the barre had fallen hard onto the floor.

"Dang, that was close," one of the boys said. The others clustered around, talking excitedly.

I rushed to Tater, the kicker, who was once

more red-faced and this time mortified, too.

"Are you okay?" My vision seemed to stutter as I tried to make sense of what I'd seen. Tater turned to me, shoulders slumped.

"I didn't mean to, Ms. Argie. I'm so sorry."

"Your foot's not cut?"

"No, I'm okay."

I stared at my barre, its graceful length tilting crazily, one end on the floor, surrounded by shards of broken mirror. I didn't know what to say. Little girls don't smash things.

Trying not to think of how much it was going to cost to replace, I turned my mind to adjusting my teaching style. "Everyone, come to the middle of the room. It's time to do center work."

I explained how balance was important to football, and about the role that abdominal and back strength played. "Your legs are part of the equation, too."

This time there was no grumbling and no snide laughter. The boys concentrated, eyes on their reflections, as they reached the edges of their endurance in deep pliés, heels lifted, followed by excruciating slow ascents to standing position.

I made them work every bit as hard as I'd

worked at their age, and although I'd had years of dance behind me, most of these boys had been playing football since they were toddlers. The training showed in their endurance and the way they all worked together once they got serious.

I only wished that they'd gotten serious without wrecking my wall.

Thirty minutes later, they were gone. Exhaustion and ennui crept over me as I swept up broken glass. At least the floor wasn't damaged. I could've bought a brand new Mercedes Benz for what that floor had cost.

I cleaned up the glass, carefully going over the floor with a dampened paper towel to catch every tiny splinter. As I tossed away the last glittery paper towel, I remembered that I needed to call Fred Mabry with a report.

The phone rang as I was reaching for it. My heart skipped as I noted the 212 area code. New York City. "Hello?"

"Argie?" The soft male voice was familiar, but the tentative tone was strange.

"Peter?"

It was as if my ennui had reached back into my past. Peter Allison had been my partner in the New York City ballet. After I left, he'd changed partners and although he'd promised to keep in touch, he hadn't.

"Yeah. Do you know how hard it was to track you down? The number you left was disconnected."

"My old cell phone. I lost it." I laughed shakily. It was surreal to be talking to Peter. Like a phone call from my past life. "How have you been?"

"Fine. I'm leaving the New York Ballet and wanted to tell you about it."

"You aren't retiring, are you?" At thirty, he wasn't a kid, but he was still strong.

"Are you kidding? They'll have to drag me off the stage." He chuckled. "I've got a new venture. I'm moving to the Modern Dance Cooperative, and I want you to join me."

For a second, I forgot to breathe. "Would you repeat that, please?"

"Join me. At the Modern Dance Co-operative. We were a great team, Argie, and if I announced that you'd be dancing with me again, everyone would go wild." He sounded excited, buoyant. The way I'd sounded so many years ago when I'd called Mom's hospital room to announce that I'd been chosen to dance in the corps at the New York City Ballet. Mom hadn't lived to see my rise to principle dancer, but the fact that I'd met my goal to be a professional ballerina had brightened her last days.

That seemed to be a theme in my life — the good moments were marred by sadness and troubles. Right after I opened the dance studio in Mossy Creek, my neighbor at the funeral home up the hill started a war, determined to shut me up or shut me down. And now that I was finally settling into my new home, here came an offer to return to my old life.

Except I hadn't settled in. I still had doubts about whether I'd truly been accepted by the people of Mossy Creek.

No! I refused to go there. Coach Mabry sent me the football team for lessons, didn't he? Valerie was digging in my garden, wasn't she? My classes were full, weren't they?

I *would not* let Peter's suggestion throw me into a tizzy.

Still, the broken barre hadn't upset me this much.

"You can't say you haven't thought about it," Peter continued. His voice lowered to a seductive purr. "I'll bet you haven't cut your hair."

I ran my hand down my long ponytail. Ballet dancers wear their hair long to make it easier to style for different characters. Wigs are awkward when you're dancing. I don't know why I hadn't cut my hair. It was a nuisance to care for, but it had been a part of my life for a very long time.

"You'll make enough money for a decent apartment. I promise," he continued. "And there will be minimal travel."

"You always said that, and it was never true."

"Come to New York this weekend so we can discuss it. I've got a sponsor who'll put you up at the Plaza."

Peter always did know how to chase the money. "Thanks for the offer, Peter, but —"

"Don't say no," he said quickly. "Not before you've had the chance to think about it."

I sighed. "I can't get away this weekend, but I *will* think about it. I'll talk to you later."

"Argie, please let me —"

I placed the phone back in its cradle without letting him make any more promises.

The next morning I received bad news. The repairmen could deliver new mirror panels, but not for two days. And it would take as much as two more days to install them. I'd have to find another place to hold my classes. I called Fred and explained the situation, and he promised to come up with a solution for his team. Then I spent a couple of hours calling parents to cancel ballet classes for my youngest students. Most were relieved, since just about everyone was busy with Homecoming activities.

Jeff, the injured player, hobbled late into my three o'clock Pilates class and was instantly smothered by a wave of sweaty female sympathy.

"You poor baby. Sit down and take the weight off your ankle," Louise Sawyer said. Others echoed advice.

"There's nothing wrong with his ankle," I told them.

"What happened, honey?" Louise asked.

Jeff looked around, clearly embarrassed to be surrounded by women in tights and shorts. "I fell the wrong way during practice week before last. My physical therapist agrees that Pilates might help." He looked heartbreakingly hopeful. "I just want to play against Bigelow. I don't care if I play Harrington at Homecoming, but I want to clobber Bigelow."

I looked at the calendar that hung by the door leading to my apartment. "That's two weeks away? If you rest your foot, you might be able to play. I can get you started with some light stretching, Jeff, but I'll need to speak to your therapist."

He handed me a business card. "He said you'd want to talk to him."

I glanced at the card. The address was in Bigelow. "You don't think this guy is a secret Bigelow High fan, do you?"

Jeff's eyes widened, and the women hooted.

"Just kidding, Jeff. No medical professional would deliberately give you bad advice." I hoped it was true. "Let's get back on the floor, ladies. Plank time."

The women groaned and Jeff looked at me, brows furrowed.

"Get on your tummies, then lift up onto your elbows and toes, back straight. We're going to hold it for sixty seconds."

More groans. "Jeff, you're excused because of your toe."

"Oh, I can try it, Ms. Argie." He followed the others, laying down, but wincing as he assumed the position. Then he lifted the injured foot, leg straight. The women behind him gasped, which caused others to turn and look, their usual complaints forgotten.

"Holy cow. A three point plank," Spiva Quinlan said, using her observance as an excuse to sit up.

"He's not even breathing hard." This from her sister, Pearl Quinlan, who wasn't breathing hard, either, mostly because she was still on her stomach.

At one minute I called time, and those

who were still in position collapsed gratefully, except for Jeff, who went to his knees and slid his legs sideways so that he could sit up without flexing his injured foot.

When we finished the class I took Jeff aside and asked him if he would consider coming to more classes. I'd never seen my students work so hard to keep up. He said he'd think about it, probably because several ladies kept trying to set him up with their granddaughters. I sent him off with a tube of sports cream to rub on his foot.

The next morning, I headed to Mossy Creek Books and What-Nots to pick up a couple of DVDs I'd ordered from Pearl. She'd changed into work clothes by then.

"Hey Argie. The FedEx guy dropped off a box for you while we were in class. He was looking for the Wisteria Cottage but couldn't find it listed." She held up the distinctive white corrugated box with red and blue markings.

"I wish they'd get that fixed. Apparently when you Google 'Wisteria Cottage' you get some retirement community near Atlanta. Thanks for holding it for me." I took it, paid for my DVDs and realized that the three other customers in the store had edged closer, eyes on the box.

"It says it's from New York City," Pearl offered.

Katie Bell's eyes snapped with interest.

"Don't weigh much. What do you reckon it is, Argie?" Rainey Cecil seemed puzzled, and certain that I would answer.

"I'm not sure what it is, and I don't recognize the return address." I lied, since the address was Peter's, but I didn't want to stop and explain my life, especially in front of Katie Bell. I tucked the box under my arm, grabbed the box with the DVDs and turned. "Thanks!"

Katie Bell stood between me and the door, eyes locked on the box. "I heard the football team destroyed your studio. What are you going to do now? And this is on the record. I'm including the story in the next edition of the *Gazette*."

I fought the irritation that had been brewing ever since the broken mirrors and dented floor.

"Okay, I give. I'll open the box now. And the studio is not destroyed," I added through gritted teeth. "It just needs a little work."

I flipped the box on edge, searched for the tab and ripped it, tearing the box open. Papers slid to the floor, fanning out — brochures announcing the Modern Dance

Cooperative's new principle dancer, with Peter's face smiling brilliantly in glossy color.

Pearl picked up the brochures, uncovering the eight-by-ten black and white photo below it.

Peter, dashing in his velvet *Swan Lake* doublet, held his partner, tall and sleek on pointe, leaning back over his shoulder with one leg wrapped backwards around his waist, long black curls spilling over his arm.

"Why, Ms. Argie, that's you!" Rainey seemed surprised, although my former life was no secret. Maybe it was my past displayed so enticingly in Peter's embrace that brought out the heightened interest.

Eager hands reached for the photo, which was signed in decisive black strokes, "Until we dance again."

"Yes, that's me." I gathered all the papers and the photo. "These brochures are for my former dance partner's new venture. Modern dance. I can't wait to see him perform again."

"Is he gay?" Katie Bell asked.

I sighed. For an old-fashioned town, they sure asked a lot of personal questions. "No, he's straight. He loves women. All women. He's very Russian that way. And don't get any ideas. We were never an item. More like brother and sister."

Rainey was leafing through the brochure. "Would you teach modern dance? I can't dance on my toes, but I'll bet I could do this if I worked at it."

"Sure, if enough people are interested." I'd never thought of offering modern dance. I'd envisioned my dance school full of baby ballerinas who would grow to love dance, some of them enough to make it a career. I'd soon discovered that the only way my studio would succeed is with adult classes. I'd started with ballroom dancing, then expanded to Pilates. It would be good to add another class.

Only one problem. If my classes grew larger I'd have to build an addition and maybe hire another teacher. Did I want to? Maybe I was foolish to let the opportunity Peter offered pass me by. I could postpone teaching and dance professionally for another ten years.

Thoughts spinning through my head, I left the bookstore and headed back home.

I parked at the far end of the studio's gravel lot. My so-called new garden was a disaster. Sad, disturbed, pungent clods of dirt covered the area that used to be orderly patches of weeds. Not beautiful, but a weed whacker had kept it under control.

Why couldn't anything in my life be tidy? I walked into the studio and went straight to the stereo and turned it on, careful to keep my eyes away from the shattered mirror. The wall above it held shelves of CDs, carefully organized alphabetically by composer.

I slipped a disc from its plastic case and fed it into the CD player's slot.

The rich sound of Dvorak's twelfth string quartet filled the studio. Energized by the familiar music, I quickly changed into black calf-length tights and a leotard and tied on a short wrap around dance skirt.

Shoes were not needed for what I had in mind. The brochures that Peter sent had done exactly what he'd intended. I itched to stretch my legs and torso, to follow the choreography of the dances shown in the photographs. I stretched a little, then restarted the CD and went through the steps I remembered of the solo I'd danced at the *Festival du Dance* in Paris.

At first I was careful not to look towards the wall that had held the barre, afraid that seeing that damage would take me out of my mood, but then my muscles warmed and I slid through all the sequences I remembered, and lost myself to the movement, improvising where I forgot the steps.

The CD ended and changed to the next. I barely took a breath before the first act of *Giselle* began, favorite music for my little ballerinas' barre work, and I danced that too, stopping briefly to dig my newest pointe shoes from their box in the closet and tie them on.

The contrast was obvious to me from the first *entrechats quatre.* From knees to hips, I could feel the unsubtle hints that it was time to quit.

A movement at the window caught my eye. My football heroes grinned and waved through the glass. I'd been so lost in the music that I hadn't noticed the hours dancing by. I laughed and unlocked the door. The cool fall air hit my sweat dampened skin and I reached for the cardigan that hung on a coat hook rack just inside.

"You dance real pretty, Ms. Argie," Tater said. He handed me an envelope. "This is from my Dad. I'm sorry about your wall."

"Thank you, Tater." I slipped the envelope into the cardigan's pocket. "Leave your shoes outside, guys. You were standing in manure there under my window."

As they busied themselves with their shoes, I turned away and slid my finger under the envelope flapping, tearing it open. Inside was a check with a sticky note in the middle that read, "Sorry about what my boy did. Hope this is enough. Ed." I peeled off the sticky note to reveal the amount: two thousand dollars. It would more than pay for the mirror and the barre, and I appreciated Ed's fast response, but maybe Tater needed to do some work around the studio, a little sweat equity to pay off the debt. I'd make the repairs, then give Ed back the rest of his money and put Tater to work.

The phone rang, and I answered, one eye on my rowdy, reluctant *danseurs.*

"It's Fred. You can hold class on the practice field. I gotta warn you, it'll be noisy, but you'll have lots of room."

"How noisy?"

"Marching band and cheerleading practice. They're building the Homecoming floats there, too."

"That's okay." Actually, it sounded insane, but no crazier than it already was. Plus, no mirrors. "And when you have a moment, I want to discuss putting Tater to work around here. Can't talk now. I have to get class started."

I hung up then told the boys to put their shoes back on because we were moving practice to the football field. I thought they'd be thrilled, but instead of cheering, they looked at each other or down at their feet. "What's wrong?"

"That's where the cheerleaders practice."

"I don't get it."

"Girls," Tater supplied, filling in the silence.

And then I understood.

Despite the threat of humiliation, the team gathered on the practice field half an hour later. I didn't bring music, thinking that today we'd do without, and later the boys could bring their own and we'd dance to whatever they brought. If the school approved, or course.

The area was busy, and two nearby picnic tables were surrounded by kids working on some kind of art project. Homecoming-related no doubt. We were three days away from the big event and everybody was excitedly working away on finishing touches.

I gathered my troop of big guys together and we stretched, then started the pliés. Several of the guys looked around nervously as we exercised. Maybe a little laughter would help.

"If you feel unbalanced without the barre, stand close to another person and grab his hand. I'm sure no one will notice that you're holding hands."

The guys laughed. They were already doing ballet. No way they'd hold hands too, but they relaxed a little about doing the pliés.

For a while they looked like any athletes stretching and bending on the field, but then we started the *battement tendus,* and the girls at the picnic tables stopped to watch as the boys stretched their legs out, bare toes pointed. If the pointed toes weren't a dead giveaway that this was strange, my yells to keep their arms gracefully arched were.

"As if your fingers are being pulled by the current in a stream," I hollered, trying to be heard above the marching band's rehearsal. "Not with your fingers splayed out to catch a pass."

The girls bent over laughing, and I could see the boys cutting their eyes over to them. One by one they slowed, then stopped. I glared at the girls, frustrated. I couldn't kick them out, it was a public area.

"Ladies, why don't you help the team instead of hindering them?" I walked over to them and explained what Coach was trying to accomplish. "So if they learn to stretch their joints, their chance of getting injured will go way down."

"I think ballet is cool," one of them said.

"Why don't you join the class? Free of

charge, as long as you cheer on the football team. Which means no making fun of the players."

The girls eagerly joined the team for the remainder of the class, and though the guys didn't concentrate totally on ballet, they did make an effort, showing off for the cheerleaders until the girls had to go.

They looked reluctant to leave.

"We've got to get back to work on the float," a pretty blonde said, pointing to the picnic tables where their banner was spread out, surrounded by poster paints and empty soup cans full of paint brushes. The banner they were painting read, "Time to Ram the Harrington Eagles."

"We'll be doing a dance on the float," another girl said. "Can you tell us what you think of our choreography? We're going to dance to *Rock Around the Clock*."

I stared at her. "You're going to dance on a moving float? That's dangerous."

The girls looked at each other.

"Aw, don't bench 'em, Ms. Argie," Tater said.

"Benched!" the blonde squealed. "Tater, you're brilliant. We'll sit on the bench and dance."

I thought about what could be done on a bench. "Seated kicks, some acrobatics. Any of you take gymnastics?" From their excited nods, I could see we were on to something. "Okay. I'll help you change your dance to a seated routine. Hmm. Today is Tuesday and the parade is Saturday, right? That gives us a few days to practice. I'll make the routine simple so it's easy to learn. Can all of you come by my studio tomorrow afternoon right after school? I have an hour free just before the football team's class."

They all agreed that they could, so I turned to Tater. "And you can help them learn it once we have it done. Be there an hour before class."

He looked baffled for a minute, then a smile spilled like honey across his face.

The phone was ringing when I walked into my apartment. I was so tired, I thought about letting the machine pick up, but it might be one of the parents I hadn't been able to reach.

"Hello?"

"Did you see my package?" Peter's voice held something of the grin he always wore.

"Yes, I did." So did everyone at the bookstore. "Great brochures." I bit off my next words, afraid my fear and longing to dance would flavor my voice.

Had I made the wrong choice in moving

to Mossy Creek? It had been impulsive to quit and move here, but I knew my dancing days were almost over. I hadn't wanted to end up in a second tier company, or teaching in one of New York's many ballet schools. No way my inheritance would pay for more than a closet there, much less a building as nice as the one I had now.

But this was a chance to dance again, to regain my place in the ballet world. I was glad I'd found Mossy Creek, but I'd probably have no trouble finding someone to buy the studio. My brain was awhirl as Peter chattered on, filling me in on the dance world. I was no longer plugged in to the gossip and I managed to concentrate on his voice enough to laugh at his tales of rivalries and petty misdeeds and backstage romance.

He cleared his throat. "I got married."

I choked back laughter when I realized it wasn't a joke. "Congratulations! Who did you marry? Do I know her? You can tell I'm not in on the latest news."

"Nobody is," he said grimly. "I knew Jenny from back in Ohio. The dancers here are treating her like she's some kind of hick. If you were here, you two could be friends."

Sudden realization swept over me. His remark reminded me of his less than pleasant traits. Manipulative, Peter had always been able to get me to choose the roles he preferred, do interviews when I just wanted to soak my feet.

"Peter, you can't just buy friends for your fiancée. Is there really a place for me at The Modern Dance Cooperative? I have a studio here. Students who count on me. I can't just leave then pop back up here."

"Right. Five-year-olds who would do just as well learning from someone who's never danced professionally. You should be dancing. And if you want to teach, the students here need a higher level of teaching, the kind you can provide. You're wasted in Boggy Creek."

"Mossy Creek. And what makes you think there's no dance talent here?" I hung up on him for the second time. I swear, he was bringing out my inner Yankee.

Tater turned out to be a good teacher. He followed the girls around, pointing out when they weren't in sync, and they loved the attention.

The football team was thirty minutes late. Fred Mabry came in first, holding a little box, and with a laptop bag over his shoulder.

Several men came in right after the coach. One of them held the door open with his back as the entire football team followed.

The men looked around with what seemed to be equal parts disgust and interest. I'd seen some of them in town, but had never met any of them.

The football players seemed just as sullen as the older men.

My heart fell. I thought I'd made a good head start changing their attitudes toward ballet. Apparently, I'd thought wrong.

I looked at Fred, eyebrows raised.

"Seems some of the fathers have been razzing the guys about dancing. I thought it was time for some show and tell, so I asked them along." He leaned forward. "Hope you don't mind."

He plugged in a squat black box, then unzipped the bag and pulled out a dented blue laptop which he also plugged in, then popped open the screen came to life in the football team's colors. He saw my questioning look. "You mentioned Lynn Swann, so I had one of the teachers put together a little presentation." He moved the box, pressed a button and a bulb came on inside.

"A projector." I'd never seen one so tiny. A picture of Lynn Swann appeared on the whiteboard by the door, blank now that I'd decided to add classes and had to reconfigure the schedule usually posted there.

My heart sank. Did he think I was so

desperate for the help? Yes, I suppose I was.

"Ms. Argie, I have two clips to show, then we'll have a special guest come in."

"Okay." I went to sit on the floor, in the middle of the boys. They scooted away to make room for me.

Coach clicked on the presentation, and a picture of football star Lynn Swann appeared. He went through statistics of the famous football player, then played a short clip from a documentary about Lynn Swann.

I watched the boys' faces. They seemed only a little bit impressed. Definitely not persuaded.

When the film ended Fred smiled benevolently. "Ms. Argie, get the door. We have company."

I went to the door and opened it, wondering what he was up to. Tag Garner stood outside, grinning. He was accompanied by Win Allen, President of the Town Council, Mac Campbell and Police Chief Amos Royden.

"You must be Coach's special guests." I stepped aside and they came in, making my studio look even tinier.

Win stood to one side while Tag sent a penetrating glance around the team. "Boys, let me tell you what ballet did for me."

That got their attention. They all knew the owner of Figuratively Speaking, because he was the assistant coach for the team. They also knew he'd been a star quarterback for the Atlanta Falcons.

"I warmed my high school's benches for a year until I took ballet. It gave me the balance and footwork to be a starter."

"*You* danced ballet?" Tater's jaw hung open.

"Yessirree. And while you can't play football and not get hurt, I never had to sit out a game because of an injury." He smiled wryly. "Until that last one, of course — the injury that ended my career. But not even Mikhail Baryshnikov could've avoided those three linebackers coming at me from my blind side. I've seen the tape."

"Who do y'all think gave me the idea?" Fred asked.

"Do Mr. Mac Campbell or Police Chief Royden look like sissies to any of y'all?" Tag pointed to the two men standing behind him.

Amazed, everyone shook their heads.

"Well, they took ballet, too. For football." Tag glanced around the team. "Is there *anything* y'all wouldn't do for football? For your team? For Mossy Creek?"

Again, all heads shook.

"All right, then. Listen to Coach." Tag stepped aside.

Fred smacked his hands together. "So if these strong men — town leaders — can do ballet, so can you. Will it make you good enough for the pros? Who knows? You heard how he warmed the bench in high school. We aren't asking you to put on tutus and dance a recital with Ms. Argie." His brows lowered. "Unless you lose to Harrington."

I laughed, then covered my mouth, afraid I'd offend someone, but the dads were laughing, too. The boys pretended to look outraged, which made their fathers laugh even harder.

Fred's mouth spread in that scary grin again. "So no more arguments, right, gentlemen?" He was looking at the row of dads, who shuffled from foot to foot. "Come on, Tag, I'll buy you a coffee."

He paused at the door. "Argie, the principal asked me to ask you if you'd mind being a chaperone for the Homecoming Dance."

A chaperone. For a moment I stared at him, then turned to look out the window, where Valerie was back at work, carefully stacking corn stalks into a teepee, a wheelbarrow full of pumpkins behind her, turning the manure pile into a gorgeous garden.

I fought back silly tears. "I'd love to."

He clapped a hand on my shoulder and the two men left. The minute the door closed, the boys jumped up, ready to work. Amazing what a couple of "old" guys talking about ballet could do to make a difference. So far I hadn't motivated them to do anything. Pretty girls and tough old football players had done the trick.

After class I went outside to help Valerie, but she was almost done. I stared, amazed, at the transformation. The messy clump of manure had been raked into rich black earth, spotted with tiny shrubs and elegant arrangements of greenery I didn't recognize.

A stack of pumpkins, a couple of bales of hay and the corn stalk teepee made Wisteria Cottage look festive. Impulsively, I hugged Valerie, startling her. "It looks so great, I can't believe it."

She looked satisfied. "It came out all right. May I clean up inside? It's almost time for Pilates."

"Absolutely. Want some tea?"

She did, and I put the kettle on while she washed up and changed into her workout clothes, then I opened my mail. An envelope from Peter. Luckily, I didn't see it before, or I wouldn't have been able to sit through the ballet class.

It was another brochure, this one with a sticky note on the cover. Peter had scrawled, "No pointe shoes, no blisters. Pure dance. You'll love it." I peeled it off, crumpled it up, and tossed it in the wastebasket under my desk.

The brochure was good. A line of dancers, arms stretched behind them leaned forward, feet a blur.

I knew exactly how to achieve that pose, and what dance it came from. It was part of Paul Taylor's amazing *Promethean Dance.* Unable to resist, I ran back and forth, arms stretched up and behind me like wings, twisting and turning. I laughed as I danced the steps I remembered from a college performance. Sinewy, earthy. I could do this. Peter was right. I still had years of dance left in me. Who needed an audience?

The Pilates class straggled in, and I took aside the mayor, Ida Hamilton Walker, as she entered. "You said you wanted to take ballet, but I'm afraid it might put too much stress on your joints. But look at this." I showed her the brochure. "I can teach you this dance."

I showed her the steps I'd danced only an hour before. "You can do this, too, with practice."

Cries of "I want to try that," followed me

as I raced around my studio. I stopped, a little breathless. "Well, who's in? Modern Dance is what the class is called."

Hands shot up, and I grinned. I knew what I wanted to do, and it was energizing.

"How are the boys taking the ballet lessons? Are they working?"

"Well, it's a little early to tell. However, Coach said he was going to make ballet part of the regular football schedule. But I think I'll incorporate some Pilates in there, as well." I smiled at Jeff, who was hobbling through the door. "That class will be all guys."

He waved. "Count me in." He blushed at the good-natured laughter.

"Is it working for you?" Katie Bell was eyeing his foot.

"My physical therapist says I'll be able to play Homecoming tomorrow, if I keep it taped." He shrugged. "But I'll probably be on the bench most of the time. Coach says he doesn't want to risk it."

I wasn't going to make a big deal about it, but the minute I was done with this class, I'd make an appointment to cut my hair. Hopefully Rainey could fit me in tomorrow. I wanted to look sassy and chic for my chaperone gig on Saturday night.

I was going to take a hint from my new
garden and thrive in Mossy Creek.

PART THREE:
THE GREAT
TIME CAPSULE CAPER

Louise & Peggy, Friday morning
"Yoo-hoo! Louise! Peggy! Wait up!"

"Oh, Lord," Peggy whispered, but turned to Katie Bell with a smile on her face, muttering beneath her breath, "It's too early in the day."

Mossy Creek's ace reporter tottered up to us on red babydoll pumps with five inch heels. If I wore those things I'd be in the hospital with a broken leg. "What are you two lovely ladies up to this glorious morning?" She leaned close and whispered conspiratorially, despite the fact that we were standing in the middle of the sidewalk so people had to walk around us. And stare. "You can tell me."

I would not tell her the sun rises in the east unless I expected the information to show up in a headline in next week's *Mossy Creek Gazette.* I had no idea, however, what I could tell her that would put her off the scent. Next to her nose, the average blood-hound is nasally-challenged.

Peggy jumped in. "I'm researching a monograph for the North Georgia Historical Society. Louise is tagging along so we can have lunch after."

"Monograph on what?"

"The effect Bigelow County's original zoning regulations had on the prices of row crop and grazing land in the eighteen nineties."

"Oh." Katie Bell deflated visibly. Then she waved a hand at us. "Well, carry on." She tottered off down the street to ambush some other unsuspecting Creekite.

Once we were inside the building, I turned to her. "Did Bigelow have zoning regulations in the eighteen nineties?"

"I have no idea. Probably not."

"Are you always that quick with a plausible lie? That's scary."

"I," Peggy said, lifting her chin, "am an academician. I can be an Olympic caliber bore when I have to."

"Well, you got Katie Bell off our tail. For the moment."

"Un-huh. Probably not for long." She sighed. "Bless her heart."

We walked arm-in-arm down the stairs to

the basement where the Assessor's Office
was located.

"The Voice Of The Creek"

<u>BERT</u>: Hey, Sports Fans! This is the *Ram It Home Sports Hour* on WMOS Radio. Our first caller is Mike from Bigelow.

<u>MIKE</u>: Hey, do you losers up in Mossy Creek really think you have a football team? I hear they been going to ballet class. What a bunch of sissies! They gonna show up on *our* football field wearing tutus?

<u>BERT</u>: Hold on, there, cowboy. I think you'll find a few people in Mossy Creek who disagree with you. Wolfman, you there?

<u>WOLFMAN</u>: You know-nothing, low-life Bigelowan scumbag. Do you know how many famous football players have taken ballet?

<u>MIKE</u>: Name one . . . that anyone gives a toad's fart about.

<u>WOLFMAN</u>: Hershel Walker for one.

Chad Johnson for another. Lynn Swann. Vance Johnson. Randall Cunningham. Aklili Smith —

MIKE: Sez who?

WOLFMAN: Look it up on the 'Net, you moron. Y'all *do* get the internet in your backwater town, don'tcha? All kinds of athletes take ballet 'cause it helps with injuries or somethin'. And they *don't* wear tutus!

MIKE: Oh yeah? Well, *you* wear a tutu!

WOLFMAN: No, *you* wear a tutu!

MIKE: No, *you* wear a —

BERT: Thank y'all for that riveting and enlightening discussion! Now a word from our sponsor, Goldilock's Nail, Hair & Tanning. They're open late all week to accommodate every Creekite wanting to look their best for Homecoming!

NEW GUY IN TOWN

We cannot live only for ourselves.
A thousand fibers connect us with
our fellow men.
— Herman Melville

Coach Fred Mabry, Wednesday
I swore I'd never be *that* guy. You know what I'm talking about — the new guy in town who's so friendly you just know he's covering up for something. Well, there I was, nearly two months living in Mossy Creek and still grinning and glad-handin' around town, trying to make a good impression like I was hidin' some god-awful skeletons in my closet — which I was not. Not really.

The firestorm my arrival had caused was still pretty obvious. Winning six of the first seven ballgames of Mossy Creek High School's first football season in over twenty years had helped a whole lot, but there were still a few hard-core folks who wanted somebody else — anybody else — to coach Mossy Creek's boys in the grand ole game of football.

I'm Fred Mabry, one of the best offensive coaches ever to work between The Hedges. For you folks who don't understand that lingo, that means I was an offensive coach at The University of Georgia, working under the best coach who ever walked on a football field, Vince Dooley. But my time had come and gone on the college circuit. I never made it to head coach, never coached in the pros, but that didn't matter much. What mattered to me was that I'd coached some of the finest players in the game, players who went on to become the best quarterbacks, running backs and receivers in the NFL. And about 99.9% of those boys became good men.

Some of those players became lifelong friends. Like Tag Garner. Fine boy, he was. Seemed more like a son, not just a player. I'll tell you honestly, it was a shame about his career ending because of a bad knee, but it happens. And everything happens for a reason, I always say.

Through the years, we kept up with each other, had dinner together sometimes. I always looked forward to that. And now he'd pulled me out of retirement to coach the Mossy Creek High School football team, promising he'd hire on as my assistant. At first I didn't want to do it. And then the weirdest thing happened. I heard about the commotion created when he suggested me to the school board. Man, I'm telling you, tempers ran high.

And so did mine. Even though I didn't really want the job (or so I thought at the time), I can't tell you how it ticked me off for people to judge me without even talking to me.

I'd never inspired much conflict through the years, so I didn't exactly understand what the problem was. Still don't. I guess some folks just wanted some hot-shot young coach, bein' as how it was a new school and all. Mossy Creek High School was just ending its first year of existence. 'Course, there used to be a Mossy Creek High School way back when. Burned down is my understanding. Something about some pranksters from Bigelow High put some sparklers in the wool of the school mascot — a ram — and let it loose at half-time. Spooked a damned elephant, if you can believe that. All hell broke loose after that when the ram and the elephant both got into the school and set it on fire. Talk about a boyish prank gone bad. That sure was one.

Turns out that our illustrious governor, Ham Bigelow, nephew of Mayor Ida Hamilton Walker, was involved in that boyish prank. Might even have been the instigator. Imagine that! Talk about skeletons in your closet. To divert attention away from all that, he promised to find money for a new school in Mossy Creek. Which meant a new football team and a new coach.

So, here I am, walking into the Naked Bean before school on a Wednesday morning in October. Jayne Reynolds makes some of the best coffee the North Georgia mountains. And it's a good place to meet new folks. Everybody drops in at the Naked Bean occasionally. I met some fine people there. And if truth be told, I met some ornery ones, too. Willard Overbrook being one of the worst. Never figured out what I did to get under Willard's skin, but he always treated me like an infestation of chiggers that somehow found its way to his privates.

When I first met him, I thought he was threatening me. I mean, really threatening me. Like he was some macho guy and wanted to take on the new "kid" in town. As time passed, the sense of threat went away, but he always made it known that he would like to be rid of me, one way or the other.

If it sounds like I'm paranoid, I have to tell ya that Willard wasn't the only one who acted like I was a menace to society. Over the past few weeks, the resentment — or whatever it was — had lessened, even with Willard, but he just couldn't seem to completely let go of that anger.

Looking forward to a nice cuppa Joe before heading to school was my aim when I walked through that door. Dealing with Willard was the last thing on my mind, but there he was.

I nodded at him cordially as I passed him on my way to the counter. "Mornin' Willard," I said, trying to take the high road.

He grimaced and for a moment, I thought he would ignore my greeting. Finally he said, "Morning, Coach."

The way he used the word coach told me what he thought of my skills. Trouble is, I just don't know why he felt that way. Wasn't as if I'd taken Mossy Creek from a winning season to losing. Just the opposite. And to my knowledge, I'd never met the guy until I came to Mossy Creek.

I turned my attention to a more pleasant face. "Mornin', Miss Jayne. What's the special today?" Not that I really cared.

Everything here was good.

"Coffee and a buttered biscuit with home-made blackberry jam."

"Homemade?"

"Made by Betty Halfacre's half-Cherokee hands. She and her family even picked the wild blackberries." Jayne smiled and pointed at the neat row of jars bearing her name. They were capped with some kind of little red-checkered cloth and something that looked for all the world like a piece of straw.

"Sounds real good. I'll take it."

I sat down with the newspaper and glanced at the front page. The *Mossy Creek Gazette* was a weekly paper, so it was all about the game that would take place in two days. Harrington Academy wasn't much of an opponent, but suitable for Homecoming, I guess. I'd rather have a little more of a challenge so my boys didn't get complacent. Never do for that to happen. I've seen "sure win" games that left the players wondering what happened after getting whupped up on by a far inferior opponent. My main job this week was to keep our boys sharp.

The door opened and Tag Garner came in. "Hey, Tag."

Willard looked up from his newspaper. He nodded at Tag. This time a grin accompanied the nod.

"Hey, Coach." Tag snared the cup of coffee Jayne held out for him. "Mornin', Jayne. Good to see you."

"Good to see you. How's Maggie?" Jayne asked.

"Fat and sassy as ever." Tag grinned from ear to ear. "She's pretty worn out at the end of the day, though. Gets tired real easy."

Jayne chuckled and nodded. "How well I remember those days. Near the end of my pregnancy, I thought I'd die of exhaustion. Feet swollen, back aching. It was awful."

"Sounds just like her." Tag shook his head and ambled over to the table where I was sitting. He looked over at Willard, hesitated and said, "Comin' to the game Friday night, Willard?"

Something akin to a growl erupted from the corner where Willard sat. "Reckon so."

I glanced across the room. Willard was watching as Tag dropped into the chair across from mine.

"So, the game's on for Friday," I said. "The big one."

"Well, Coach, I'm not real sure folks around here would call the Harrington game the big one. I'd say the rivalry between Mossy Creek and Bigelow makes the game coming up in two weeks the big game."

"Yeah, I know. Folks 'round here put a lot of pressure on me about that game, but we got to play 'em one at a time. That means the 'big' game is always the one coming up." I cut my eyes over toward Willard. He'd been one of the worst. "I don't know what happened last week."

Tag grinned and shook his head. "Everybody loses one every now and then."

"We shouldn't have lost that game. No way." I looked at my watch and then over at Jayne. "Can you pack that biscuit to go?"

"Sure can." Jayne wrapped the biscuit and brought it out to the table. "Here you go. See you in the morning?"

"Yep, just like always." I rose and headed toward the door. "See you this afternoon, Tag?"

"Yes, sir. I'll be there." Tag stood up, tossed a few dollars on the table, nodded at Jayne. "I'm coming with you. I'm subbing for the art teacher today. She's got a migraine."

We walked out the door together with Willard staring daggers at me. Just can't figure that man out. "You seem to be subbing a lot lately."

"Not much going on at the store, what with the economy and school starting back. No tourists except on weekends."

I headed toward my car and then looked at Tag. "I heard what you told Jayne, but is Maggie really okay?"

A grin erupted across Tag's face that looked like the sun coming up over the mountains. "Yeah. Just ornery. The doc says the baby's not coming for another couple of weeks, but she's 'bout big enough to bust."

"Well, she's healthy. She'll do fine."

The grin sagged and Tag shook his head. "Yeah, I know. Still . . ."

He waved and stepped over the door to his Spider. I watched with a grin. That boy loved his fast cars. The flashy red Alfa Romeo Spider roared to life. Tag sped out of the space and disappeared at the end of the street where he turned toward the school. As far as I knew, he had only two vices . . . fast cars and Maggie Hart.

By the time I got to school Tag was nowhere to be seen. He was subbing because he technically had to be employed by the school in order to serve as my assistant coach. So far, it worked out fine. He usually worked down at his shop, *Figuratively Speaking.* Turned out, he had a helluva talent for sculpting action figures, mostly sports stuff like football players. But every now and again, he created something historical, like the Battle of Cowpens from the Revolutionary War. After a lot of research, he sculpted something like a diorama. Then he had the sculptures cast in bronze and limited editions produced.

Personally, I think he enjoyed teaching school. I know he enjoyed the kids. And as for football, he was the best natural coach I'd come across in a long time. The boys looked up to him. He'd been there in the trenches and they respected that.

I got out of my car and was practically attacked.

"Hey, Coach!" Greg Pitts threw his arms around me in a bear hug and lifted me off my feet.

"Now Greg, put me down, son."

"Two more days. Just two. I'm gonna be the manager." His exuberance was infectious.

"I know, I know. You gonna be at practice this afternoon? I need you mighty bad, son." I watched as he puffed out his chest with pride. Nobody seemed to pay much attention to him. He was a good kid, just a little slow. He was probably borderline for being able to attend regular school, but somehow managed to get by. I noticed a lot of the kids made fun of him or made him the butt of jokes, but he never seemed to mind. Or maybe he just wasn't smart enough to see they were really making fun of him. But he had a good heart and just overflowed with enthusiasm. After the players griped about having to deal with "the retard," I had a team meeting with them. Told them that anybody who didn't treat Greg with respect didn't play on Mossy Creek's football team. The key word being "team." My feelings about that went way back to my college days, to a time I'm not real proud of.

Some of them still groused, but didn't make a big deal about it. I didn't know much about Greg, just that he lived with his grandparents. I think his daddy didn't hang around very long after the boy was diagnosed as being slow. Then a few years after that, his mama split, too. The boy was raised by his grandparents. I was hoping to meet them, but so far, they hadn't showed up.

This would be Greg's first game as team manager. His job really consisted of getting water to the players during the game and towels for them after the game. He did the job well.

Still, he was proud to be a part of the team. I don't think I'll ever forget the day I offered him the job. He'd been standing on the sidelines watching. Our previous team manager had moved out of state. Pretty much anybody could do the job, but for some reason I was drawn to Greg. I was watching the practice from about ten yards away from him, listening to his muttering. He knew the positions and the plays. And there was a special quality about him. I suspected there was more to him than met the eye. That was when I decided to make him team manager. So far, he hadn't disappointed me, but there was a big difference between practice and the big game. I hoped he didn't get a case of nerves at the last minute.

The rest of my day went by quickly, but we had one last "appointment" scheduled with Argie Rodriguez for ballet class — a meeting with the team and their fathers. The guys had flat out refused to take ballet at first, but they'd finally relented when told how much it helped. Then some of the dads got involved and got the team riled up again. Seems like they thought their macho sons didn't need to be involved in something that sissified.

The meeting went well. Tag told the team about his own experiences with ballet and settled everybody down so we could get on to business.

Argie was a good person and a great dance teacher. She spotted right off that the boys were uncomfortable taking ballet. So she tried to make it less "sissified."

I watched the boys as they went through the routine she'd developed for them. They were getting into the swing of things today. Maybe it was nerves because of the big game coming up. I guess I was having a bit of a nervous problem, too, because my heartburn was really kicking up.

When dance class was over, we headed to the field. It took about twenty minutes to get everybody back to the locker room and another ten or fifteen to get them suited up for practice. And another ten to get them settled down. Man, they were keyed up.

Tag met us on the field. He was grinning, tossing the football in the air and catching it. "Our Come-to-Jesus meeting at Argie's went well, don't you think?"

"Yep. They're pretty as a picture. Gonna order the boys some tutus to practice in. Whadya think about that?"

A couple of the players heard me and grumbled at my attempt at humor.

"Might ought to hold off on the tutus." Tag strode forward and tossed the ball to Greg who caught it with a toothy grin. "I reckon we got some hard practice this afternoon, Greg. You gotta be sharp, man. Big game coming up on Friday."

"Reckon you're right about that." I gave a curt nod toward the field and the guys started into their exercises with Willie Bigelow taking charge.

Willie was a born leader. Come to think of it, everybody in that family seemed like a leader. I mean, you got Mayor Ida. And of course, Governor Ham. I know calling him Governor Ham might sound a little disrespectful, but as far as governors go, he makes a good hog. I got nothing but praise for Mayor Ida. That's a good looking woman who's got a good head on her shoulders. She's a little young for me, of course, or you can bet the farm I'd give Chief Royden a run for his money.

I noticed HayDay Carlisle standing with his arms looped over the rail on the bleachers. He was talking to some men I didn't know. Wolfman Washington was there, too, along with Dan McNeil from the Fix-it Shop, Win Allen from Bubba Rice's Restaurant and Nail Delgado. And standing sort of at the back of that crowd was Willard Overbrook. I half-way expected him to start something, but he seemed content to stare a hole through me for the moment.

I glanced around and the guys were finishing up their calisthenics and starting to do wind-sprints. Greg was busy filling up the water cups for the guys and placing them on the table by the bench. It was an interesting thing to watch. The boy lined the paper cups up in perfect rows, perfectly spaced. He couldn't have done a better job if he'd chalked a line and measured the distance. He might be simple, but he certainly had gifts that needed to be explored.

"Hey, Coach. Ready to go?" Tag was looking at me as if he'd called my name a couple of times.

"Yeah. Sorry. Lost in thought, I guess." I blew my whistle to get the boys' attention. I glanced from eager face to eager face as they ran to stand in a semi-circle in front of me. These were good boys. "Big game tomorrow, men."

A few of them nodded, but others chimed in with appropriate comments. Tag was studying a playbook we'd developed back in the summer. He had a strange look on his face. "Say, Coach, we need to . . . Oh . . . I'll study this further. I may have a new slant on one of the plays."

I chuckled. Tag had gotten so involved in his study of the playbook, he hadn't realized what was going on around him. He can be tunnel-visioned sometimes. "Great. We'll look at it in a minute."

"As I was saying," I began again. "Let's

make sure we are focused on Friday night. We know the plays . . . Well, maybe with the exception of the one Coach Garner has in mind. So, let's run a few plays and see what we need to work on."

The boys disbursed and lined up on the field. Tag called a few plays that were executed flawlessly. These boys were ready. They were more than ready, and that bothered me a little. I didn't want them to get complacent.

I was watching them intently, full of pride at how they were responding to the coaching they were getting from Tag and me, when Mayor Ida strode up, looking for all the world like she was about to take on a Grizzly. "Afternoon, Mayor," I said, hoping I sounded cheerful and confident.

"Hey, Fred. Looks like the boys are working hard."

"Yes, ma'am, they are. Fine group of boys."

She sighed and watched for a few seconds. "Yes, they really are. Amos is having a little problem with a couple of them roughhousing."

"I heard about that. Who knows what they were thinking?"

Ida's face softened for a moment and she chuckled. "I'd bet everything I own that

Amos knows from personal experience. Battle had a time with him when he was a teenager."

"Well, most of them are good boys basically. We'll get through this."

"We're going to win, aren't we?" There was just a bit of anxiety in her tone, though she maintained her calm exterior.

"I wish I could give you an unequivocable 'yes.' " I shrugged and glanced at the boys on the field. "You just can't really answer that question with any degree of certainty. *Should* we win? Yes. Do I think we're *going* to win? Yes. *Will* we win? I'll tell you on Friday night after the game."

Ida chuckled. "You answered that like a true politician."

"Mercy, Miss Ida. Don't be putting notions in my head."

Ida stared down the field, watching Tag and the boys practice. "You gotta win this one, Fred. I've got a little wager going on this game — and the Bigelow game, too."

"Wager? Miss Ida, I'm surprised."

"Nothing big, Fred."

"Nothing big enough to mention to Amos. Is that what you're saying?"

She leaned over conspiratorially and winked. "Let's just keep this our secret. You know how he is."

"Yeah, I know. But somehow, I'm thinking this wouldn't bother him a whole lot."

"Just a friendly wager with the mayors of the other towns. Something to make it interesting."

"Not to mention putting a little pressure on me and the team."

"Well, they don't have to know." Ida gazed downfield. "I'm so glad Tag decided to get involved."

"Me, too. He's good with the kids."

"I hear he's a great teacher. The kids really relate to him."

I watched, too, for a few seconds. "He'll be a good daddy."

"Oh, that reminds me. I stopped by here on my way from Gooseberry Farm. The produce stand is still open. Not much left, but I brought you and Tag a few things — apples, cabbages, that kind of thing. I'll just put it in your truck."

"And Tag's car?"

"Yes, well, it's easy to get it in his car. No top." She laughed as she turned to walk back off the field.

"Thanks, Miss Ida. I appreciate that." I watched as she walked past the cluster of men watching the practice. She raised her hand in farewell and disappeared behind the bleachers.

After a good workout, Tag gathered them back on the side of the field. Greg eagerly handed out water and towels as they swooped by him, grabbed a towel and water and lined up in front of me. I was about to turn and start my "One for the Gipper" speech when it happened. Luke Sylvester "stumbled" into Greg and knocked him into the table full of water cups, then onto his butt. I knew it wasn't an accident.

"Luke!"

"Yeah, Coach?" Luke grinned an absolutely transparent grin that was a challenge if I ever saw one.

"Hit the showers, son. You're off the team for two games."

A chorus of protestations rose from the other players. Luke lost his self-satisfied look. "Aw, Coach, it was an accident. You can't bench me for an accident. No way."

"I know an accident when I see one and that was no accident." Tag reached down and helped extricate Greg from under what was left of the table. "You all right, son?"

"Yes, sir, but, Coach . . ." Greg hung his head in that way he had when somebody played a trick on him. "Coach, you can't bench Luke. He's the best receiver we got. I'm all right. Um . . . I don't think he meant to hurt me."

"There . . . You see? Even the retard knows I didn't do it on purpose." The swagger had returned to Luke's voice.

"For calling Greg 'retard', you get another week on the bench. You've just taken yourself off the team for the game against Bigelow. One more time and you're off the team for good. Am I clear about that?"

Realization started to dawn on him and his face morphed from smart-aleck to contrite . . . almost. "Coach, he's right. I'm the best —"

"Best or worst makes no difference to me. I made it clear from the beginning that everybody on this team deserves respect. Even the team manager."

Tag stood there for a moment, watching. I knew this cut way into his game plan, but I couldn't let something like this happen without consequences. "Coach is right, Luke. Hit the showers."

"Y'all will be sorry when we lose." He looked directly at me, a malevolence I'd never seen in his eyes piercing me. "You think it was bad when you first came here? Just wait until people hear what you done now."

He turned and stalked off the field. I glanced at the men standing by the fence — fathers, mostly — half-expecting them to start raising hell. Not one of them said a word.

I turned to look at the team. Their jaws hung open in astonishment. "Okay, boys. Let's reconfigure those offensive plays. We're not going to have Luke, so we need to put Tater in."

Tag took the ball immediately and began to discuss the new play he'd come up with earlier. Turns out, with that particular play, Luke's absence might not make much of a difference.

When I was sure Luke had time to clear out of the locker room, I dismissed the players. Some of them were helping build floats and would take a quick shower and then come back to stuff tissue paper into chicken wire or whatever the cheerleaders had planned.

Tag watched me carefully as I strode into my office and slammed the door. He waited until the boys were leaving before he knocked lightly.

"Come in," I called.

"Um . . . I'm getting ready to head home. You want to stop by for some supper? I don't know what Maggie has planned, but —"

I gazed at him, realizing that he was looking for an invitation to sit and discuss what had happened. I'm not sure I was ready to talk about it, but I guess I owed him some sort of explanation. "Hang on, Tag. Have a seat for a minute."

He obliged and drew up a folding chair, spinning it neatly in front of him until it faced backwards and sitting down with his hands folded over the chair back. "What's on your mind, Coach?"

"We've been friends a long time. I guess it's time we talked about this."

His brows knitted together and a serious demeanor overcame his usually cheerful smile. "Okay. So talk."

"Years ago, long before I met you . . ." I swallowed hard. This confession wasn't going to be easy and I knew it. I'd never spoken about this with anyone and had felt guilty for the past thirty-five years because of it. "Look, I hate to mess up our friendship telling you this, but it's been eating away at me for years. I need to tell somebody. I'd rather it be you than somebody else."

"So talk. I'm not somebody who's going to —"

"I know, I know." I swallowed hard again, wishing I had a drink. Something alcoholic . . . anything alcoholic. "I haven't had a drink in thirty five years."

"Congratulations. Is . . . is that it?"

"No, I wish it was as simple as that." I glanced at the ceiling fan spinning slowly above me. "Look, Tag. I'm not proud of this, God, I wish it had never happened."

"Coach, I've known you since I was eighteen years old. I've never known a more honorable man. It can't be that bad."

"Yeah. It can." Memories flooded over me, that horrible night. I squeezed my eyes shut, trying to block out the vision that swam before me. It was useless. Better tell him and get it over with. "I killed a boy."

"What?" His eyes opened wide, the horror visible in his face.

"Not literally. But my actions contributed to his death." The words began to tumble forth. "He was retarded. Cecil Atworth. He hung around the campus all the time, particularly around the practice field where we were playing. We teased him all the time. Unmercifully."

I couldn't help it. A tear slid down my cheek. I glanced at Tag. He was still there, listening attentively. That he hadn't jumped up and bolted out the door was something I considered a good sign. "I was probably one of the worst. I was cocky. I was perfect, or so I thought. Star football player. Good looking. Popular with girls. Hell, life was

129

handed to me on a platter. I was too stupid to realize it at the time. I was a bonafide smart-ass."

"Coach, look, I —"

"Let me *say* this, son. And if you're going to look for excuses for me, don't. I don't deserve it." I sucked in air and leveled a gaze at him. Tag was a good man. I was lucky to have him as a friend. "That Saturday night, we won . . . big. We were on top of the world. Had a few too many drinks after the game, celebrating with fans who wanted to buy us drinks. We beat Alabama by twenty-four points. As we left the bar, Cecil came up to me grinning his foolish grin. God, what a dopey look he had on his face. Maybe he'd had a couple of drinks, too. I don't know. I was leaving with Mimi Francis, the head cheerleader. Cecil clamored all over me, clapping me on the back and trying to hug me. I shoved him. He fell backwards into the dirt. A couple of other guys who'd come out with me were laughing and carrying on, making fun of him. When he tried to get up they shoved him back down.

"That dopey look turned into anger. He glared at us and swore to get even. He grabbed his rickety bicycle and pedaled off, heading across the street. He probably never saw the car coming. It was speeding. Cecil never had a chance."

"And that's it? Something you did when you'd had too much to drink, when you were a kid?"

"Tag, that kid is dead because of me."

"No, not really, Fred. You may have started it, but the other boys finished it. Were they football players, too?"

"No. I didn't know who they were."

Tag sighed and shook his head. "That's a tragedy. Were you charged?"

"Hell no. I was a star football player."

"Yeah, but if there had been a direct link between you and Cecil's death, you would have been charged for sure."

"Maybe."

"Look, Fred, I know you'll never be able to forget it happened, but you need to stop beating yourself up about this. It happened twenty-five years ago.

"Time doesn't alter what happened and it doesn't . . . it's never taken away the guilt." I buried my face in my hands, unable to look at Tag's earnest face any longer.

"Fred, this is about Greg, isn't it? About Luke tripping him and making fun of him. It's not about you, not anymore. I've seen what you've done over the years. I've seen the work you've put into Special Olympics.

Everything happens for a reason. That tragic accident years ago changed you. It made you a better man, a better coach."

I raised my head and stared at him, surprised that he hadn't declared he never wanted to see me again. It was almost like I wanted him to. I wanted the punishment for what I'd done. He sat straighter and crossed his arms. "Now, are you coming to dinner or not?"

"You're still inviting me? If Maggie knew, she'd —"

"She'd what? Put her arms around you and tell you to forgive yourself? That's exactly what she'd do. And Maggie's smart about things like that."

"What time?"

"Come now. We have some planning to do anyway. We can do that while she finishes supper."

I swiped at a tear that trickled down my cheek. Imagine if my boys could see their intrepid coach with tears in his eyes. I'd never be able to discipline any of them again. "All right. Let me get my stuff."

Tag went out to make sure the boys were gone and the locker room cleaned up. I followed almost immediately.

We walked out the door of the locker room and into the sunset. It was one of those beautiful moments, when the sun was sinking below the horizon and the sky blazed with colors. Somehow I felt lighter. Talking with Tag had been the right thing to do.

"Oh, Tag, Ida left some produce in your car. I meant to tell you earlier."

"I saw you talking to her. She had a hard look on her face and I thought something was wrong." He chuckled. "Just like her."

"I'll tell you about the rest of it at dinner." I turned to walk toward my truck and spotted trouble. Willard Overbrook was standing by my truck, arms crossed like he was about to bust a gut.

Tag glanced at him and then back at me. "Need some help?"

I dragged in a deep breath and shook my head. "I can handle Willard."

Tag nodded and strode away. I noticed that when he got to his fancy sports car, he reached in and pawed through the bag of produce Ida had dropped in. He was obviously delaying his departure until he could determine what was on Willard's mind.

Can't put it off any longer if I'm gonna make it to dinner, I thought, and headed toward Willard. "Hey, Willard. What can I do for you?"

He watched me approach, glanced at Tag

and then back at me. "I got something to say. A score to settle, I reckon," Willard said.

My first thought was to call for Tag, but something about Willard's face stopped me. "What would that be?"

He spat tobacco across the next parking space and then faced me again. "This ain't easy, Fred . . . er, Coach."

"What's that, Willard?" I tilted my head Tag's way. "I'm having supper with Tag and Maggie and I don't have much time."

"It won't take much time. I been meanin' to talk to you ever since you got here. Now, I'm glad I didn't."

Anybody could see the conflict on his face. He looked like a tortured man. I knew the feeling. "Sometimes, it's best just to say what you got to say and get it off your chest. Clear the air."

To put Willard more at ease, I called to Tag. "We're fine. Go on home to Maggie."

"You sure?" Tag eyed Willard dubiously.

I waved him away. "I'll be along directly."

As Tag started his engine and drove out of the school parking lot, Willard stood straighter and squeezed his eyes shut. When he opened them, they were glistening with tears. "Maybe I should come back."

I reached out and gripped his arm, trying to reassure him. "Talk to me, Willard.

What's troubling you?"

"I was at Georgia when you were there. You were the big man on campus that senior year. We won the Alabama game."

"That was a great win, all right. Tag and I were just talking about that . . . that game."

"It's what happened after the game I want to talk about."

My palms got sweaty. Had Willard overheard the conversation? "Yeah? After the game."

"Yeah. I saw you and your date leave and followed you out. I admit I was jealous. She was a looker, you were popular. You had everything, seemed like." He took out a pouch and put a pinch of tobacco in his mouth. "I saw you push that boy."

"Look, Willard, a lot of time has passed. I know I shouldn't have done it. I wasn't thinking right and I'd had too much to drink."

"I guess. But I had more to drink than you did." He squeezed his eyes shut tight for a moment and then looked directly at me. "I kicked that boy. We did. My bully buddies and me."

I was totally stunned at his revelation. "Are you kidding me? You were there? I didn't even know you were at Georgia when I was."

"Yeah. I was there. I'm not proud of what I done. Fact is, that night haunts me to this day."

"Well, it's something that's not far out of my mind either."

"But you weren't the one who hurt him so bad he jumped on his bike and tried to get away. I'm responsible for that boy getting killed that night." He looked down at his feet and I saw a tear slide down his cheek. "I was a freshman. When I realized what happened, I dropped out of school."

"Willard, we were . . . we were just kids ourselves."

"Don't make no difference. Never should have happened. I was raised better than that."

There was no disputing that. And I had no answers for him. I'd just said pretty much the same thing to Tag. "Look, Willard, let's go —"

"I know you got to go, just let me finish." He watched me a moment as if to see if I was going to run or leave anyway. "I've lived with that thirty-five years. I figure God got even with me, though. I've been paying for my actions for years now."

"Paying for it? What do you mean?"

"Greg. Greg is my grandson. I figure God wanted to teach me a lesson, so he gave me a grandson that's like that kid was. That Cecil kid."

"Greg is your grandson? He's a great kid. I made him team manager. Willard, for God's sake, he's not a punishment for something you did all those years ago!"

"Anyway, I saw and heard what you did today. I been watching to see how you treat him. I gotta say, I was expectin' you to ignore him or make fun of him."

"Make fun . . . Do you know how much time I spend with Special Olympics? I'm on the Georgia Board of Directors. I volunteer countless hours and contribute a ton of money and —"

"Yeah, I heard about that. But to be honest, that ain't got nothing to do with how you treat somebody when the spotlight's not on and the cameras ain't rollin'."

"Willard, if you've got a complaint about the way I've treated Greg, I need to hear it. I've gone out of my way to —"

"Nope. That's what I'm telling you. When I heard Tag say he'd recommended you as coach, I lost it. I started a campaign to get rid of you before they ever hired you. I guess part of it was guilt on my part or I thought you might remember me and start something. I'm here to apologize because I misjudged you."

I could only stare for a few seconds before my brain kicked in and I nodded. "Thanks, Willard, that means a lot."

"And I really appreciate what you did for Greg today." He stuck out his hand and I shook it. "But you don't really have to bench Luke. I want us to win that game. Greg wants us to win that game."

"You know, Willard, I want to win that game, too. But not at the expense of a good kid's life or even his feelings. When I told the team that Greg was a part of the team, I meant it. I won't tolerate Luke acting that way to anybody. He's benched. The team will pull through this, but a lesson needs to be taught here. Everybody has value. We're a team. Those boys might think it's cool to pick on a helpless kid. I don't, and it's stopping today."

Tears streamed down his face as he nodded. "Greg worships you. From the minute you first came, he kept telling me that you were a great coach. And when you made him team manager, well, that boy thinks you hung the moon. You got a friend for life. Two friends. Greg and me. If you'll have me."

I clasped his arm and nodded. "I'm honored to have friends like you and Greg. Thanks for telling me about this. It made both of us feel better. What we did all those years ago wasn't right, but look at the differences we've been able to make in many people's lives because of that night."

His lips curled into a smile and he wiped his eyes on his flannel shirt sleeve. "I reckon I'll see you in the mornin' at breakfast then."

"I 'spect so. I'd be pleased to share a cup of coffee with you anytime."

Willard turned, headed over to his truck and climbed in. As the engine roared to life, he stuck his hand out the window and waved. I just stood there, amazed. I felt better than I had in years. Maybe it was sharing that episode with Tag, maybe talking to Willard. But whatever it was, I smiled and jumped into my truck with a light heart. My guilt for that night would never go away, but because of two very different men, it didn't hurt so much anymore. Healing comes when we least expect it. And at times, from the strangest direction.

I popped a Tums in my mouth for that dratted heartburn and headed for Tag's house, feeling more like a Creekite than I ever thought I would. Before I got out of the parking lot, this old Creekite was humming "Glory, Glory to Georgia."

I felt like I'd come home.

PART FOUR:
THE GREAT
TIME CAPSULE CAPER

Louise & Peggy, Friday morning

The assessor's office was hidden in the far end of the basement and manned by Felicia Wren, who matched her name, small and brown, but definitely not shy.

"The dragon at the gate," Peggy whispered as we walked up to the counter.

When I asked to look at the old plans for the football stadium, she peered at me over her thick bifocals. "Why?"

I was going into confrontation mode when Peggy edged in front of me, gave Mrs. Wren her sweetest smile and said, "I'm writing a monograph for the North Georgia Historical Society on ways the old football stadium reflected Mossy Creek culture and how the fire changed things. I need a copy of the site plot, please. I'll pay for the copy."

"Indeed you will. They're way back there somewhere." Felicia pointed toward the Mammoth Cave of deed boxes and file cabinets behind her.

"May we come look and save you the trouble?" I asked.

She glared at me as though I had demanded she turn her firstborn son over to the Mongol Hordes. "Go sit. It'll take me a while."

I didn't see why. Certainly the new contractor would have needed the old plans to avoid cutting sewer or gas lines. But we sat. And sat.

A large black and white cat stalked out from between the rows and began to turn figure eights around my ankles. "I'll bet this place is mouse heaven," I whispered.

Peggy leaned over to pet the cat, which promptly tumped over on its back to have its belly scratched.

"Don't do that. It's probably flea-ridden and diseased."

"Bigelow is perfectly clean and disease free," Felicia said. She slapped a long cardboard tube on the counter and brushed a cobweb off her shoulder.

"Bigelow?"

"He's more competent than anybody else named Bigelow I've ever met. We have *no* mice."

Mossy Creek Gazette

Volume VIII, No. Three   Mossy Creek, Georgia

HOMECOMING ROBBERY ATTEMPT FOILED BY FAST-THINKING TELLER
by Jess Crane

A man walked into the Mossy Creek Savings & Loan yesterday and slid a hand-written note across the counter to veteran teller, Ann Stroud.

On the back of a deposit slip, he'd written, "this iz a stikkup. Put all yore muny in this here bag."

Trouble was, he'd written it on a Bigelow National Bank deposit slip.

"Noticing the wrong deposit slip, I studied the young man and assessed the situation," Stroud said. "That's when I told him he had the wrong bank."

According to the Bigelow County Sheriff Harlan Bigelow, the alleged robber had first gone to Bigelow National Bank. While standing in line waiting to give his note to the teller, he began to worry that someone may have seen him write the note and might call the police before he could reach the teller.

So, the criminal left Bigelow National Bank and drove into Mossy Creek. After waiting in line for several minutes at the Savings & Loan, he handed his note to Stroud. After reading it, the teller determined that this robber was perhaps "a few sandwiches short of a picnic."

She told him that because his note was written on a Bigelow Bank deposit slip, she could not honor his demand. He would either have to fill out a Mossy Creek Savings & Loan withdrawal slip or go back to Bigelow National Bank.

Feeling defeated, the man said he understood and left.

Stroud promptly called the Mossy Creek Police, but the criminal made it out of town before he could be apprehended. MCPD alerted the Bigelow Sheriff's Dept. who arrested the man a few minutes later — still waiting in line at the Bigelow National Bank.

Stroud was given a raise on the spot. "I'm going to donate my raise to the new Mossy Creek High School Stadium," she said.

EVERYBODY KNOWS

You can never go home again.
But the truth is you can never leave
home, so it's all right.
— Maya Angelou

Jayne Reynolds, Wednesday
"Where Win?"

I heard the plaintive question at the same time a small hand tugged on my apron. Glancing down, I had to suppress a smile at the sight of my three-year-old son standing arms akimbo, his lower lip stuck out in a petulant rant. Or as close to a rant as Matt ever got, knock on wood.

Oh, don't get me wrong. He could throw a tantrum with the best of children. But he wasn't whiny or mean or manipulative. Usually just tired.

As Matt's question sunk in, I checked my watch. Six-thirty. Only a half-hour until the Naked Bean's closing time. But an hour past the time when Win said he'd come by to take Matt and Glinda to play in the park.

"I don't know, Matt," I said honestly. "It's not like him to be late."

Win Allen and I had been dating steadily since The Great Mouse Hunt, as we'd come to call it. We fell into place in each other's lives as naturally and easily as I'd fallen in love with Glinda, the dog Win had found to squelch the mouse population that had exploded when Dan McNeil's crew had opened up a wall to consolidate the Naked Bean and Beechum's Bakery.

"Yip!"

Think of the Devil.

I glanced over to Matt and Glinda's play area in a corner near the new opening connecting the former bakery and the Naked Bean.

A tiny ragamuffin of a dog, coarse reddish-blonde hair sticking out in all directions, sticky-up Yoda ears, waited indignantly on the mat she and Matt shared in playtime. Fearing Health Dept. retribution, I insisted she be as far away from the food as possible, and she was very good about staying put. However, when Matt left her there, she was not shy about voicing her displeasure.

How come he gets to go over there and I don't?

I shook my head and smiled. I'd been a dyed-in-the-wool cat person all my life, yet here I was, communicating psychically with a dog.

"He pwomised to push me on the swing," Matt complained.

"I'm sorry, sweetheart, I was laughing at Glinda, not you." I reached down and picked him up. "I'm sure Win can't help being late. You remember what week it is, don't you?"

"Homecoming." He said it in a parroty, sing-song tone. At three, "Homecoming" didn't mean much except it was keeping "his" Win away from him.

"That's right," I said. "And since Win is President of the Town Council, he has a lot to do this week. Remember him telling us that on Sunday?"

Matt nodded, but his lower lip did not un-pout.

"I'm sure he'd be here if he could," I said, but as I glanced out the window and saw darkness creeping in, I felt concern creeping in, as well. If Win were going to be even five minutes late, he'd call.

"He's okay."

I turned to find Ingrid Beechum covering a tray of leftover oatmeal chocolate chip cookies. Since Betty Halfacre had baked

146

them earlier in the afternoon, they'd be okay to sell tomorrow morning. After noon, they'd go into the "3-for-1" sale tray. I was not surprised that Ingrid had overheard my conversation with Matt. She possessed bat ears and could hear any conversation she wanted to within 50 feet. "How do you know? Did you hear something?"

She shrugged. "No, but as you said, it's Homecoming week. Even though the official festivities don't start until tomorrow, I'm sure he's busy putting out fires. This is Mossy Creek, after all."

I'd lived here long enough to get her meaning. One thing Mossy Creek had never been accused of was being boring. Too many eccentric Creekites running around. A few of them probably shouldn't be left without supervision, but we Southerners can't bear to lock up our beloved crazies.

"Do not worry, Miss Jayne," Betty said from the other side of Ingrid. "He still loves you."

Shock rendered me immobile. Betty had worked at Beechum's Bakery — as Ingrid put it — "for donkey's years." A half-blooded Cherokee, Betty possessed the legendary Native American reticence. On an average day, I rarely heard her speak more than half a dozen words — all of

which were work related. "Need sugar."
"Cake fell." That kind of thing. For her to
voice an opinion with such conviction was
totally unprecedented.

"Oh, close your mouth," Ingrid said as
the bell on the door jingled, signaling a
customer coming or going. "You and Win
have been dating nearly six months. This
can't be a surprise."

I guess my jaw had actually dropped, and
I obediently shut it. "It's just that . . ."

"Just what?" Josie McClure had entered
just in time to hear. "Ingrid, don't put those
Macadamia Nut Brownies away yet. Daddy
asked me to bring him half a dozen."

"Nothing," I said quickly. "Matt, look
who's here!"

"And no, I'm not going to eat even one,"
she added defensively, placing a hand on
her round belly. "Doc Champion told me
I'd gained another three pounds."

"Josie!" Matt raced around the counter.

Josie's cousin, young Monica Mitchell,
had come in with her. She carried a long,
black bag carefully folded over one arm and
swung it away from my son's charging path.

Despite a seven month baby bulge, Josie
lifted Matt into the air, then hugged him
close.

I handed a sugar cookie across to Monica

and Josie, hoping to distract them from the conversation they'd overheard. A true Creekite, Josie thrived on town gossip. Not that she passed around anything mean-spirited. Still, she could tell a tale.

Josie broke her cookie in two and handed half to Matt.

"What do you have there?" I asked Monica.

"It's my formal for the dance on Saturday night."

"Especially . . ." Josie paused for effect, "for her Homecoming Queen dance with King William Bigelow."

Monica blushed. "I'm not Homecoming Queen yet. And Willie isn't King yet."

"But he will be," Josie said firmly. "And you'll be his Queen."

"Just imagine," Ingrid said. "A Mossy Creek Homecoming King named Bigelow. I never thought I'd see the day."

Josie nodded. "It just doesn't seem right, does it?"

Intellectually, I understood the Mossy Creek hatred of all things "Bigelow." The feud had started well over a century ago when the Georgia Northeastern Railroad chose Bigelow over Mossy Creek and subsequently, Bigelow became the county seat. Over the years, the feud had been fueled by star-crossed lovers, high school fires, rampaging elephants and just plain cussedness.

But even though I understood it, I didn't have the emotional connection to the fight that homegrown Creekites had.

"Willie is not a Bigelow," Monica said hotly. "I mean, his name is, but he loves Mossy Creek as much as his mother. That's why he chose to play his senior year for Mossy Creek instead of Bigelow."

Her vehemence surprised me, but I also saw bleakness in her eyes. I glanced at Josie, who gave me a tiny, comprehending nod. So, Monica was in love with Willie Bigelow, the star of the Mossy Creek High School football team and most popular boy in school, but he wasn't in love with her.

I studied Monica from a fresh perspective. To me, she'd always been Josie's little cousin. Having been raised mostly by Josie's parents, Monica had been pushed along the same Beauty Queen runways as Josie had been, but with more success. Now I realized why. She was lovely, with the same thick, chestnut hair as Josie, but with much more regular features.

Josie was my best friend and I loved her dearly, but nothing about her face warranted all the beauty contests LuLynn had pushed her into. Monica, on the other hand, had a classic, unspoiled beauty that would take her far. Certainly far enough to win the notice of Willie Bigelow.

"I hear he's a fine young man," I said. "But there are several other fine young men who could be crowned King. Don't count them out."

Monica smiled wanly. "But Willie will probably win. He's the captain of the football team, and the most popular guy in school."

"He's a really good football player, too, I hear," Ingrid said. "Does he have any interest in Georgia?"

Monica nodded. "They're top of his list."

"I approve," I told her. "Both my husband and I were Dawgs, and I remain a Bulldog fan to this day."

"Me, too." Ingrid set the bag with John McClure's brownies on the counter for Josie to pick up when she was ready to leave.

"Why, Ingrid, I never knew you went to the University of Georgia." I didn't know that she'd gone to college of any kind.

"Yep. Home Ec. major. How did you think I became such a good baker?"

I shrugged. "Didn't know. I guess I assumed you went to a baking school, or learned on the job. Betty, did you go to the University, too?"

"No'm," Betty replied, nodding a Ingrid. "Ingrid taught me."

"Well, I'll be. Ingrid, you constantly amaze me."

"As well I should." Ingrid winked at Monica. "So, Monica, are you gonna show us that dress, or is it a state secret?"

Waiting to be asked, Monica unzipped the dress bag then looked around for a place to hang it.

"Over there on the door jamb," I said, lifting Matt, who'd come back around the counter.

As Monica carefully settled the fancy hanger on the trim of the opening that had joined Beechum's Bakery and the Naked Bean, I exchanged smiles with Josie.

"We went to Atlanta today to pick up her gown," Josie explained. "It had to be altered. Mama insisted that Monica have a dress that no one around here has seen."

Monica slid her hand into the bag and drew out the shimmering, silky folds of a strapless goddess gown. It was a deep green with gold trim.

"It's the school colors," she said unnecessarily. It being the first Homecoming in twenty years, the town was draped in green and gold.

It was a lovely gown and we all ooohhhed

and aaaahhhed with the proper amount of enthusiasm. Even Matt was entranced by the beautiful dress.

Glinda, too. Before I'd noticed, she moved next to me to gaze up at the gown as if she beheld a fairy princess. She was so cute, I reached down and patted her head, then sent her and Matt back to their play area.

"So . . ." Josie pulled me a little aside. "What did Ingrid not consider a surprise?"

I barely contained a groan. I thought we were long past that conversation. Ever since Josie got pregnant, though, she was even more protective of her friends and family. "It's nothing. Just something Betty said."

"Betty spoke?" Josie exclaimed. "That's remarkable in itself."

"Tell me about it." I said as I rolled my eyes and headed back behind the counter. We had a lot of work to do tonight.

"Why is she still here, anyway? Isn't she usually gone by now?"

I nodded. "She leaves after the baking's done, usually midafternoon. But tonight we're making what we're taking to the bake sale tomorrow. We'll be here late."

"Do you need me to take Matt for awhile?"

"I don't know. Win was supposed to have been here over an hour ago, but I haven't heard from him."

"We saw his car over at the dance studio on the way in."

"The dance studio?!"

She nodded. "There were a bunch of cars there. Mac Campbell's. Amos's squad car. And a lot of . . . you know, now that I think about it, they were cars owned by fathers of the football team."

"The football team? At the dance studio? What in the world?"

"I'm sure you'll get the story when Win gets home," Josie said. "Now back to what Betty said. What was it? She's Native American, you know. Many of them have a strong connection to the cosmos."

I felt like rolling my eyes again, but I knew better. Josie got a little kooky sometimes with all her feng shui and astrology, but she was right about so many things.

"Betty told Jayne not to worry that Win has been so distracted this week, that he still loves her," Ingrid said as she passed by.

I nearly groaned, but Josie seemed deflated.

"Oh, is that all?" she said. "Everybody knows that."

"Everybody —" I choked. "How could everybody know that when neither Win nor I have mentioned the word? Not even once!"

"What?" Josie and Ingrid echoed.

It was my turn for an eye-roll. "You heard me. Neither one of us has said . . . those words."

"But it's so obvious to everyone who sees you together," Josie insisted.

"Even I know it," Monica said, turning from her concentration on getting the gown back into the hanging bag just right.

"So do I," called Judge Campbell.

"So do I," called Yvonne Clay and her mother, Myra.

The three were the only customers still in the shop.

"We all just assumed that *y'all* knew," Ingrid said. "Well, you all can just un-assume," I announced to everyone. I felt trapped and wanted to lash out at someone, but apparently I'd have to strangle the entire town. "The man doesn't even call when he's going to be late, for Pete's sake. How can you possibly say that he —"

The bell on the door sang across the room and as if he'd heard us talking about him, Win blew into the shop on a blast of cool October air. "Hey! Sorry I'm —"

He stopped short as he realized that everyone in the shop was staring at him. His gaze darted around to everyone, several times. "What's going on?"

"Nothing," I said brightly. "Absolutely nothing."

I passed a murderous gaze around the room. One by one, they all caved, clearing their throats and looking away. Josie helped Monica gather her dress bag, then shuffled her out the door, throwing a "Call me!" over her shoulder.

"Win!" Matt launched himself at the man who'd become a virtual father. Why hadn't I noticed?

Win caught Matt and lifted him for a hug. "Hey, buddy! Sorry we missed the park, but have I got a story to tell you!"

"What?" Matt demanded.

"I'll tell you while I whip us up something to eat." He placed Matt back on the floor, took a moment to pet Glinda, who'd been dancing around his feet, then came over to give me a kiss, as was his habit every time we were apart.

Feeling everyone's gaze on us, I gave him my cheek.

He kissed it, then pulled back with a brow raised and a look that said we'd discuss it later. "You want something to eat?"

I shook my head. "We'll be awhile. I'm going to order a pizza for Betty, Ingrid and me."

He nodded. "Matt and I are going to have

156

grilled cheese and tomato soup."

"Yay!" Matt cried.

Feeling the excitement, Glinda yipped and wagged her tail furiously.

Win led them both through the door that led to my newly renovated upstairs apartment.

Though the fare sounded mundane, I knew that "grilled cheese and tomato soup" to Win meant smoked Gruyere on Artisan bread and soup made from fresh tomatoes. All the ingredients were upstairs. He'd brought them over last night. He often cooked for Matt and me in my new kitchen, which Dan McNeil had completed two months ago. We just as often ate at Win's house. All four of us. As if we were a family.

Judge Campbell and the Clay ladies left very quickly after that.

"Are you nuts?" Ingrid asked when I came back from locking the door and dimming the lights in the dining area. She stood behind the counter, chopping pecans we would use later that night in one treat or another.

I glanced pointedly at the marble counter. "So you could chop me up, too? What kind of nut do you think I am? Pecan? Peanut? Macadamia?"

She waved her chef's knife at me. "A crazy

nut. Maybe I *should* chop you up. It might bleed the stupid out of you."

"Gee, thanks. I think the world of you, too."

My sarcasm left her undaunted. "You know I love you, but if you can't see what's right in front of you . . ."

"What?" I asked when she didn't finish, to see if she would back down.

I should've known better. "Well, then you might just lose him."

"Why? Because I want to take it slow? He obviously wants to take it slow, too. He hasn't said anything about his feelings, either. Much less mentioned *love.*"

The truth was, we haven't had time. Between our jobs, my renovations and Win's successful campaign for President of the Mossy Creek Town Council, we'd only had time for five one-on-one dates. Our together times had mostly consisted of attending some town function, grabbing a bite to eat, then putting Matt to bed. Unless we'd left him with Ingrid, which happened as often as not.

"We haven't even . . ." I couldn't finish.

"I know." Ingrid said. "Who would know if not me?"

I felt as if I had to explain. It seemed odd for a couple who has been dating for almost six months not to have been intimate. "At first, we hadn't wanted to give Dwight a reason to question Win's morals. We were under such a microscope."

Ingrid nodded in complete understanding. "What couple in Mossy Creek isn't? But a candidate for President of the Town Council, well . . . Believe me, I understand."

"And since the election . . ."

"It's okay, you know," Ingrid said softly. "In fact, I applaud you both for waiting. In my day, people didn't sleep together until they were married."

"Matthew and I did, but only a few weeks before."

"It's okay, either way," Ingrid said. "I will love you no matter what. But . . . you *are* in love with him, aren't you? It really does seem as obvious as the noses on your faces. *Both* your faces."

"I . . . I . . ."

"Okay, then answer this — can you definitively say that you aren't?"

I thought about that for a really long moment. So long, she went back to chopping. Just as she poured another batch of nuts onto the marble slab, I answered softly, "No, I can't."

PART FIVE:
THE GREAT
TIME CAPSULE CAPER

Louise & Peggy, Friday afternoon

Two hours and a lunch later, we took our rolled-up copy of the yellowed plot with us and drove to the site of the football stadium.

"What on earth?" I said. I had expected bulldozers and bush hogs and such, with their attendant remoras of pickup trucks. The equipment was there, but not in use at the moment. Instead, there must have been twenty cars in the overgrown lot, some of which I recognized. They were *not* contractors.

We parked beside a beige SUV. The tailgate was up and a man was standing beside it holding a shovel. Dwight Truman, our recently displaced Council President and not one of my favorite people.

"What is all this?" Peggy said.

"We're here to give you a hand," he said with that smarmy smile that I found so irritating. "Can't have you pretty ladies digging up half of Mossy Creek looking for that capsule, now can we? You leave it to us men." He pulled on a pair of pristine gardening gloves and walked toward the newly cleared field.

"What capsule, Dwight?" I called after him.

He waved a monitory finger at me. The gesture was even more irritating than the smile. "Can't keep something like that a secret. Y'all go have you a Co-Cola and come back. Bet we'll have it all cleaned up and waitin' for you."

"So much for nobody knowing it's missing," I said.

Peggy dragged me away before I could do something regrettable about that finger.

"Bet he thinks there's something nasty about him in that box," I said, the moment we were out of earshot.

"What? Evidence he cooked the books on the Homecoming decorations?"

"Why not?" I glanced over my shoulder. "If he does find it, what odds do you give he'll open it and commit all the secrets to memory to use in the next election?"

"Not with all those other people watching, he won't."

Since we were obviously not needed in the digging department, we unrolled the old stadium plot on the hood of my SUV, weighted it open with Diet Coke cans and started looking for 'x marks the spot.' So far as we could tell, there wasn't one. "Surely somebody marked the location where they buried the thing," Peggy said.

"They buried it after the fire, remember," I answered. "Everybody who could fight the fire had fought it, so they must have been worn slap-dab to a frazzle. Who knows where Amos and his friends buried the thing. They probably drove their pickup truck as far into the stadium area as they could get, dug a hole any ole where, dumped it in and drove away. They may have planned to come back the next day, but with the fire, nobody bothered. Besides, things look different at night. And they sure as heck look different twenty years later."

"How big is this box anyway?" Peggy asked.

"Bigger than a bread box at any rate. But digging even a yard away from it wouldn't necessarily uncover it."

"Maybe it rusted away to nothing."

"Nope. That I do remember. Big deal was made about how it was stainless steel lined with lead to preserve everything perfectly. Probably weighed close to a hundred pounds."

"This is a waste of time. We need to talk to whoever actually headed up the team that buried it."

Mossy Creek Gazette

Volume VIII, No. Four   Mossy Creek, Georgia

HAVE YOU SEEN THIS COW?
by Katie Bell

Homecoming festivities have been interrupted by a bovine emergency.

Eddie Brady filed a "missing cow" report at the Police Station yesterday, stating that his best milker, Matilda, ran through a hole in the fence caused by last week's storm.

The photo below is Matilda. If you've seen her in the past few days, please contact Eddie or the MCPD.

Matilda was last seen crossing South Bigelow Road by a very surprised Judge Campbell, who was returning from a law seminar in Atlanta. "She just darted out of the woods rightin front of me. It was, oh, about six-thirty. She paused for an instant, as if assessing my level of danger, then scooted into the woods on the other side. If I'd known she was a runaway, I'd've called Eddie and Amos."

Until Matilda has been located, Police

Matilda, favorite cow at Brady Farm, is missing.

Chief Amos Royden asks drivers to take it down to 35 miles per hour for the first few miles south of town.

In the meantime, Eddie is setting up a hayrack on the south leg of Mossy Creek. The pen will not only be stocked with hay, but with John McClure's prize bull named after singer Waylon Jennings.

"Don't know if we'll catch her," McClure said. "When a cow gets away, she can get onery *and* smart. But ol' Waylon here's gonna give it the ol' bullish try!"

Hunters are urged to look before they shoot!

BAKE SALE BLITZ

The reason women don't play football is because eleven of them would never wear the same outfit in public.
— Phyllis Diller

Lucy Belle Gilreath, Thursday
"No, no. More like this," Inez said. My wizened grandmother stretched out her arm, leading with the heel of one arthritic hand, and cradled her oxygen bottle in the other, pigskin-style. She was striking the Heisman trophy pose for the benefit of young John Wesley McCready, just turned ten years old and football-crazy.

If there was a more unlikely Heisman contender than my pulmonary-challenged, five-foot-tall grandmother, I couldn't imagine him or her. John Wesley, on the other hand, had potential as a future player. The stocky little guy was beside himself with excitement over the Homecoming game against Harrington Academy.

"Are you and your Grandma Inez going to the game, Miss Lucy Belle?" he asked me.

"We sure are," I said. "We're going to get there extra early so we can sit on the 50-yard line."

Mossy Creek hasn't had a Homecoming Game in over twenty years — mostly because we haven't had a high school since that fateful fire way back then. Even though I'd been a graduate of Bigelow High School, it was because I had no choice. Mossy Creek High School didn't exist back then. So I was really looking forward to this game. The bake sale was part of Homecoming Week. Since it was to benefit the high school Booster Club, hopefully it would be a fun and profitable part of it.

The weather was crisp and clear here on the town square, which was decorated with the school colors and all the other fiery hues of autumn in the South. The leaves in the old oaks were a blazing crimson and gold, and orange pumpkins were stacked high beside crates of red, ripe apples.

The smells of the bake sale were enough to make your mouth water. Fresh cakes and pies, plus all manner of confections — especially fall treats like candied and caramel apples — vied for buyers with savory standbys like boiled peanuts and crispy pork rinds.

Somebody's boom box played the Mossy Creek High School band's rendition of the beloved fight song, and you could hear old friends greeting each other over the squeals of little kids in the ring toss booth and the laughter of older children trying to dunk their favorite teacher in the dunk tank.

John Wesley had begun the afternoon helping his mother set up the booth for the Mount Gilead Methodist Church. After awhile, his mama worried that his non-stop questions were fraying the nerves of the other members of the ladies' auxiliary, so she told him to take a walk. John Wesley, you see, is blessed with an inquisitive nature and the gift of gab. I considered him a kindred spirit and wasn't in the least troubled by his philosophical queries.

So after he was banished by the Methodists, he volunteered his services to me and Grandma Inez. As he stacked the jars of chow-chow into smart pyramids, he shared his gridiron goals and asked us our thoughts on the game and favorite players.

"Herschel Walker," Grandma intoned dramatically. "Now there was a star. He had class. Never celebrated in the end zone; just handed the ball back to the ref when he scored a touchdown. And he won the Heisman for the Georgia Bulldogs in 1982. Now you try that Heisman pose."

John Wesley tucked his football under one arm and lunged forward, mimicking the famous collegiate trophy stance. Inez and I applauded our approval.

"Why do they call Harrington Academy a prep school?" John Wesley wanted to know.

"Because that's where they prepare you to be a snob," Inez said.

Inez was particularly sensitive to snobbery. She reserved her most venomous populist ire for folks she considered uppity and — as she termed it — "forgot where they came from." People like her arch-nemesis, Ardaleen Bigelow. She and her cousin Ardaleen had been engaging in games of one-upmanship for as far back as anybody can remember.

The last two anti-Ardaleen stunts she'd enlisted me in had almost landed me in the pokey, so I'd vowed to keep my nose clean in the future. I was getting a little long in the tooth to let my grandma talk me into illegal plots, although the siren song of her schemes was hard to resist.

"I'm playing in the Rotarian league," John Wesley said proudly.

I opened a box of fried pies for the youngster to arrange on the linen-draped table I'd covered with butcher paper. "Offense or defense?"

"Defense. I love to hit!"

"I'll bet you do," I said as I caught him eyeing the baked goods. "Here, arrange these pies across the front. And pick one out for yourself. A growing defenseman has to keep his strength up."

Inez put her oxygen bottle back into the harness which she wore around her neck like a metal papoose. Decades of smoking unfiltered Camels will do that to you. She was still pretty spry all-in-all. In fact she was so busy cooking and filling orders for our chow-chow business, she'd lost enough weight to get around a lot better than she used to.

"John Wesley, try one of those pies with the scalloped edges and tell me what you think," Inez said.

After a moment's deliberation he picked the biggest one and took a bite. "Chocolate!"

"That's her specialty," I said. "Grandma makes a paste out of cocoa, sugar and butter and uses that in the pies instead of the usual fruit filling. She heaps it onto the rolled-out pastry, folds it over, seals the edges and fries it up real crisp."

"It's great, Miss Inez," John Wesley said. "Whatever you're charging for 'em ain't enough."

"Why thank you, young man," Grandma said proudly. "I won the bake-off at the county fair a few weeks ago with that recipe."

"She beat out her cousin Ardaleen again," I said.

"The governor's mom?" John Wesley asked between bites.

"The very same," Grandma said, a competitive gleam in her eye.

"She's on quite a winning streak, especially where Ardaleen is concerned," I said. "And you can bet that cousin of hers is going to pull out all the stops next year." The two of them were cut out of the same ornery, competitive cloth, but I wasn't going to say that out loud. Not around Grandma.

"I've got to be ready," Inez said seriously. "I'm going to be doing some talent scouting here at the bake sale."

"What does that mean?" John Wesley asked.

"It means she's going to be tasting all the samples she can get her hands on for ideas on a new baked item or a pickle or preserve for next fall's entry," I said.

John Wesley looked troubled. "You mean Miss Inez is going to steal someone's else's recipe?"

"Oh, no, child," Inez said. "I'm just looking for what you might call . . . inspiration. And scoping out the competition. There's a lot of good cooks in this county. Most are better than Ardaleen, and several are almost as good as me. Why, I'm convinced Ardaleen's maid Ruthie does most of the work behind her entries anyway."

"Grandma doesn't believe in false modesty. Or false anything else for that matter," I said to John Wesley.

"Just keeping it real," Inez said with a shrug.

I sometimes thought it was Grandma's ongoing feud with her cousin that kept her alive and kicking. Some elderly people live for their grandchildren, their hobbies, or whatever else they held dear. Inez, in her mid-80s now, lived to kick butt, pure and simple. She was as contrary as a mule and would argue with a sign post. But she was also a hell of a lot of fun. Even though the fair had only been over for a couple of weeks, she was thinking toward next year. That's what you call focus.

She'd already been sniffing and tasting

around the other booths as they were being set up. Samples of pickles, preserves and baked goods would be given out right and left and she'd make sure she tried them all. Right now she was peering down the walkway, eyeing a table being set up about five booths down from us. She wore her customary pull-on stretch jeans and the vintage Mossy Creek High School hoodie sweatshirt she got out whenever the weather got nippy. "Hog-killing time," she called it.

"I think I'm going to mosey on down yonder," she said. "I heard someone say that Clementine Carlisle's apple butter may be good enough to ease my chow-chow out of contention in the condiment competition at next year's fair. I've got to scope it out, see if I can find out any secret ingredients. It's starting to get crowded in here, anyways. I'm going to keep things on the down low."

"The low down," I corrected with a sigh. My aged, lily-white and Lilliputian grandmother had developed a fondness for hiphop slang, and it just doesn't get any funnier than that. Unless it's her notion that she could sneak up on anyone unnoticed. Even though she was short, she was built like a bowling ball and came on just as strong. In the interest of skulking around incognito, she pulled the hood of her sweatshirt over her head right down to her black and birdlike little eyes, pulled the drawstring really tight and tied it in a bow.

Off she went, her cherubic face tightly cinched up in green fleece with her breathing tube strapped across her nose, her oxygen bottle slung over her shoulder. She could use the same clever disguise at Halloween in two weeks and call herself a maniacal Martian munchkin. As she disappeared into the gathering crowd, John Wesley and I just looked at each other and shook our heads.

"I'm glad you're interested in football," I said. "But what about academics, John Wesley? Are you still doing well in school?"

"Sure am. I've got straight A's so far. I have to write a paper for social studies about our Southern culture, so I've decided to write it on Homecoming."

"Good choice. Homecoming is about as Southern an event as there is — besides rattlesnake roundups, Brunswick stew cook-offs and tent revivals. What are you going to say on the subject of Homecoming?" I asked.

"I haven't decided," he said. "I thought maybe I'd interview other folks about what they thought and then use it in the paper. It's due on Monday. So what does Homecoming mean to you, Miss Lucy Belle?"

I closed my eyes for a moment and took a deep breath of the fresh autumn air. They say that your sense of smell triggers memories better than any of your other senses. Sure enough, aromas of the boiled peanuts, cotton candy and freshly-popped popcorn on sale nearby brought back memories of Homecomings past. The town square was decorated with bundles of Indian cornstalks tied up with twine and bales of hay strewn with autumn leaves. Pots of gold chrysanthemums were on sale everywhere.

"First off, Homecoming comes at my favorite time of year," I said. "I love the fall when the air gets nippy and it's time to get out your soft, comfy sweaters and boots. The mountains hereabouts are so pretty with all the changing leaves. You can go on hikes and bike rides without getting all hot and sweaty and then drink hot chocolate with friends in front of a roaring fire."

"I love fall, too," John Wesley said. "Besides football, I think I love the candy apples best. And popcorn balls all sticky with butter and corn syrup."

"And then there are all the events. Homecoming brings all the pageantry of high school football, the parade with the marching band, the floats, the cheerleaders, everything. But the best part is getting together with old friends who've come back into town for Homecoming, roasting hotdogs and marshmallows over bonfires after dark, laughing about old times when we were young and full of promise."

"I like all that stuff, too," offered the youngster. "I guess I don't understand why people leave Mossy Creek to begin with. So they can do the coming home part of Homecoming?"

I reached out and ruffled his hair. John Wesley was a firm believer in the town motto, "Ain't goin' nowhere and don't want to."

"Sometimes people have to move away to find the kind of jobs they want," I said. "I did that for many years. But wherever you go, it's hard not to leave your heart right here in Mossy Creek."

"Oh, I remember. You were a computer programmer."

"That's right. But when Grandma's and my chow-chow business took off, I quit that programming job and moved back to Mossy Creek where I belong."

"I'm never going to leave," John Wesley assured me. "If my friends like Little Ida or Timmy or Clay decide to move away when they grow up, I'll be here to welcome them back for Homecoming."

"Good for you, pal," I said.

"Psst!" I heard Inez hiss from somewhere over my right shoulder.

I turned around to see her waddling along as fast as she could, holding aloft a mason jar, a woman and a girl in tow.

"That's my friend, Melissa," announced John Wesley, indicating the little redhead.

I recognized the girl and her mother. Melissa Henderson and her mother, Maria. Their family were migrant farm workers who'd come through town last year and wound up working for Hope Stanton at the Sweet Home Apple Orchards in Bailey Mill.

When they reached us, Grandma looked left and right before seizing my elbow and thrusting the Mason jar into my hand. "You've got to taste this," she said in a conspiratorial whisper.

"Is it Clementine's apple butter?" I asked. Then I peered through the greenish-blue glass of the jar and knew better. Whatever it was, it wasn't apple butter. The murky, red contents looked like some of the more unsavory specimens my old high school biology teacher kept on the shelves of the lab when I was in school. In particular, it looked like the specimen Eddie Brady had given her after one of his hunting trips. The label, hand-lettered on a strip of adhesive tape stuck onto a mayonnaise jar, had read simply: "squirrel innards."

"Go ahead," Inez urged. "Taste it."

"Uuuuh," I heard myself moan. I managed a smile for Mrs. Henderson, who grinned up at me with sweet expectation. Gingerly I unscrewed the cap and saw to my relief that the jar held a crispy-looking stack of spiced apple rings afloat in a tantalizingly aromatic red sauce swimming with cloves. I snagged the piece on top with my forefinger and thumb and took a bite. My taste buds came alive with delight. "This is wonderful."

"That recipe is off tha hook, yo," Grandma insisted, poking her finger toward the jar.

I took a sniff of the contents. "I see the cloves, but I can't rightly tell what that other sweet-hot flavor is coming from. What else am I tasting? Cayenne and sugar? Ginger and honey?" I held out the jar for John Wesley to sample a ring.

"It's a whole bunch of them red-hot candies all melted down," Mrs. Henderson said proudly. "It's my own recipe. I've been working on it for years."

"Genius!" declared Inez, who indicated the small case of jars the woman carried. "Mrs. Henderson here brought these jars to sell right out of this here box. I told her we would buy every one of them, but I've got an even better idea than that." Turning to the woman, Inez continued, "Would you be willing to sell me that recipe, too? I want to refine it a little and enter it in the county fair next year."

"That is, unless you want to enter it yourself," I put in hastily.

"Of course," Inez said, rolling her eyes as if that went without saying.

"We won't be around here by then anyway," Mrs. Henderson said with an eager and faraway look in her eye. "My husband's cousin has asked us to work with him on his new fish farm down in Pensacola, so any money you want to give me for that recipe would come in mighty handy."

John Wesley looked so stricken I thought he was about to choke on his apple ring. "You're leaving?"

"Yeah," said Melissa. "Daddy said we'd be close enough to the beach we could go swimming every weekend. Isn't that great?"

"Uh, I guess."

John Wesley would never make a decent poker player. I could see clearly the question in his eyes: *Why would anyone ever voluntarily leave Mossy Creek?*

"It was great living here," Melissa said. "I

reckon this is the longest I've ever lived anywhere in my whole entire life."

"Everybody's been so nice and kind," Mrs. Henderson said. "We'll always have fond memories of living here with y'all, won't we, girl?"

"Sure will," she agreed.

"We'll miss ya," Inez put in, rubbing her hands together. "Lucy Belle, get your checkbook out."

"Will do." I grabbed my purse from the cardboard box stashed under the table, fished out my checkbook, jotted down a brief but legally binding statement on the memo line of the top check and filled it out. I let Inez see the amount and after her nod of approval I handed the check to Mrs. Henderson.

The pretty little woman blinked her blue eyes once, twice, and finally found her voice. "Do you mean it?"

"Sure do," I assured her. "But just to make sure you understand, you're giving us the rights to sell your recipe as a product in our line if we ever decide to."

"That's mighty fine," the woman said, fanning herself with the check. "I'd be proud to see y'all sell it along 'side your chowchow. This money is going to let us set up housekeeping in style. My kids will all be able to have brand new school clothes and shoes, too."

"And books!" Melissa put in.

"All the books you want, honey," her mother assured her.

"You have my word that if our Piggly Wiggly distribution deal goes through for our whole line, we'll give you a big bonus, so you be sure and keep in touch, you hear?"

I gave Mrs. Henderson a business card with instructions to write to us when she and her family got settled in Florida, and with one last word of thanks, and a kiss on the cheek from Melissa to John Wesley, they disappeared into the crowd.

"Wow, this has been productive day already," I said. "And the sale is just now officially open. John Wesley, let's see if you're as good a salesman as you are a football player. Are you ready to help us move this chow-chow and these fried chocolate pies?

He nodded, but I could tell his heart wasn't in it. I put my arm around his shoulder. "Don't worry about your friend. When we get her address you can write to her. I'm sure her mom won't mind."

"Yeah, I guess," he said with a sigh. "I just can't understand why the Hendersons want to leave when they have such a good home right here."

"Some folks long for the open road, son," Grandma observed. "They've got what's called the wanderlust. No matter what good a home they've got, they crave to see what's just over the next hill or around the next bend in the road. It's just who they are. Do you understand?"

"I guess," he said.

"Why, I was hoeing in the field one time while my uncle Lee was plowing. He dropped the reins and said he was going to the house for a drink of water. He left the mule right there in the middle of the row, her trace chains just a' droopin'. I didn't see Lee again for seven years."

I smiled, having heard this story many times growing up.

John Wesley's eyes grew wide. "Where did he go all that time?"

"He was traveling all over the country, doing all kind of things for a living, married a woman and eventually left her. You name it, he did it."

"What made him come back when he did?"

Grandma scratched her head through the sweatshirt hood. "I don't rightly remember."

"Maybe it was Homecoming," I suggested with a wink for my young friend.

John Wesley grinned and reached into the

mason jar for another spiced apple ring. He and Inez had matching red stains around their lips and I probably did, too, but I didn't care. Those apple rings were delicious.

I was looking right at Inez when I saw her stiffen. Afraid she was fixing to have one of her spells, I said, "Grandma, are you all right?"

"Quick! Hide the rings!"

I stuffed my checkbook down beside the jars and slid the box under the tablecloth before I figured out why I was doing it. When I straightened up, I saw.

Ardaleen Bigelow was standing stock still twelve feet away from us. She was dressed in a casual but expensive pantsuit and Italian flats. Her hairdo was a retro beehive affair, a tacky off-note that clashed with her otherwise stylish ensemble. Over her shoulder she carried a voluminous designer bag out of which poked the fuzzy, bow-festooned head of her vicious little dog Pierre.

As a breed, the Shih Tzu are said to be sweet and loving animals. Pierre, on the other hand, was a tiny hellhound. I figured years of enduring the indignity of being dressed up like a sissy had turned him into five pounds of fractiousness. He backed his ears and bared his teeth the instant he recognized me.

To say I had a history with this hideous creature — the dog, not Ardaleen — would be to say that Ham Bigelow was a bad governor. That is, a vast understatement.

And Grandma Inez had a longer and more checkered history with her cousin Ardaleen that went back fifty years to an incident in which Ardaleen stole a prize-winning chow-chow recipe and the heirloom pepper pods that went with it.

The two women faced one another, squaring their feet and glaring. Passersby instinctively stepped aside as if the two elderly women were gunslingers about to draw on each other and they didn't want to be in the crossfire.

"Ardaleen," Inez drawled. "What are you doing here?"

"It's Homecoming, or haven't you heard?" her cousin sneered. Her dog pulled back its lip even farther, revealing a double row of sharp teeth.

"Oh, I know it's Homecoming. What I can't figure out is why you'd bother coming home to Mossy Creek. You've been ashamed of your roots ever since you threw in with the Bigelows."

"This is like the Hatfields and the Mc-Coys," John Wesley whispered to me. "I read about them one time."

"They're a lot like that," I agreed. "Only with more hate and less bloodshed."

"You're just jealous because you came from the poor branch of the Hamiltons. Y'all stayed stuck here in Mossy Creek while I actually made something of myself."

"Ha! It doesn't take much effort to marry into money," Grandma said. "Just a little flirtin' and a little luck."

Ardaleen gasped, and Pierre clawed at the bag with his painted toenails, itching to get out of his confines — and sink his fangs into my shin bone, no doubt.

"Why you — you ridiculous-looking little redneck, you."

"That does it, hussy! This bake sale ain't big enough for the both of us!" Grandma pulled the sweatshirt hood off the back of her head, causing her thinning white hair to stand out in all directions in a bristly, static-charged halo. I caught her by the shoulders as she started to charge the governor's mother.

"Grandma, get a'hold of yourself," I hissed in her ear. "You see that state trooper coming up behind Ardaleen yonder? He's her bodyguard, the one that almost wrestled us both to the ground when we got caught crashing that garden party to steal back the pepper pods. You are not going to get us arrested right here amongst the bundt cakes and cheese straws!"

"Let go of me." She tried to wrest herself away from my grasp, but lapsed into a coughing fit. "This ain't your fight," she wheezed.

"The hell it's not," I said. "Any fight of yours is a fight of mine. Always has been. Always will be."

"Bless you, child," Grandma said, genuinely moved. It was one of those special moments in the lives of grandmas and granddaughters.

Or it would have been, between normal grandmas and granddaughters, that was.

I made the mistake of turning Inez loose. As soon as I looked back at Ardaleen, who wore a maddening smirk of triumph, I knew I'd made a mistake. It was clear from the look on Ardaleen's face that she thought she'd gotten the last word. I knew my grandma well enough to know that she would never let that stand.

This was not going to end well. Kind of like that Bigelow Mercedes and its trunk full of fireworks that time. Or was it a Cadillac? You'd think I'd remember a thing like that inasmuch as I could have been charged with criminal destruction of property and all.

Quicker than you can say Jack Robinson, I heard Grandma yell, "John Wesley, go long! Go long!"

John Wesley took off as fast as Hershel Walker, the end zone stalker. He took a zigzag route in and out amongst the crowd of onlookers and right past Ardaleen as she dipped a celery stick in a sample jar of tomato aspic and brought it toward her lips.

Inez threw John Wesley's football in a wobbly spiral, but her aim was true. It struck Ardaleen in her beehive hard enough to spin her around and startle Pierre into a yapping frenzy. I wondered if there was any way to get dog pee out of a designer bag lining. You can think of the strangest things in a time of crisis.

As she stopped spinning, she faced us, her hairdo at right angles to itself, her face red with outrage, and her suit red with tomato sauce. The trooper, who had caught up with her by then, must've decided that she'd been shot. At least that's why I figured he knocked her completely to the ground and lay on top of her.

As Ardaleen screeched and the rather dim trooper wondered why he hadn't heard a gunshot, I took the opportunity to get Grandma out of sight. My hand shot to her cheek and jerked her by the plastic tubing that ran across her nostrils and hooked behind her ears. Her heart and mind — not to mention the rest of her elfin body — soon followed the way of her sore nose. "Ow!" she hollered. I shushed her and guided her under the table as gently and quickly as possible.

Then I made sure the long tablecloth hid her completely and stood upright again to assess the chaos. John Wesley had retrieved his ball and the last I saw of him, he'd cleared the square and was running down the sidewalk. I could see him in the distance, getting smaller and smaller as he approached the horizon. Derned if that little fella wasn't going to make a fine running back, just like old Herschel.

As soon as I could tell that Ardaleen, the trooper, and even Pierre were all unhurt, I backed into the booth space, grabbed the cash box and the half-finished jar of spiced apple rings, lifted up the table cloth and settled in beside Grandma.

We munched on the apples and — in hushed tones — brainstormed ideas for tweaking the new recipe that we just knew would make us a fortune. Then we listened quietly as Ardaleen raged and the trooper asked people in neighboring booths where the troublemakers had gone.

"Why do you think that Ardaleen came to Mossy Creek in advance of the Homecoming game?" I asked.

"Are you kidding? She's here to steal the best recipes, of course." Inez sniffed.

"Or maybe it has something to do with the time capsule. I wonder if there's something embarrassing to the Bigelows in there that she wants to try and hush up . . ."

Grandma's eyes widened as she finished my thought. ". . . or get rid of completely."

We were jarred out of our speculation when a fuzzy black nose peeked under the tablecloth and quivered with recognition.

"Uh-oh," Grandma said.

"Oh, crap," I said. I offered Pierre an apple ring, and he snapped at my fingers instead.

Grandma reached for a box of the chocolate pies.

"No!" I whispered. "You can't give a dog chocolate. It could kill him."

"But it's Pierre," Grandma hissed, "the most godawful dog in the history of, of dogdom."

"There's got to be a better way," I said.

"Yeah, I guess you're right," Grandma allowed. "I'd go a fer piece to show up Ardaleen, but even I wouldn't murder her dog no matter what a sorry specimen he is."

That's when I remembered Pierre's reaction to the pepper pods he'd gotten hold of at the ill-fated garden party. His eyes had watered and his mouth foamed. I had to dunk the poor little devil in Ardaleen's swimming pool to get him some relief. I hated to do to him what I was gonna do, but he should have remembered that I was nobody to mess with.

Pierre began to growl, so I had to act fast. It would be only a matter of moments before Ardaleen or the trooper would lift the linen and find us. With our history of mayhem where the Bigelows were concerned, it was going to be hard to keep Grandma and me out of lockup. I reached up and over the table for a jar of the chow-chow, hoping nobody saw my disembodied hand.

Why, oh why had I let John Wesley stack those jars so high? I had to raise myself on my other hand to reach one. When I grasped it, I took the top off as fast as I could, dipped in my forefinger and flung about a spoonful of chow-chow in Pierre's direction.

It landed on his nose. His growling stopped, and he looked at it, which made him go cross-eyed. The chow-chow was stern stuff, and all it took was a good whiff to set him to yelping. I don't even think he got any up his nose. I thought again about remembered aromas being best at bringing back memories. Judging from Pierre's reaction, I believe the memory of his humiliation at the garden party came back to him in a rush.

The dog disappeared out from under the cloth and took off. The sounds of his yelping, Ardaleen's screeching, and the trooper's hollering got farther and farther away until we figured it was safe to come out of hiding. By that time, everybody was going about their business as if nothing had happened.

I craned my neck to see if I could see any sign of them in any direction. I couldn't. They hadn't disappeared quite as fast as John Wesley had, but they were good and gone. "Do you think they'll be back?"

"Heck, no," Grandma said. "Ardaleen will be too embarrassed to show her face in here again. I'd say we're safe."

I had to laugh at that. Nobody, but nobody, was safe around Inez Hamilton Hilley when she was riled up, not even me I figured, when she heard what I was about to tell her. "Even though she deserved it, I hope you haven't ruined her whole Homecoming experience," I dared to say. "Everybody should have a nice Homecoming in Mossy Creek, don't you think?"

I looked down at Grandma for her reaction, half expecting to have to take off running myself. She grew thoughtful for a moment, grinned a crooked grin and actually agreed with me.

"For shizzle," she said.

PART SIX:
THE GREAT
TIME CAPSULE CAPER

Louise & Peggy, Friday afternoon

"You have to understand," John McClure said. John was captain of the Mossy Creek football team that year. "We never got to finish the game. I don't even remember which ones of us rescued the box from the gym when the school started burning. By the time we got the fire under control it was nearly morning and we were exhausted. There were still hot spots around the football field."

"Why bury it at all?" Peggy asked.

John drew himself up and glared at her as if she were responsible for the fire. "It was a symbol. It said, 'We're still here. We're doing what we planned.' Most of all, 'we'll be back.'" He leaned back into his recliner with a satisfied grin on his face. "Were, too." He took a swig of his beer. Peggy and I had stopped for lunch at the café, but it was still much too early in the day for us. Actually, I was surprised to find John at home. Maybe he was taking an extended lunch. How often he did that I had no idea.

"All this time after, I don't remember anything we put in 'cept a Rubik's cube. You remember those?" he asked.

"I never could do them," I said.

Beside me, Peggy huffed. No doubt she did them in her sleep.

"John, you must have some idea of what part of the field you buried it in."

"Far away as we could get, would be my guess. Down past the restrooms, maybe. Hard to tell in the dark."

"Men's or women's?" I asked. "Think, John. Visualize." I dragged out the plans we'd copied and spread them on his coffee table. "Anything look familiar?"

He glared at the map, then shook his head in frustration. "Shoot. I don't even remember driving home. Good thing Amos's daddy was too mixed up with the fire to check on us. Way he laid in wait for us on weekends, we knew not to drink and drive. Most of the time."

"How about the girls? Would any of them remember?" Peggy asked.

"We took them home after the fire started. Didn't even get to crown the Homecoming queen. LuLynn has never forgotten that.

She still bitches about missing her chance at glory. Wish I could be more help."

"You can help by not mentioning this to anyone, even LuLynn," I said.

"Let it stay buried. Lord only knows what's in it. Even after all these years, some of those things could bite us in the butt."

"Including you?" Peggy asked.

He shrugged. "Even LuLynn's worried. I'd rather not take a chance. Leave it. Box's probably rusted away to nothing anyway."

"One can but hope," Peggy breathed.

Mossy Creek High School Drama Dept.

Presents

Romeo *& Juliette*

a play by **William Shakespeare**

Starring
Savanna Whirley & Harley Cooper

Directed by Hermia Lavender

**Thursday
7 p.m.**

**Mossy Creek
High School
Auditorium**

**Adult: $5
Children: $2**

*The Mossy Creek
High School
Booster Club
will be taking
donations at the door
so come prepared
to give!*

*You don't want
to miss it!*

*This is <u>not</u> the
average rendition
of
Romeo & Juliette!*

MOSSY CREEK BY
ANY OTHER NAME . . .

To look backward for a while is to
refresh the eye, to restore it, and to
render it the more fit for its prime
function of looking forward.
— Margaret Fairless Barber

Hermia Lavender Belmont, Saturday
Few things move slower in a small town like
Mossy Creek than change. Molasses from a
jar, or Miss Eustene Oscar driving her old,
blue Buick down Main Street right when
you happen to be in a hurry. Paint drying,
maybe.

Consistency is a virtue with the people
of Mossy Creek. Just look at how long Ida
has been mayor or how long that silo has
been sitting empty on her property at the
edge of town, ever since Punky Hartwell
got his eye knocked out in that unfortunate
Fang and Claw club prank. Things don't
evolve much. And I suppose there's nothing

197

wrong with that.

But unlike many of the Creekites twice my age or better, I've gotten to see the world from a different angle. And not just because I went to school in Athens. No, novelty is in my blood. I thrive on it. My mama, Anna Rose Lavender, even named me Hermia after the character in *A Midsummer Nights Dream.* Drama you could call it. But what can you expect when you're the daughter of a movie star and a theater director, for heaven's sake?

I suppose even with as much as I love this old town, I've never really fit in among the Creekites the way other native sons and daughters have. That's why I wasn't surprised the day Seth Taylor walked up to my locker our Junior year of high school and asked me out on a date. See, Seth was a Bigelowan. Now, you may recall that there's an unspoken but iron-clad rule that Creekites don't associate with Bigelowans. But I couldn't help it. Even though dating Seth was forbidden, I was infatuated with him. Who knows? Maybe that was part of the attraction. At least, at first.

All of our dates, of course, were top secret. We could never be seen in public together doing something normal like going to the movies or out for ice cream. No, our dates took place in the woods. In the wide open spaces of country between Bigelow and Mossy Creek. Sometimes we'd wander far enough to see Yonder, or spend lazy afternoons on inner-tubes on Mossy Creek. But it was always secret.

Seth used to tell me he thought the feud between our towns should come to an end, that he imagined us someday introducing each other to our families and walking hand in hand down the street. It was a wonderful idea. Wonderful that he was bold and forward-thinking enough to dream such a thing.

But it wasn't meant to be.

One night Seth was on his way to meet me at Mossy Creek, where the two forks circle around and meet near South Bigelow Road. It was raining, one of those hard rains that makes you stop and stare in wonder. I was already there waiting, soaked to the bone. Thank goodness it was the middle of summer and hot enough for steam to be snaking up from the stones around the lake. And so I waited. And waited. Waited until the rain cleared and the moon hung high in the night horizon, big and white enough to light the forest in shades of silver and grey. I waited until the warmth had left the ground and dew took its place, until my teeth chattered and my stomach sank. I waited until the tears came, ushered in by the certain feeling that something was very wrong.

Funny how sometimes you just know things. There's no reason for you to, no rational logic that could lead you to believe a certain fact. And yet, sometimes there in the pit of your stomach a knot forms, and your heart has somehow learned the truth. That was how I felt that night.

The night I knew my Seth had died.

I think that's why I didn't cry at first when Seth's brother, Evan, found me soaking wet, walking down Hamilton Street in the middle of the night. I hadn't known that he knew about Seth and me, not until Evan took me in his arms and just held me. We both stood there in the pouring rain like that. Now that I think back on it, I suppose that was kind of strange. Evan had always seemed very shy. He and I had hardly ever said a word to one another. Besides a nod or a random, passing smile, it had been like he hadn't known I existed. Until that night, when everything changed.

That was the night I grew up. The night I became Juliette.

Evan turned into one of my closest friends after that. It was difficult to mourn in secret, but Evan helped me through it. A year later

I graduated from high school and left straight for Athens. They have an amazing drama program at the University of Georgia and I knew, more than anything, that I wanted to teach drama. Evan came to visit me, even attended some of the plays I was in. But I had left Mossy Creek behind me.

There's something about small towns, though, that keeps pulling you back. After four years of college, I was ready to come home. Fate, ever faithful, was in agreement that I should return. The new Mossy Creek High School needed a drama teacher. So I came home, eager to inspire young Mossy Creek Thespians.

I believe my job is my calling. I wouldn't trade it for the world.

Most of the time.

The Saturday rehearsal before Homecoming week, however, was one of the more frustrating times.

"Harley, you big hick, if you don't figure out how to land on your mark before you say that line, you're going to ruin the whole show." Savanna Whirly glared at Harley from across the stage. "How am I supposed to kiss you if you keep avoiding me?"

Harley Cooper, for all his height and bulk, looked like he wanted to cry. "I'm not ruining anything. We've only practiced this scene a couple of weeks."

"Well, we don't have forever. The Homecoming play is Thursday. That's five days from now." Savanna sneezed for the fifth time in two minutes and then held up five fingers in Harley's face as if doing so would better get her point across. "I still think someone else should play Romeo."

I placed an understanding hand on Harley's shoulder and glared my disapproval at Savanna until she looked away with a self-righteous teenage huff. "We can't be this way towards one another, y'all. A play is just like life, it goes so much smoother when we all work together."

Savanna threw her hands on her hips, looking every bit like an exasperated badger. Her nose was red from sneezing, and her face was pale. Figured the girl I cast as lead in the play would come down with a cold a week before production. Hopefully she'd be over the worst of it by Thursday. "That's what you said at the beginning of the semester. And our first play was awful. Everyone walked out."

Harley actually nodded in agreement. "Yeah, even my mom left before the third act. And my part wasn't 'til Act Four."

I took a deep breath as the other students crowded around the stage and started putting their two cents in. I'd already gotten an earful from my department head and the school principal over my last play's less than stellar reviews. Apparently just because a play was a hit in Athens, did not mean it would score points among Creekites.

Personally, I would have just chalked it up to a lesson learned. But Principal Blank wasn't quite so forgiving, considering the play was supposed to raise money for the school's big Homecoming celebration. No one in attendance had donated a cent other than the two dollar admission price — except, of course, Evan. After production expenses, the school actually lost money — forty-two dollars and sixty-one cents to be exact. Not all that much on the grand scale, but Blank said it was the principle of the thing. I was up for review, the kind that determined whether or not they'd renew my contract in the spring. This was not good.

That's why I'd decided to do *Romeo and Juliet* for Homecoming. The timeless play was always a hit.

"Look, you guys. I know we've been working hard. There's a lot riding on the success of this play for all of us. But I promise, if we can all just come together and give one-hundred percent here, I know we'll be a hit this time. The classics have always been a huge success in Mossy Creek."

The class conceded amid grumblings and mutterings of disaster. Luckily the bell rang for lunch. I needed a break. This play absolutely had to be a victory. Not only did my job depend on it, but this was the first Homecoming in twenty years for Mossy Creek High School. I wanted to contribute, and ticket sales and donations were really the only way I could.

I needed magic to happen. Mossy Creek had been preparing for the Homecoming celebration for months now, ever since we found out about the groundbreaking for the stadium. This was big. Really big. And somehow, even though classics like *A Midsummer Nights Dream, The Importance of Being Ernest* and *Romeo and Juliette* always were met with open arms among the critical masses, it felt like something new was in order, something special to commemorate the event.

I'd tried to be creative last spring, however, and as the kids so graciously reminded me, current plays were an acquired taste. So *Romeo and Juliette* it was.

But as I left the school that afternoon, I still wasn't satisfied. Not that there was time to do anything about it. The play was in four days. There wasn't time to teach the kids anything new. I would just have to keep my fingers crossed that Shakespeare would come through for me the way he had for my parents.

On the way home, I ran into Evan at the Naked Bean as I tried to relax over a cup of coffee and a slice of chocolate pie. But as Evan slipped into the booth and smiled across the table at me, I knew it was his company and not the coffee that soothed my nerves.

He had an easy way about him that I could only imagine came from being in the woods so often. He made his living as a hunting and fishing guide for tourists visiting the area. He spent more time outdoors communing with nature than anybody else I knew. The peace from living such a lifestyle seemed to just seep out of him and touch any and everyone who knew him.

"What's up, Mia?" He smiled at Jayne as she neared with a coffee pot. "You don't have that pre-performance glow I'm used to seeing a few days before opening night."

I took a sip from my cup and debated just how much I actually wanted to unload. I was used to having things under control. Luck was on my side more often than not, but this time I wasn't sure.

"Come on." He slid the plate of chocolate pie Jayne placed on the table closer to my side. "I don't see that look very often, but when I do it's a pretty good indication that I need to go in search of either tissues or chocolate or both."

I laughed. Evan could always make me laugh.

"So what is it, then?"

I sighed and took a bite of pie. "Okay, so opening night is five days away. Technically, not even five full days, since we don't have a Sunday rehearsal. I settled on *Romeo and Juliette* because I thought it would be a safe bet, but now I'm not so sure. I feel like I should have done something a little more special. I don't know, something a little more Mossy Creek."

"I see." He sat back in the booth and smoothed a hand through his dark hair. He hadn't shaved that morning, maybe in a couple of mornings for all I knew. He wore a white fishing shirt with the sleeves rolled up to his elbows. He steepled his large, tanned hands in front of his face as he looked at me with genuine consideration in his hazel eyes. Scruffy was a good look for Evan Taylor, if I did say so myself.

"So make the play about Mossy Creek."

"What?" I coughed on half-swallowed coffee. If I was a comedic actress, you'd swear it was a perfect spit-take. "No, Evan, there's no way I can assign a whole new play with only four days to rehearse. There's just no time."

"Yeah, I guess you're right." He reached across the table and swiped a forkful of pie. "It's a shame though. Creekites love hearing all about themselves."

"Spoken like a true Bigelowan." It was strange how sometimes I forgot Evan was from Bigelow. He was such a good friend, it was easy to forget the feud between our towns even existed.

"Wait a minute." I set my coffee mug on the table with a thud so loud I saw Jayne look over. "You just gave me a brilliant idea."

Evan chuckled. "That's what I'm here for." He raised his eyebrows. "What was it?"

I grabbed a pen from my purse and started jotting notes on a napkin as I spoke. "What if I turn Verona into Mossy Creek?"

He sat up in his seat, interest shining in his eyes. "You mean set the play in Mossy Creek instead of Verona?"

"Exactly!"

Evan rubbed the whiskers on his chin. "You're aware that *Romeo and Juliette* usually doesn't end well? I mean, this is not a happily-ever-after kind of play. What exactly are you trying to pull off here?"

I paused a moment in my excitement. He did have a point, but these were only minor details. "Evan, don't you see? This is my chance, a golden opportunity to show Bigelow and Mossy Creek how ridiculous the feud between them is. And it'll pay tribute to Mossy Creek. It's the perfect Homecoming play."

Evan chuckled, finished off the last bite of pie. "I suppose the Creekites won't be able to resist. The Bigelowans, either. Be sure to run an ad in both papers." He tapped the table with his fingertip. "Imagine, Bigelowans showing up at a Creekite fundraiser, especially one for the football team. You know the hullabaloo that's going on about Mossy Creek's new coach. I wouldn't be surprised if one of the more avid Bigelow football fans didn't have a contract out on the guy. Talk about job security. You'll go down in history if you pull this off."

I swung my purse strap over my shoulder and scooted from the booth. "Thanks for listening. As always, you are my muse." I popped a friendly kiss on his handsome, scruffy cheek and promised to keep him posted. I had the perfect idea. Now all I had to do was make that idea a reality.

Luckily, I had all day Sunday to figure out how.

"All right guys, everyone line up at the lip of the stage and have a seat. I've got a surprise for you today." My second period students looked at me like I had a screw loose.

Savanna sneezed and raised an eyebrow as she lounged back on the stage floor. "You do remember that the show is in three days? I mean, do we really have time for surprises right now, Miss Lavender?"

"You tell me." My father stepped out from behind the stage curtain to gasps of awe and applause from my students.

No time for a surprise, my foot.

The students stared starry-eyed at my father. They'd seen him around town often enough, but to have him there in their presence, his attention solely focused on them, was a dream come true for more than one of them.

Little Nancy Cartwright was visibly shaking with excitement and her face turned red as a ripe tomato. "Beau Belmondo!"

Dad stepped right into the scene without hesitation. "Class, I am here because Miss Lavender has had a brilliant idea for your

Homecoming play and I'm going to help you make it a hit. Can you do it?"

The students all nodded in unison, each of the girls with dreamy doe eyes, each of the boys swimming in awe mixed with envy. It was ideal. If we were going to pull this off, I was going to need complete attention and concentration from the students. The plan was going perfectly so far. I couldn't have asked for more moldable clay. If only I could drag their attention away from my father.

The students didn't even look in my direction as I gave them the second piece of good news. "I've been in touch with your teachers, and you're excused from your third and fourth period classes for the rest of the week."

It took a moment for my words to sink into the thick heads of teenagers lost in movie star fantasies. When it did, cheers broke out. Harley looked as if he might actually cry with joy.

I whistled to calm them back down. "All right, let's get to work."

Dad winked at me. "This is gonna be fun."

The next couple of hours went by in a blur of activity, bustling excitement, a barrage of questions, and only some confusion. It wasn't hard to make the kids see the similarities between Mossy Creek and Shakespeare's Verona. The feud between Mossy Creek and Bigelow was as fresh in their lives as the feud between the Montagues and Capulets. The symbolism they got. It was finding consistency in the changes that tripped everyone up.

We decided that we would sack the old Shakespearean wardrobe the drama department had been using since I was a kid in favor of the students' own clothes. We changed the last names of Romeo and Juliette to Bigelow and Hamilton. And best of all, in a moment of epic clarity, we changed the ending. Romeo and Juliette were no longer destined to die, at least not in my version. Instead, Romeo and Juliette would be successful in their scheme and be embraced with open arms by the Creekites and Bigelowans.

This was my drama class. I was making the rules now.

Of course, I had to convince Eustene Oscar of that. She had been the ringleader of the mass exodus that nailed the coffin in my last play. And true to form, here she came marching into the school theater, right after lunch, right in the middle of rehearsal. Well, she wasn't exactly marching. Her walker sort of prevented a genuine march.

Apparently, the Mossy Creek Social Society was terrified that I was corrupting the town's children with highfalutin' city notions.

"I've heard through the grapevine that you're doing something strange down here, Hermia Lavender. I never in all my years would have imagined that your sweet mother, Anna Rose, would raise such a free-thinking, hippy . . ."

The old woman's words died off as Harley and Savanna spoke lines from Shakespeare's third act of *Romeo and Juliette*. Her paper-thin eyelids blinked hard beneath translucent eyebrows. For a moment I was sure she was going to cry.

"Why, that's *Romeo and Juliette*."

"Yes, it is," I agreed.

Several moments passed before her teary gaze turned back to me. "I played Juliette the year my high school did this play." She looked back at the stage with a wistful expression. "I'm sorry I interrupted. Hopefully, this will teach these children some wholesome values."

It took every ounce of my being not to point out to Eustene that *Romeo and Juliette* was a play fraught with deceit, bloodshed, prejudice and even a love scene. Instead, I just nodded with a smile. "Yes, my father is here with me, helping to make sure the play is a success."

Miss Eustene mumbled something as she gave me what I could only assume was the Social Society's blessing and approval before turning around her walker and leaving for her Garden Club meeting.

Always respect your elders. That was one quality Anna Rose had taught me well.

I rejoined Dad on the stage and tried not to let Eustene's visit distract me from my mission. The kids certainly hadn't. They gave the rehearsal revisions their all, even suggesting new lines, and by the end of the day the play was taking on a definite Creekite flavor. Dad seemed impressed with the kid's ability to pick everything up and according to Evan, who showed up that afternoon, we were destined for certain success.

But there were still quite a few bugs in the works. The week ahead was going to be long.

Mossy Creek glistened in the moonlight as I crept barefoot to the water's edge, lulled to a strange peace with the sound of water rushing over stones slick as glass. There was something magical about crisp fall nights in Mossy Creek. Maybe it was this spot, the same where I'd waited for Seth those years ago. It was strange how time had carried away so many details of him. I couldn't quite picture his face anymore, recall his scent or the sound of his voice. But his spirit I remembered easily. His passionate ideas of good, solid, respectable living. Of peace and respect between Mossy Creek and Bigelow.

Maybe my play would help see those dreams fulfilled, be the spark that lit the fire.

I could only hope. It was clear to me now that if the play failed I would probably lose my job. The Creekites would either love or hate my rendition of *Romeo and Juliette*. And who could blame them?

But what better way to celebrate our heritage than with a message of hope? What better way to usher in a new era for our school at such an important event as Homecoming? Possibility. Renewal. Changing for the better. I was taking a tragedy and turning it into a Happily Ever After. It was perfect. At least I thought so.

The breeze tickled the trees and swept my hair about my face as I waded a step into the shockingly cold water. I stared up at the sky a moment. My mother, Anna Rose, had told me often of the fairies she believed lived here in the hollows by the creek. She said they appeared to usher in new life, new hope. I hadn't seen any fairies yet. But then, in my experience, magic came when your faith was almost spent.

I still had faith — in myself and in Mossy Creek.

Mossy Creek was bustling with activity Thursday morning as Evan walked with me to The Naked Bean to grab coffee before school. Everyone was hard at work preparing for the big Homecoming events that were to take place over the next couple of days up until, and even after the game, win or lose. Tents were already being constructed to house the bake sale, raffles and side-walk games of all kinds. Landscapers were placing pots of gold chrysanthemums and hanging school banners from light posts all around the square. The energy was high, and I couldn't help but join in the excitement.

I dug through my bag and pulled out a fresh heap of fliers advertizing the play. Evan had already spent the last two days hanging them up all around town. Tuesday I'd managed to find the time to order an ad to run in this week's edition of both the Mossy Creek and Bigelow papers. It was a gutsy move, but with any luck we'd have a good enough Creekite turn out that I wouldn't have to rely solely on my drama student's parents for success. I still hadn't gotten on all of their good sides since my last play.

"You're nervous." Evan shook his head with a sly smile. "Don't be nervous, Brown-Eyed Girl. There's too much good karma floating around your head right now for this not to be successful."

"I hope you're right."

He opened the door to the coffee shop for me. "I am."

We had a seat in a booth that looked out over the square. I couldn't recall a time in the past when the square had been so done up, other than for Christmas, of course.

A Bake Sale was scheduled for that afternoon on the square, then the play afterward.

Surely with all the excitement, Creekites and Bigelowans would be lined up out the door tonight, anxious to get in on the festive play. I'd made the ad in the papers big and bright, with red, flowing letters announcing a celebration of Creekite and Bigelowan heritage the likes none of them had ever seen before.

"Seriously, Mia. No one is going to be able to resist this." He held up one of the fliers I'd handed him. They were the same as the newspaper ad. "Get the worried look off your face and enjoy your breakfast.

You've got a long day ahead. You need your fuel." He took a bite of a doughnut.

"You're right," I said as I took a bite of coffee cake and let myself enjoy the sunshine and the aroma of coffee wafting through the coffee house. "Thank you for coming to all the practices. It was nice having you there and it gave Dad someone to talk to during down time."

"No problem." He chuckled. "I never thought I'd know Shakespeare so well. I think I could recite the play in my sleep."

Fifteen minutes later it was time to get the ball rolling. "All right, I'm off to school." I dropped some money on the table. "Dad's gonna come to class again today to try and help smooth out the kinks. It's amazing the way those kids worship him." I took one last sip of coffee before slipping out of the booth and heading toward the door. "They've never seen him first thing in the morning with sleepy eyes and bed head. Not exactly Hollywood hunk material if I do say so myself."

Evan was still laughing back at the table as I walked past Jayne on my way out the door. She gave me a wink and nodded meaningfully at Evan. I stopped abruptly and glanced back at the handsome guy finishing my breakfast.

"Evan?! No," I told Jayne, "we're just friends."

She smiled, clearly not believing me. "Sometimes that's the best start to a lasting relationship."

I shook my head and just smiled as I stepped out of the Naked Bean and off to school.

Ten hours and four cups of coffee later I was standing at the entrance of the high school auditorium watching the parking lot fill with curious Creekites, and yes, even Bigelowans.

So far so good.

But the question was there. Had they come to see the play out of celebration for Homecoming? Or had they come to see the latest disaster that was becoming my career?

I suppose it didn't really matter. The point was they were there, and all the kids and I could do was give it our best shot. It didn't matter how many times I'd performed or directed in Athens, my stomach was twisted up in knots and my hands were shaky. Granted it could have been the excess amounts of caffeine, but I was nervous, no doubt about it.

The play started right on time. The students didn't miss a beat. Each line was enunciated as if I was at a Broadway show, the Southern twang of their voices somehow adding a definitive Creekite flair to Shakespeare's prose.

The entire play went along without a hitch. The audience laughed when they were supposed to laugh, cheered when it was right to cheer, and gasped when circumstances called for it.

The sword fights were epic, each of the boys dressed in their favorite jeans and plaid shirts, their sleeves rolled up to their elbows, handkerchiefs on their heads. They fought with wooden swords as the girls cheered them on from the side, decked out in cutoff shorts and gingham tanks.

Harley and Savanna managed a believable Romeo and Juliette despite their real life disdain for one another. That is — right up until the final act.

Savanna had already drunk her potion meant to put her to sleep and was lying atop a very well-made funeral bed, looking every bit as dead as a doornail. Vacant expressions are something of a strong suit for Savanna if I do say so myself. Harley was doing a stellar job, finally looked as though he was comfortable on stage, maybe even enjoying himself.

And then Savanna sneezed.

Not just a little, understated sneeze. This was a whopper of a sneeze, the likes of which made audience members jump in surprise. Harley hesitated a moment, but continued on in with his lines.

And then another sneeze. And another. And another.

Savanna sat up and looked at the audience, cheeks glowing almost as red as her nose and she rolled off the bed in a rush and ran backstage without a word.

Harley stared at the place Savanna had vacated, his face as white as a sheet. He stood frozen, and I could have sworn he was going to burst into tears. I'd never met a boy who cried so often or as easily as Harley. But he was such a big guy none of the students dared make fun of him. But to cry in front of the whole school, in front of the mixed Mossy Creek and Bigelow audience, would ruin the poor kid.

I couldn't let that happen.

Savanna still stood backstage in the throes of a sneezing fit. None of the other students knew her lines well enough. I had to step in. Without another thought I rushed onstage and lay down on the funeral bed. I winked at Harley, willing him to continue his lines.

But he just stood there. White faced, chin

quivering. I was too late. I saw a single, glistening tear trickle down Harley's cheek as he ran from the stage, clear and present terror plastered across his face.

Murmurs and chuckling broke out across the theater as I continued to lie on the bed, hoping Harley would step back on stage. But moments passed and nothing happened. And just as the notion that I was ruined for good crept into the forefront of my mind, just as I considered standing up and thanking the audience for coming and apologizing for the mishaps, just as I gave up hope, a miracle happened.

Evan hesitated at the edge of the stage. I'd never seen him speak in public. Usually he was the quiet, mysteriously handsome guy in the back of the room, taking everything in. But now there he stood, a strange and exciting courage evident in the set of his chin, in the sparkle of his eye.

He leaped onto the stage with a flourish and winked at me before reciting the line left hovering in the theater by Harley, who I could hear quietly sobbing behind the curtains.

Evan would be my Romeo.

He stood close to me, his voice full of passion as he spoke his lines over my funeral bed. He was flawless, and as I peeked down at the front row, there sat my mother and father, their eyes gleaming, no doubt remembering the night Dad had come to my Mom's rescue in almost the same way.

It was fate.

"Arms, take your last embrace! And, lips, O you the doors of breath, seal with a righteous kiss, a dateless bargain to engrossing death!"

Evan threw his arms around me, lifting me close to him as he recited what would have been his last line. But this was my play now. This was no tragedy.

I opened my eyes and reached up to touch his smiling face, trying not to look out over the gasping crowd.

"Romeo."

"Juliette, you're alive!"

And then it happened. He kissed me. Oh, he was supposed to. But this was a high school play. A little peck on the lips, that's what I expected. But this was a kiss. Among the cheers and laughter of the Creekite and Bigelowan audience, a real kiss.

The kids entered on cue. The Bigelowan and Creekite characters of the play cheered at the sight of Juliette alive and in the arms of her Romeo. And as I looked up at Evan's smiling face, something inside of me came alive, as well.

"That was amazing." Principal Blank actually grinned at me as he shook my hand in congratulations. "You sold out every seat in the house and we've collected outstanding donations for the new stadium."

"The standing ovation wasn't bad, either," Dad chimed in from over my shoulder. "I even saw Eustene Oscar leap to her feet."

Principal Blank chuckled. "Yeah, it was an impressive night." He patted the money-bag full of the aforementioned donations. "Keep up the good work, Miss Lavender."

I breathed a sigh of relief as he walked away. I could hardly believe the success of it all. My job was safe, and everyone had loved the play. Creekites and Bigelowans alike, beneath one roof. The feud wasn't over in one night. But it was a small step in the right direction.

Mom pulled me into another giant hug. "You should come over for pie and ice cream."

Dad grinned. "Bring Evan, too."

Mom elbowed him in the ribs. "You don't have to bring anyone, dear."

I giggled, heat rushing to my face at the look in Dad's eye when he mentioned Evan.

"No, it's all right. If I see Evan I'll invite him. I'll be along soon."

After another set of congratulatory hugs, my parents left and I sighed another breath of relief over the emptying theater. I scanned the crowd for Evan. He'd disappeared right after the show, before I'd even had a chance to really thank him. But it was okay, I knew right where I would find him.

Mossy Creek rolled softly, singing its sweet music beneath the moonlight once again as I crept near. Barefoot, my blue jeans rolled up to my knees, I waded out into the shallows, letting the cold creek roll and eddy around my legs, reveling in the feel of the world moving on its own. That was part of what I loved about the place. It was always there. No one made it happen. You couldn't command the creek to flow or the trees to bend and sway with the wind, to reach down and touch the water with their gnarled and aged fingers.

No this place was alone, unto itself. No matter what happened elsewhere, here it was always the same. And when I thought of home, it was this place that came to mind.

I leaned down and felt the cold water with my fingertips, let the stress run out of me into the creek. I'd done it. I'd saved my job, my reputation, broken fundraising records. But I'd also brought two towns together in celebration. Whether they liked it or not, Bigelow was a part of Mossy Creek heritage and visa versa. It seemed only fitting that they should somehow be a part of the biggest town celebration in twenty years.

Having stood up on stage, hearing the laughter, the gasps, the applause, you couldn't tell which cheers came from Bigelowans and which from the Creekites. They all blended together. And it had been beautiful. Just like Seth and I had always imagined.

"Mia."

I turned at the sound of Evan's voice. He stood at the edge of the creek, and I could barely make out the crooked smile on his lips.

"You did it, Mia." He came closer, close enough that he reached out and tucked a stray strand of hair behind my ear.

I shook my head. "No. *We* did it. Evan, I don't know what I . . . I couldn't have done it without you."

"It was the right thing to do. Harley never woulda lived down busting into tears on stage."

"And I never would've lived down another flop." I reached out and took his hand. "You saved the entire night. You saved me." I gave him a teasing look. "Romeo."

He took a step closer, the creek rushing around us and between us, turning us into part of it, part of the magic so embedded in the very soul of the place.

"May I kiss you?" he whispered.

His words lit something inside of me and I couldn't hold back a smile. "You didn't stop to ask the first time."

He stepped forward, so close I could feel his warmth. Yet he made no move to touch me. "But you never said whether you liked it."

"Oh, yes," I whispered. "I liked it. I most definitely liked it."

He chuckled, looking more handsome than ever in the sparkling moonlight, as he pulled me close and pressed his lips to mine.

For the first time in a long time everything felt right, felt as if it was the way life was supposed to feel. For the first time I felt like I belonged, safe and loved and destined for Happily Ever After. I'd managed to turn a tragedy into a story of hope. And not just the play. I'd finally found my place in the world.

As Evan took my hand, I could have sworn I saw the fairies dancing here and there among the swaying, moonlit trees, welcoming me home.

PART SEVEN:
THE GREAT
TIME CAPSULE CAPER

Louise & Peggy, Friday afternoon

But of course we couldn't leave it alone. We were given a mission and come heck or high water, we'd finish.

"Let's drive back to the stadium," Peggy said. "Maybe somebody actually stumbled on it with all that digging. They haven't had time to abscond with it, if so."

Nobody had found it. Everyone had gone home in disgust, apparently. I was sort of expecting to find Katie Bell's car, but either she hadn't caught on to Peggy's lie yet or didn't want to mess up those pumps.

At the far end, a bulldozer rumbled as the driver shoved his front loader into a pile of scrub pines.

"Look, Peggy, everybody's dug holes down by the men's bathroom. But John said he thought it was the women's side. Maybe we can get the bulldozer guy to dig a little at that end."

Football fields don't look that big on TV, but even when I'm training the Bouviers for sheepherding I don't do that much walking. Peggy, however, does. She reached the bulldozer before I did, yelled loud enough to get Wolfman Washington's attention and signaled for him to shut down the engine.

"What now?" he called down. "I already chased them folks off from down there. Acted like they was digging for pirate treasure. I just got this dang field halfway smooth. Don't y'all let me see no shovel down thisaway."

So much for asking him to dig up the entire end of the arena.

"Not pirate treasure," I said in the voice I use to cajole my plumber into fixing the leak today instead of next week. "Just one little bitty old steel box."

"What kind a' box?"

I spread my hands, guessing that the box would be less than a yard across. "Probably about this big. Kind of heavy. It's got some real important papers in it."

"What kind a' papers?" he asked. His voice dripped with suspicion.

Peggy stepped up. "Important to the town of Mossy Creek. If we could just get you to use your backhoe to dig . . ."

"Ma'am, I have excavated until I am blue

in the face. You got any idea what a concrete block does when it gets burned? It breaks up, is what it does. And in near thirty years all them blocks have been covered up with brush and trees and roots and dirt and I don't know what-all."

"You have dug in this area?" Peggy asked.

Wolfman lifted his hard hat and ran his hand back through his buzz cut. "Halfway to China some places to get them footings out."

"And what did you do with what you removed?" Peggy asked.

I caught my breath and looked around, expecting to see piles of debris where I saw only piles of scrub trees.

"Took it to the dump like I was supposed to. Code says you can't leave that junk sitting around. If you knew how many copperheads I have done run over . . ."

"In the debris that you moved, did you by any chance see a steel box?"

"Lord, I may have."

"Think, Wolfman. It's important," Peggy said.

"There was some old metal lockers, I remember that."

"Not lockers. A box," I said. Did he want money for information? My handbag was locked in the car, and I didn't want to go back to get it. Besides, if we bribed him, he'd be likely to tell us what we wanted to hear.

"Maybe," he said. "Could'a been I picked it up with all the other junk. Can't say for certain."

"But it's possible?"

"Well, yeah. Sure as shooting ain't buried around here, I can tell you that. I had to go down a couple of feet to break the footings loose."

"And you take everything to the dump?"

"Somebody does. Wouldn't do to drive my dozer all the way out there."

"When did you do this?"

"Couple of weeks ago, maybe."

"So it would be close to the surface?" Peggy kept up her interrogation. Just like Sherlock Holmes.

"Could be. Most of the construction debris goes into a single area in the dump."

"Where?"

Wolfman grinned. "No idea, ma'am. Don't go out there myself. Ain't sanitary and it smells to high heaven."

Peggy reached in her pocket, pulled out a twenty-dollar bill and handed it up to the man. "Thank you. You've been very helpful." She turned to me. "Come on, Louise, we're going to the landfill."

"Not tonight we're not. It's late. I have to get home to fix Charlie's dinner and take the honey bunnies for a walk. We can start tomorrow morning early."

"Cutting it close, Louise. Today's Friday."

"You don't truly think we'll find it, do you?"

"Not really, but we have to go through the motions."

"The motions can start tomorrow morning. I'm whipped."

Mossy Creek Gazette

106 Main Street • Mossy Creek, GA 30000

From the desk of Katie Bell

Lady Victoria Salter Stanhope
The Clifts
Seaward Road
St. Ives, Cornwall, TR3 7PJ
United Kingdom

Hey, Vick!
Just a quick note to update
you on all the Homecoming
goings-on.

The best gossip floating about
town is that a letter was sent
to Police Chief Amos Royden
about mysterious items added
to the time capsule buried by
the last graduating class of
the OLD Mossy Creek High
School. Rumor is that every
single "extra" thing added
twenty years ago incriminates
someone. Everyone's in a
tizzy, I don't have to tell

ya! Kinda makes ya wonder what-all folks have to be worried about, doesn't it?

It's gonna be interesting, and that's the truth. But don't worry! I'm on the case and I'll keep ya posted!

Katie

HOMECOMING HEADACHES, HOMECOMING HEARTACHES

Homecoming means coming home to
what is in your heart.
— Author Unknown

Win Allen, Thursday

"Where's Jayne?" I asked loudly. My words
had to carry above the din surrounding The
Naked Bean's booth at the bake sale.

Betty Halfacre looked up from the cash
box. She regarded me for a long moment,
unblinking, then turned and unhurriedly
counted change to Eleanor Abercrombie for
her cookie purchase. After closing the box,
she looked at me again. "Jayne isn't here."

I returned her gaze. This short, round
half-Cherokee woman could've exchanged
places with Marilyn on *Northern Exposure*
without any loss of vacant stares on either
side. But the mind behind the stares definitely wasn't blank. I enjoyed engaging her
in conversation when I could, just to see

235

who would blink first. "I can see that. Do you know where she is?"

Betty didn't still blink, but her attention was pulled away by Derbert Koomer, who cleaned out their stockpile of vanilla brownies. As I watched the exchange, I wondered if he was going to mark them up and sell them at his *I Probably Got It* store at the crossroads.

When his purchase was complete, Betty turned her attention back to me. "No."

I was so amused by her classic American Indian taciturnity, I couldn't help but chuckle. The humor was unexpected, and felt good after the week I'd had. So good, I leaned across the goodie-laden table and planted a kiss on Betty's cheek. "Thank you."

She didn't act surprised. "You're welcome."

Somehow, Betty could always zero in on what people needed, and knew exactly how to give it to them. I envied her that trait.

"Jayne and I have been missing each other all week." I glanced around at the crowded square. Seemed as if everyone in Mossy Creek was there. I even spotted a few Bigelowans in the throng, mingling easily with the Creekites wandering from table to table. "I've barely seen her."

"I know," Betty said.

She had such a odd tone in her voice that I turned back, but her attention had already been claimed by Bert Lyman. I exchanged a nod with the owner of WMOS, who handed a dollar to Betty for one of Ingrid's famous chess pie squares.

What had Betty meant by that cryptic comment?

I waited while she helped Bert, but then she turned immediately to another customer. Since she seemed determined to help everyone but me, I stepped away from the table and glanced up and down the aisle fashioned from festooned tables laden with Mossy Creek's best baked goodies, canned goods and crafts. The aisles wrapped three sides of the Mossy Creek Town Square. Vendors from other close-by towns were also there.

Aurrie Putney from Yonder was selling various cheeses that her husband, Burke, made on their dairy farm.

LuLynn McClure and her daughter, Josie Rutherford, from Bailey Mill sold dried wildflower arrangements. Feng shuied, no doubt.

Most of the Bailey family who ran Sweet Hope Apple Orchard, also in Bailey Mill,

237

had bushels of their famous Sweet Hope apples.

A cousin of the Bailey family, Clementine Carlisle, was selling her usual apple butter, and seemed to be doing a booming business.

Nancy Daniels from Lookover displayed her sewing expertise with aprons, potholders and such decorated with appliquéd Mossy Creek Rams.

They were flanked by Creekites like Camel-smoking Inez Hilley who stood over a table of fried pies and chow-chow alongside her granddaughter, Lucy Gilreath. Residents of Magnolia Manor had a table with various mountain crafts. There were many others, including parishioners from every Mossy Creek church selling all varieties of goodies and crafts.

Most of the proceeds would be donated to the Stadium Fund. And most of the county was there to support the cause. I'd seen people I rarely see, and some I didn't know. Some of those were, no doubt, fall-tree visitors who'd happened upon our quaint festival. All were welcome, and all were welcomed by the friendly Creekites selling their wares.

I let the warmth of their camaraderie wash over me. It went right to my heart, then filled my whole body. I loved this town. I thanked the good Lord every day that he'd led me there years ago when I'd been searching for a place to belong. Of course, I hadn't known at the time that I was searching for anything more than a little peace and quiet. I'd found peace, but this town was anything but quiet. Especially now that I'd been elected President of the Town Council.

What had I been thinking? This week had been a baptism by fire, with Creekites coming at me from all directions with every possible kind of "emergency."

Like the argument over who was going to lead the caravan of vehicles from the parking lot of the new high school to the stadium in Bigelow, where we had to play our football games this season.

Or the brouhaha over Amos's decree that no personal bonfires would be allowed. It didn't matter to some folks that the town was planning a massive one at the pep rally just before everyone left for the game.

Or the letter that had just arrived that had changed the time capsule buried twenty years ago into a time bomb.

All of that when all I wanted to do was spend time with Jayne and Matt.

Jayne.

Just the thought of her caused the heat coursing through me to deepen. A huge part of my feelings of belonging — of having found my home — was due to Jayne, and to her son, Matt.

I brought my attention back to the crowd. Where the heck were they?

"Win!"

I turned to find Bert Lyman wiping crumbs of chess pie square from his face. "Hey, Bert. How's it going? Have you seen Jayne?"

"I *did* see her, about an hour ago. She was here at the Naked Bean table." He shrugged. "Perhaps her little tyke needed a nap."

I relaxed. "Yes, of course. We're planning to attend the play tonight, and Matt's going with us for as long as he behaves, so Ingrid can go, too. You going to the play?"

"Wouldn't miss it," Bert said. "Have to review it for my Mossy Creek Culture Hour on Sunday morning. I've been hearing rumors about it. Looking forward to seeing it, especially after the flop last spring."

"It wasn't that bad . . ." I trailed away. Even I couldn't say anything good about the disaster the spring play turned into. "Okay, it was. Poor Hermia. She tried so hard."

"And with *her* parents . . ." Bert shook his

head. "The expectations were high."

"Yes, well, guess I'll head over to Jayne's and see if —"

"Just a second, Win." Bert grabbed my jacket sleeve and leaned in. "What's this buzz I hear about the time capsule?"

I held back a groan. What had it been? Four hours? The Mossy Creek grapevine was working overtime. "I don't know. What did you hear?"

"Something about secrets. Something about a massive time-capsule hunt."

I shook my head. Bert certainly had a flair for the dramatic. "Hardly massive. We can't find the capsule, so Ida suggested we set the town's two best amateur sleuths on its trail — Louise Sawyer and Peggy Caldwell. That's all there is to it."

Bert gave me his best you-can't-fool-an-old-journalist stare. "Is that right?"

"Bert," I said with warning in my voice. "Don't make mountains out of molehills."

"Me? What can *one person* do?" he asked, clearly affronted.

"A lot," I answered. "And *one person* with a radio station can stir up a mess of trouble. You wouldn't want to do that in the middle of Homecoming week, now would you?"

"Are you trying to suppress the press?" He stuck a finger in the air. "The truth must be told! The First Amendment says so."

"I'm not trying to suppress anything except widespread panic," I said.

"Aha! Then you admit there's a reason to panic."

"That's *not* what I —"

Suddenly Bert stiffened as he caught sight of something behind me. "LordAMercy!"

I turned to see what had captured his gossip-loving attention. Ardaleen Bigelow was meandering down the row of booths. She was dressed to the hilt, as usual, and carried her vicious little Shih Tzu, Pierre, in a huge bag hanging off one shoulder.

"What's wrong?" I asked, turning back to Bert. "Ardaleen has the right to come . . ." I trailed off as I realized that Bert was glancing between Inez Hilley and Ardaleen. Mortal enemies.

Ardaleen hadn't spotted Inez yet, but from the hard look on Inez's face, something bad was about to happen.

Win Allen, ordinary citizen, wanted to flee.

Win Allen, leader of the Town Council, couldn't.

I groaned as a football sailed past me.

Even though everyone else in the audience sat enthralled by the novelty of *Romeo and Juliet* being told from a Mossy Creek/

Bigelow perspective, Matt fell asleep in my lap a few minutes after the play started.

When Ingrid noticed a few minutes later, she leaned over and whispered, "I should take him home."

"I'll do it," Jayne whispered from my other side.

I shook my head emphatically. "This play is too good to miss. He's not making a fuss, so he's fine right where he is."

A laugh from the audience drew my attention back to the stage in time to see Romeo entering Mt. Gilead Methodist Church instead of the Verona Cathedral. There he spoke with a teenager pretending to be Reverend Phillips, not Friar Lawrence.

A moment later, I felt Jayne's gaze and turned to find her searching my face. I smiled and wanted to reach for her hand, but Matt held it down.

Jayne attempted to return my smile, but the effort was clearly half-hearted.

"What's wrong?" I whispered.

She shook her head and returned her attention to the stage with a quiet, "Nothing."

I knew enough about women to know that Jayne's "Nothing" held volumes of meaning.

The play receded as panic seeped into me.

Something was wrong.

Suddenly every odd moment in the last week played across my mind. Things seemed to have changed last night when I'd been late picking up Matt. Was that it? Was she mad because I felt I needed to accompany Tag to the football team meeting at the dance studio? I'd been so tired, I'd put Matt to bed, then fell asleep waiting for Jayne. I woke the next morning on her sofa, and stumbled into the kitchen to find her and Matt eating breakfast. She said she'd hated to wake me, so she covered me up and let me sleep. I recalled what I'd thought then were distant tones in her voice. I'd put it down to my own lack of coffee, and had beat it home to shower and shave.

And today, I hadn't seen her until I picked everyone up to go to the play.

Then I recalled Betty Halfacre's cryptic comment that afternoon about how little I'd seen Jayne. But then, Betty was always cryptic, so I hadn't read that much meaning into it.

Was that it?

I searched my memory for any other possible transgression, but could only conclude it was the lack of attention during the past couple of weeks.

I had been feeling so comfortable in our

relationship, so certain of Jayne's feelings, so certain of my own, that I'd assumed she'd understand I had duties to the town now that I was President of the Town Council. She'd helped me campaign, for Pete's sake. Encouraged me to run. Celebrated when I won.

Had Jayne changed her mind, now that we saw what this new job was going to require of me? Of both of us? Was Jayne the type of woman who had to have her man's attention 24/7?

No, that wasn't Jayne. That type of woman would've searched for a new husband almost as soon as her husband had died. Not only had Jayne waited three years, but she'd had to be cajoled into dating. I'd finally resorted to bribery, finding a dog to solve her mouse crisis.

No, Jayne was far too independent to *need* a man. That was one of the traits that had drawn me to her. Winning the heart of such an independent woman had turned out to be incredibly satisfying, because I knew without a doubt that she was with me because she wanted to be, not because she needed a man around.

Then my own phrase caught my attention — *winning the heart.*

Had I won her heart? I'd never considered

things in quite that way. I never knew that I wanted her heart.

But now I knew with absolute certainty that I did.

And that begged the question — did she want *my* heart?

She'd never said anything. But then again, neither had I.

We'd fallen into such a comfortable relationship so quickly, that it seemed a given that we were a couple. That we were a couple in love.

In love.

A keen sense of wonder flooded through me. My heart felt like a hot, whistling pressure cooker. How was it possible that no one around me realized I might explode at any moment?

I'd never been in love before. I'd never felt such gratitude, awe and incredible lightness of being. I'd never felt as if there was a physical connection, like a tendril of energy linking me to her, and also to Matt. I loved both of them so much I knew I'd do anything to keep them well and happy.

Including resigning from the Town Council, if that's what was bothering Jayne. I felt instinctively that it wasn't, but I had no idea what else it could be.

Unless she'd found someone else.

A moment of fear shot through me at that possibility, then I realized how impossible that was. The Mossy Creek grapevine was too efficient. If there were someone else, I'd have heard.

That eased my mind somewhat, but I felt the need to make that physical connection real.

Shifting Matt to the other side, I reached for Jayne's hand. As I wound our fingers together, she glanced at me.

I wanted to tell her right then that I loved her, but knew it wasn't the right place. Instead, I held her gaze and smiled with all the warmth inside of me.

She seemed to relax a little, and she returned my smile.

I felt the pressure cooker ease just a little.

Jayne unlocked the door to her apartment, then turned as if to take Matt from me.

I pushed past her and went up the stairs.

"I can put him to bed," she said, following. "I know you've got a busy day tomorrow . . ."

There was no plaintive tone in her voice, so I still had no clue if that was what was bothering her. Even so, I was determined to find out. But first things first. "I like doing it. Why don't you pour us a glass of wine?"

"Wine?" she asked as if she'd never heard of the stuff. "Really? This late? Don't you have to — ?"

"It's only ten o'clock, and I have to spend time with my lady." Realizing that I'd made it sound like an obligation, I turned to face her. "I *want* to spend time with my lady. I've missed you."

Her face brightened and softened at the same time. "I've missed you, too. *We've* missed you."

I grinned, then turned toward Matt's bedroom. The work on Jayne's apartment over The Naked Bean had been completed a month ago. She'd added a large master suite and a new bedroom and bath for Matt in the space she'd taken in over what was formerly Beechum's Bakery. I made quick work of changing Matt into his *Bob the Builder* pajamas.

"Night-night, Win," Matt murmured as I tucked the blanket around him.

I leaned over and placed a gentle kiss on his forehead. "Goodnight, little buddy."

I wanted to promise that I'd find time tomorrow to help him build something with his Legos, but I knew I'd be busy from dawn until late into the night. Besides the pep rally and the game and who knew what else would crop up, I still had a business to run. And Saturday was going to be even busier with the parade in the morning and the dance in the evening.

"Sunday, little buddy. I'll be here all day Sunday."

But Matt was already fast asleep.

I entered the living room to find Jayne already seated on the sofa. A tray sat on the coffee table with the opened bottle of wine and two half-filled glasses. I sat and grabbed them both. Offering one to her, I clinked mine against it.

"To us," I said simply.

She frowned slightly and took a sip of her wine, murmuring, "To us."

"Okay, that's it." I took her wine from her and placed both glasses back on the tray. Then I faced her. "I'm sorry I haven't had much time to spend with you and Matt this week, but I have obligations now that I'm President of the Town Council."

"I know that." She looked offended. "Have I said anything about you not being here?"

"No, but you're acting all . . . weird. Like you're mad at me."

"I'm not mad. Not at all. I know you've been busy. We've been busy, too. I would never resent the time you give to the town. Never."

"Then what is it?"

"I . . ." She looked away. "I'd rather not say."

"Tough. You have to."

"This is *my* problem. Not yours."

I lifted her chin. "Jayne, this is me and you. Your problems are my problems, and vice versa. We share everything, including problems."

She blinked in surprise. "We do?"

"Absolutely. At least, I hope so. I want to know anything that's bothering you. Even if it's something stupid I've done or not done. *Especially* if it's something stupid I've done or not done."

"It's just . . ." She looked away again. "I . . ."

"Jayne, please. I've never known you to be so uncertain. You usually tell me exactly what's on your mind. Right now, I'm imagining all kinds of bad things, so please tell me which one of them I need to worry about."

"No, it's nothing like that. It's . . . Okay. You asked," she warned. "The entire town seems to think we're . . . well, that we . . ."

"What? Sleep together?"

"Well, some of them might, but I told Ingrid we haven't."

"Do you want to? I haven't wanted to

push it, especially with Matt in the picture. We've been in such a fishbowl, with the election and all. But I'm certainly all for it. Have been for months. No, strike that. Years!"

That made her smile. "Really? Now who's keeping things from who?"

I shook my head. "That's a discussion for another time. Tell me, what does the town think we are?"

She took a deep breath. "In love."

"Aaahhhh . . ." Relief washed through me. Finally, something I could deal with. I took both of her hands in mine. "Aren't we?"

"Are we?"

"Well, I am. Aren't you?"

"Well, yes, I guess I am. We've just never mentioned it before."

She looked so serious, I chuckled. "You're right. Let's take care of that. Jayne Austen Reynolds, I love you."

Her smile was warm and wonderful. "And I love you, Winfield Jefferson Allen."

"There. It's official. You can tell Ingrid and Josie they were right."

She chuckled. "They'll be relieved to know."

"I'm relieved to know, too," I said softly.

She smiled. "Me, too."

"Now we can start planning our future.

Are you ready yet to become engaged?"

"Is that a proposal?"

"Unequivocally. But if you want the proper words, here goes . . . Will you marry me?"

"You know what?" she asked brightly. "I think I just might."

I shook my head. "Sorry. The proper question needs the proper answer. Is that an unequivocal yes?"

"Yes." She wrapped her arms around my neck. "Yes. Yes. Yes!"

Emotions I'd never known existed swept through me, and I kissed her with every one of them. "Now, about that other discussion . . ."

PART EIGHT:
THE GREAT
TIME CAPSULE CAPER

Louise & Peggy, Saturday morning

"Charlie, I need your old fishing waders."

My husband looked up from the cross-word puzzle in this week's *Mossy Creek Gazette,* adjusted his bifocals so that he could actually see me, and said without a hint of curiosity, "In the storage closet in the garage. You need a rod and reel, too?"

"I'll take what I need, thank you."

He went back to his puzzle. "Louise, what's a seven letter word for insane? Starts with a 'b'."

"Bonkers," I said and headed for the garage. I pulled two of his yellow hard hats off pegs. He uses them when he consults at construction sites. I unearthed the leather welder's gloves he used when he took up building metal bird cages, added the waders and suspenders, a couple of respirator masks he used when he varnished his furniture, plus two pairs of the goggles he wears when he cuts wood. I've known Charlie long enough to realize that his lack of curiosity about my doings is a game he plays to drive me nuts. So I ignore him. I didn't even go back to tell him goodbye.

The honey bunny Bouviers were dying to go with me and fascinated by the stuff I accumulated on the back seat of my SUV, but I hardened my heart, suckered them into the back hall and shut the door on them. The last time I let them dig, they'd unearthed a dead body. I put my small cooler of cokes and iced tea on the back seat along with a roll of plastic bags and called Peggy on my cell phone. "I'm on my way. You ready?"

"As I'll ever be."

Peggy practically scuttled down her back steps and dove into the passenger seat of my car. She had on her gardening hat, gardening gloves, a heavy long-sleeved denim shirt, baggy jeans and her knee-high rubber muck boots.

"Do you have any idea how ridiculous we look?" she asked.

"We are going to dig in a garbage dump. I'm not wearing Donna Karan."

The Bigelow county dump is far enough away from Mossy Creek that its odors don't waft to the good folks who live here. Part of it has already been turned back into a landfill and planted with grass and wildflowers. If everyone recycled, we'd still generate a great deal of debris, but most people still don't.

Even this far from the Atlantic, flocks of gulls aided by crows and turkey buzzards searched for edibles among the debris. God's real cleanup crew.

When I was growing up — which was before DDT was outlawed — dozens of buzzards roosted nightly in a dead tree in my grandfather's pasture. Then they all but disappeared. Now, they're back on duty, cleaning up road kill, so we don't have to. I know they look ugly on the ground, but when the day is clear, I swear they go soaring for the sheer joy of it.

We, however, are not buzzards. I find no joy in the mess we leave behind. Nor in the smell. Nor, as it happened, do I go in for scaling small mountains.

"My Lord, Louise, where do we start? This thing must be thirty feet tall." Peggy sounded as appalled as I felt.

At least thirty feet tall. Maybe more. And unstable. I wished now we had brought the dogs. I couldn't see them running for help like Lassie if we were buried alive, but they might attempt to dig us out.

"Look at this logically," I said.

Peggy snorted. "That'll be a first for you."

"Don't start. If we walk around the base, we can tell where they've been dumping recently. Wolfman said construction debris would be in its own area. Surely we'll recognize it."

"Uh-huh. Can't we ask somebody? Doesn't anyone oversee this dump?"

"Not on weekends. We're on our own." I started off to my left. Charlie's waders were hot, the feet were so big they flopped like clown feet. If Peggy hadn't grabbed me, I'd have taken a header in the first twenty steps. I had no wish to land face down in a welter of rotting food, filthy plastic and broken glass.

"Take those things off before you break your neck," Peggy said.

"But . . ."

"Don't you have your sheepherding boots in the car?"

"My good leather ones?" I squeaked.

"They'll scrub up with saddle soap. Go put them on and lace them all the way up to the knee. This place is probably crawling with snakes."

My favorite animal. I stashed the waders in one of the plastic trash bags. I'd have to sterilize them before I put them back in the sports closet or Charlie would kill me, and the smell would drive the dogs nuts.

I had to run to catch up with Peggy.

Over the next couple of hours we twisted our ankles, banged our knees, suffocated in our masks, endured sweat running down our faces from under our hard hats, and became so used to the stink that we barely noticed it. I kicked two garter snakes out of our way and saw one diamond-patterned tail as thick as my wrist disappear into an old washing machine. The birds flew away from us, but landed again the moment we'd passed.

"I feel like Luke Skywalker in the trash compactor," I groused. "This is useless and it's long past lunchtime. In October without daylight-saving, it'll be dark in a couple of hours. If we don't find the thing in the next twenty minutes, nobody else is going to find it either, agreed?"

"Agreed. I'm too old for this," Peggy said. She is in much better shape than I am, although she's a good ten years my senior.

"Look," I said, pointing halfway up the hill. "Isn't that some broken concrete blocks?"

Peggy shaded her eyes without touching her face with her gloves. "Looks like an old 'y' painted on that one. For Mossy, maybe?"

I felt a frisson of excitement.

"You want to crawl up there and check or you want me to?" Peggy asked.

"I'll go." I didn't want to, but I felt I owed Peggy that much. She's older than I am. So, using my gloved hands — thank God for Charlie's welders' gloves — and my feet, trying to keep my knees off the ground, I climbed. I froze several times as whatever was underneath me shifted, or when I heard the scrabble of something alive. "Do rats still carry the plague?" I called down to Peggy.

"Not in North Georgia."

Finally, I reached the pieces of concrete and tried to move them. They didn't budge.

"I need a lever," I called down.

"To your right," Peggy called back. "A piece of rebar."

At first I missed it, then I saw it sticking out like a lance ready to impale me. I braced my feet and pulled. It didn't budge either.

Then it did. Fast. Suddenly I was holding the end of six feet of steel rebar flailing in mid air.

Me too.

I went over backwards and slid head first down the mountain. Peggy may have screamed. I definitely did. Above me I saw the whole pile begin to sag and shift. I must have removed some sort of key that had been holding everything in place.

I sailed the rebar to my left as hard as I could from flat on my back, and clutched at God-knew-what to slow myself down. I don't think I was sliding fast, but it felt like Mach 2.

The rumbling above sounded like an avalanche. In a sense it was.

Suddenly I felt Peggy's hands under my shoulders. She yanked me to my feet and dragged me back and sideways as hard and fast as she could manage.

"Run!" she shouted.

I ran.

It was a very small avalanche. The whole shebang stopped about four feet from the bottom of the pile. The mess it had dislodged lay strewn around the ground. The man who looked after the dump would not be happy about the mess we made. I didn't plan to tell him about it.

"You hurt?" Peggy hunkered over with her hands on her knees.

I gulped air. I do not even want to consider what my blood pressure was, but my adrenaline would have powered a supersonic transport. I shook my head. "I don't think so."

"Then let's go see if you dislodged anything of value."

"Not likely with our luck."

She grabbed my arm and glared at me. "Louise, we are due!"

We climbed across the muck very carefully. With two of us, we could move the broken concrete. The pile seemed to have subsided as much as it planned to.

By the time we shoved fifteen or twenty pieces of block down behind us, I was ready to quit. My whole body ached, I could feel a dozen scraped places I hadn't been aware of in the throes of my adrenaline rush, and the aftermath of fear had set in.

"Give me a hand here," Peggy said. She didn't look much better than I did. Cement dust caked her face, but the runnels of sweat had cut so many paths in it she looked striped. I'm sure I did too.

God in heaven, we were two old ladies! We were definitely bonkers to do this.

But I shoved with her. Then we sat down on the nearest flat piece of concrete. "I quit," I said. "The dumb box is gone forever and I, for one, am glad."

Peggy struggled to her feet. "One more."

"No! We're going home. I'll call Ida from the car and tell her we failed. She can shoot us if she wants to, but not before I stand under the shower for about a month."

Peggy turned over the piece of concrete we sat on. It slid down and barely missed my ankles.

"Hey! Watch it."

She just stared down with her mouth gaping.

"Don't you dare have a stroke on me!" I swore.

She pointed. "What's that?"

Moving our sitting block had revealed a gap. "Another damn block. See? White, dusty?"

"Metal." Peggy said. She reached down into the hole and brushed the cube. Underneath its dust coating it was dark gray.

Ridiculous! We couldn't have found it. I don't think either of us had ever truly believed we would.

Getting it out wasn't easy. We had to find my rebar and pry it up before we could remove it. Eventually, it sat on the ground at our feet like a square metal toad.

"I'm calling Amos," I said, dialed his cell phone and listened. "Says he's not available, whatever that means." I left a message anyway. "Amos, we found it. We're at the dump. Come get it."

"Call Ida," Peggy said. So I did. Same thing, not available.

"Great. We're not supposed to call Sandy

or Mutt. What about Win?" I glanced at my watch. "He'll no doubt be in the throes of early dance disasters. Looks like Amos or Ida would be waiting, if they wanted the damned thing so bad." I rubbed my gloved hands together and hunkered down. "It's getting dark. I'm not staying here waiting to hear back from them. The dance starts in an hour."

"We have to wait," Peggy said. "We can't lift the thing ourselves, and Amos wants to be the one to open it. Let's go sit in the car."

"I'm hungry. We missed lunch."

"Suck it up." She pulled me up and I stumbled behind her to the car.

"When Amos deigns to answer my call, he can drive on out here, tuxedo or not. I'll be delighted to tell him what to do with that box," I said.

"You get very grumpy when you're hungry."

"Like you don't." I started to climb into the car, then looked at my nice leather seats and at the state we were both in. "Wait a minute. I've got an old blanket the dogs use. We can cover the seats so we don't have to fumigate them."

I went around, opened the tailgate and pulled out the tattered old blanket.

"Not too clean," Peggy sniffed.

"As compared to what?"

"What's that?" she pointed.

"My two-wheeler. I've given up toting fifty pound bags of dog food in my arms."

"Bring it."

"What? Where?"

"We're going to load that box onto your two-wheeler and take it to the police station," she said.

"Who's this we?"

"Come on, Louise. We can do it. It's not that heavy."

"Then what do we do with it?"

"We are going to dump it right in the middle of Amos's desk," she said with satisfaction. "Then we are going to forget it ever existed."

WMOS
R A D I O

"The Voice Of The Creek"

Are y'all Creekites ready for more football?

We've had 7 great games so far this season, but the one tomorrow night is special — and y'all know why! If you don't, then you're either dead or from out of town. Because as every good Creekite knows . . . THIS IS HOME-COMING!

Kick-off is at 7 p.m. at the — pffft bleeeccchhh — Bigelow High School Stadium. But we can't help it so be that as that may, we're gonna win and we're gonna win BIG!

The Harrington Eagles are 3 and 5, and we're 6 and 1. That's right! Only ONE in the loss column. How about that for a first season?

Before that, though, everyone's gonna meet at the site of our future stadium for a GI-NORMOUS pep rally.

This is gonna be the first Homecoming pep rally for a Mossy Creek Football Team in 20 years. Mossy Creek fans are gonna spur our Rams to victory, helped along by the Rams cheerleaders, Rammy the Ram mascot, the team's coaches and the Mossy Creek High School band.

The pep rally runs from 4:30-6 p.m. at the newly cleared Stadium Field. They'll have games, giveaways and activities for all ages. It's free so y'all come on out and bring the whole family!

After the pep rally, we'll convoy down to Bigelow for the game. Won't that be a sight? Trucks, cars, SUVs and probably an RV or two tagging along behind the team bus.

We're singing the fight song the whole way, so don't forget to roll down those windows and let the world — but especially Bigelowans — hear your melodious voices!

QUEEN FOR A DAY

Homecoming means more than
kings and queens.
— Author Unknown

Christie Ridgeway, Friday
Leaning back against the grill of Mom's '67
Mustang and extending my arms, I felt a lot
like the girl in the movie, *Titanic,* running
away from a past I didn't want and a future
already laid out for me.

"Christie," my father had been saying for
as long as I could remember. "It's four years
at the University of Georgia for you, followed by two years at Harvard Law School.
Won't that be great?"

Great? Ha.

Those were *his* plans for me. *My* choice
involved four years at home attending North
Georgia State with a major in journalism. I
had less than a big-fat-zero desire to study
law. All I wanted was to stay in Mossy Creek

and write for the *Gazette*.

I wasn't one of the many kids at school whose main ambition was to leave Mossy Creek for Atlanta or other places so different and so far away from this small town buried in the North Georgia mountains.

I have never felt buried here. I felt nourished. I felt kinship with the people here. I felt a deep sense of *home*.

With a heavy sigh, my gaze fell across the tract of land that had been almost cleared in anticipation of tomorrow morning's groundbreaking. It was the site of the much-anticipated, much-discussed new football stadium for Mossy Creek High School. The first football field in over twenty years.

I'd parked close by what would one day be an end zone, trying to find a peaceful spot away from the hubbub of Homecoming festivities. The field was a flat expanse of red Georgia clay, mostly cleared by bulldozers in the past couple of weeks of the overgrowth that had strangled it for years.

This field would once again reclaim its destiny, but it just reminded me of another direction in which I was being pushed, rather than a direction of my own choice. Another destiny thrust upon me by my over-ambitious parents.

They had their heart set on me being the first Mossy Creek Homecoming Queen in twenty years. Mama had been the Homecoming Queen the year *before* the school burned down. She'd been claiming for twenty years that she was the last crowned queen of Mossy Creek, and technically, that was true.

LuLynn Lipscomb — now McClure — had been announced as the queen the year after Mama won, but before LuLynn could walk from her place in the Homecoming Court to the dais set up at one end of the football field, the Mossy Creek Ram had run across the field with its tail on fire and all heck had broken loose. People had scattered in all directions, so not only had LuLynn not been crowned that night, the crown itself had somehow been lost or stolen in the hullabaloo. So she'd never been crowned Queen.

I wasn't there, of course, but I'd heard the story many times from my parents and others in the community. I loved that story. It's part of what made Mossy Creek unique.

Mama liked the story, too, because it gave her bragging rights as the last crowned Homecoming Queen. Now she wanted even more bragging rights for me to be the first crowned Queen after her.

The trouble was, I had a shot at it.

If it sounded as if I wasn't exactly excited about it, you're right. For two reasons.

First of all, the Homecoming King and Queen crowned tonight would be presented on the Bigelow Football Field. Because the Mossy Creek Stadium wasn't ready, our home games were being played at the stadium in Bigelow. Both schools' schedules had been arranged to allow that. And in my opinion, there was something wrong about the Mossy Creek Homecoming King and Queen being crowned in Bigelow, Mossy Creek's arch rival.

But the biggest reason I wasn't excited about the possibility of being Homecoming Queen is that my best friend, Monica Mitchell, is also a candidate for Queen. I want her to be Queen. She needs it more than I do, for two reasons.

Monica's aunt is LuLynn McClure, the uncrowned Queen from twenty years ago. LuLynn and Monica are very close because LuLynn took Monica in while her mother did a stint in the army. Now, LuLynn is not one to suffer silently, so both Monica and LuLynn's own daughter, Josie, helped Lu-Lynn through her years of . . . well, let's just say she went through a period of nipping into the cooking sherry because of it.

After that, LuLynn entered both girls in every beauty pageant in four counties. Josie hated every one of them, but Monica loved them. She'd even won a few — Miss Perky Pigtails in Cherokee County when she was seven and Miss Amicalola Falls just two years ago.

Even so, Monica remembers very well her aunt's depression over never being crowned. When it was announced that she was in the running for Homecoming Queen this year, along with me and Nancy Bainbridge, she became determined to win for her Aunt Lu-Lynn.

According to Mom and my Great-Aunt Adele Clearwater, Monica was my most serious competition.

Aunt Adele was just as determined as Mom that I was going to win. She made that clear when she bought my dress back in September. A horrible lime green thing with puffed sleeves. I secretly returned the dress in October and bought one that a girl in . . . oh, my *century* might wear.

Being introduced as a candidate for Homecoming Queen didn't mean nearly as much to me as it did my parents. But it was tradition, and Mossy Creek lived on tradition. And I loved Mossy Creek. That was the only reason I had any interest in it at all. And though it seemed strange that the Mossy Creek Homecoming Queen would be crowned at the Bigelow stadium, until the Mossy Creek stadium was complete, there wasn't any choice.

So that ambivalence and reluctance to break my mother's heart were the only reasons I hadn't withdrawn so Monica could win for sure.

It being the first Homecoming game in twenty years, everyone was excited. Emotions were running high. This would be the last season they'd play a game on the Bigelow field, except in competition.

The Mossy Creek First Annual Homecoming Bake Sale had been held yesterday on Town Square. The festival started after school with the ladies of the town setting up booths selling various yummy concoctions. There'd been artists of all sorts with booths, too, selling everything from colorful quilts to sock monkeys to striking paintings and crafts of every description.

The football game was tonight, with the crowning of the Homecoming King and Queen. Tomorrow morning there would be a parade and the Homecoming Dance was scheduled for tomorrow night.

As if he was trumpeting his own approval, the man running the motor grader on the field below gave the clutch and gas a boost, and the machine made a lunge as he threw up his hand and waved at me. I recognized Wolfman Washington and waved back.

The roar of the motor grader almost covered up the ringing on my cell phone. I'd been ignoring it for over an hour. The phone at home was probably ringing off the wall since my friends couldn't get me on my cell. The team's last minute football practice would soon be over.

Knowing I might as well get caught up with the messages, I flipped the phone on.

It rang immediately, a merry rendition of "Here Comes Santa Claus." I didn't have to look at the caller ID to know Monica was calling.

"Where are you, Chris?" she demanded. "I thought you were going to give me a ride home, but I don't see your car."

"I'm over by the new stadium." I turned back toward the Mustang. "Where are you? I can —"

Suddenly, Monica appeared on the path up to the school. We flipped our phones off simultaneously.

"It's about time I found you," she said, then scrunched up her nose. "What are you doing here? It's so . . . dirty."

I looked back over the field and smiled.

This was home. This was Mossy Creek. So many of my friends didn't understand why I didn't want to leave, not even for college. Including Monica.

"I'm just . . . thinking."

"You've been doing a lot of that lately. What about? College, again? Today of all days? Geez, you were accepted by six schools and you still can't decide where to go."

"That's right. It's a big decision."

"Why not go where your dad wants you to go? Most of your friends will be in Athens."

I shook my head vehemently. "I'm thinking about studying journalism online. Then I won't have to go anywhere."

"I just don't understand why you don't want to get out of this place." But she said it without rancor. We'd had this discussion before, many times. "I'd go in a heartbeat."

"I know . . ." I started to explain, then I let my voice trail off.

"*I* know," Monica said with a stony look. "You don't want to leave Willie."

There it was, the second reason I wanted Monica to be Homecoming Queen. If she won that, maybe she'd be okay with my having Will as a boyfriend. We'd both been in love with him since we all attended Bigelow

Junior High, but for some reason, he liked me instead of her.

Since that wasn't the reason I didn't want to leave Mossy Creek, Monica's comment made me want to scream. How could my best friend not understand? But she didn't, no matter how much I tried to explain. Maybe it was easier for her to believe that. Whatever the reason, I picked another topic to release my ire. "How many times does he have to tell you that he prefers to be called 'Will?' "

"Hey, y'all!"

As if he'd heard us talking about him, John Bigelow Jr. — Will — appeared on the path to school. "Will! What are you doing here?"

"After practice, I thought I'd wander down and see if they've made any progress. Then I saw your car." His eyes traveled past us, over the future gridiron. "Do you realize that I will have finished high school without ever playing on Mossy Creek Field?" He stared across the expanse of red dirt, then seeming to dismiss his reverie, he glanced back at us. "Hey, shouldn't y'all be primping for Homecoming court?"

"Shouldn't you?" I returned with a bit more bite than I'd intended.

"I'll be wearing my football uniform."

"Which will be dirty and smelly by half-time," I said. "And we'll be in formals."

"Yep." His grin was unapologetic.

"We were discussing college." Monica changed the subject smoothly. "What about you, Willie? Have you decided where you're going for your next college weekend?"

"My parents are taking me down to the Citadel the first weekend after football season," he said, ignoring Monica's use of the boyhood name he was trying to shed. He was pragmatic about it, I knew. The whole town still called him Willie. Probably would for years to come.

Monica nodded. "That's cool. You're a Bigelow, and a smart one."

"What would *you* rather do?" I asked quietly, hearing the underlying tightness in his voice. He sounded like me.

Will kicked at a clod of red dirt and looked off down the field. "I'll probably do what Dad wants me to. How about you, Monica? You never talk about your future."

"Doesn't matter. Can't afford college." Monica slung her backpack over her shoulder and grimaced. "Maybe I'll hock my crown, if I win. That might buy a couple of pairs of jeans and some shoes. Not too many college classes, though."

That's when Wolfman Washington's grader

lurched forward. The machine threw a football-sized lump of hard mud toward them.

Will pulled me and Monica out of the way, though there really hadn't been much danger of us being hit. He'd learned the manners of a Southern Good Ol' Boy young.

"Nice save," I said with just the right a touch of teasing sarcasm.

"Ah, Wolfman doesn't know how to throw." He grinned. "If I head for the Citadel like Dad's pushing for, I'll show those guys how to shoot."

"You're going to be a soldier?" Monica asked, dismay clear in her voice.

"No, I'm planning on becoming a cop. *The* cop in Mossy Creek. Amos, get ready to retire!" He placed an arm around my waist. "But I'd rather give Miss Christie the best guy in Georgia's freshman class. Of course, that means I'd have go to Georgia. But that's what I want, not my Dad."

Feeling uncomfortable in front of Monica both with Will's words and his loose embrace, I stepped away and headed for the Mustang. "Come on, Monica. We'd better get on home and get dressed. I'll bet my Mom and your Aunt LuLynn are having a cow . . . each."

Monica was quiet on the drive to her house. I knew she was upset because of Will's behavior.

Both of us liked him, though my feelings went beyond like. In fact, the first time he'd kissed me, I didn't think I'd be able to breathe the entire rest of the day. But I had. But when I told Monica about it, the jealousy had emerged full force.

I never thought that we'd argue over a boy. All our arguments through the years had been minor and brief. Even now, everything was still okay between us — unless Will was around. When he'd asked me to be his date for the Homecoming Dance, Monica had been astonished and then livid. When he'd given me a wink at Homecoming court practice that afternoon, I saw flash of pain shoot across her face.

I wish I knew how to tell Monica that I wanted her to be Queen, in a way she'd believe me. But she might know that I wanted to give her that because I didn't want to give her Will. And it was the truth.

But I also wanted LuLynn McClure to see her niece crowned and perhaps, begin to let go of *her* resentment. One way or another, LuLynn would finally have a crown in the family.

"Here you are," I said as we pulled up at

her house. "I'll see you at the game. Don't let your mother use too much hair spray. You don't want your hair to stand up like a sail tonight."

Monica was clearly not amused. "Thanks for the ride." She exited the car and closed the door a little too hard.

"Bye," I called, but there was no reply. So I drove home, my emotions torn in two directions.

I was estatic that Will clearly returned my feelings. We'd become a couple and it just felt right. But I hated what this stupid competition was doing to my friendship with Monica. History seemed to be repeating itself. Jealousy loomed over us. Who would become Homecoming Queen? She cared about it, and I didn't. And I had no control over the outcome.

Three hours later, the Homecoming Court was lined up in full regalia at one end of the Bigelow Stadium parking lot. We were waiting for Aunt Adele's carriages. Someone — probably Aunt Adele — had suggested the Homecoming Court ride into the stadium in the harness carriages she and some of her friends drove.

Our parents, who'd brought us, stood around in a group a little ways off, snapping pictures and generally looking proud and happy. Principal Blank stood with them, looking just as proud.

"Stand by me," I said to Monica, reaching for her hand. At least we were speaking again. That was one thing about Monica, she never could hold onto a *mad.*

She lifted the skirt of her evening gown with one hand and grabbed my hand with the other.

Will, dressed in his football uniform, smiled at them. "The prettiest girls in the whole state!"

The boys were lined up behind the girls. Each girl would ride with her escort in one of the carriages. Will was my escort. Tater Townsend was Monica's.

The first of the harness carriages pulled up then, and Aunt Adele said, "Hey, girls. You're all so beautiful! We're going to show you how to mount and dismount, so it won't look so clumsy at half-time."

"We're not going to be clumsy at half-time, Aunt Adele," I said with forced hauteur. "We're *Princesses.*"

"Yes, you most certainly are." She leaned over with an admiring smile. "Still, even Princesses can fall on their faces when they're wearing long dresses. Even though you're only dismounting on the field, you need to practice getting in and out. One of you lucky girls will have to get back in for your triumphant Queenly circle of the field." She looked directly at me as she spoke, then glanced behind her as the rest of the carriages pulled up. "Let's do it! Men, your job is to help your lovely lady look good as she steps into her carriage. Then you have to follow her without falling on *your* faces. Your shoulder pads are as awkward as her high heels."

The first girl in line stepped carefully toward the mounting pad.

"Get in, ladies," Will called, taking my hand. "We've got to do this quick. Coach needs us in the locker room."

Monica pushed at the errant strands flying wildly about her face. Evidently she'd listened to my jesting advice and had forgone the hairspray. "Whoever came up with the idea we'd ride these harness thingies was nuts." She noticed Aunt Adele's glare. "Oh, sorry, Miss Adele. Your idea? Great!"

"Don't worry, Monica," Will said. "You'll be fine."

"Yeah, well, you know Aunt LuLynn. I'm her last chance to wear the crown."

"My Dad's the same way. He might not say so, but he wants me to be King as bad as your aunt wants you to be Queen."

"Whoever wins will have to parade around the stadium in an onion with a seat!" I frowned as Aunt Adele's horse skittered, making the tiny harness carriage skitter and bounce right along with it.

All the horses seemed skittish with the teenaged group jostling around to find their carriage and practice entering and exiting gracefully.

The principal showed up then and added his instructions to those of the carriage drivers.

Will put a hand around my waist as I stepped onto the stool by Aunt Adele's carriage. He whispered softly, "That's it, my lovely Lady Christina."

We practiced getting in and out several times. It wasn't easy, but Will helped with his strong arms and easy manners. When we felt we'd mastered it, we stood back to watch the others.

Tater and Monica weren't having such an easy time. Tater looked awkward as a Knight in Shining Armor and Monica was getting frustrated with him.

Suddenly their four legged stool twisted, throwing Monica onto the carriage bench in a frothy heap. She screamed. The carriage careened forward and Monica tumbled off behind it. She hit the pavement with a thud and rolled under the body of a pickup truck parked on the other side.

Will rushed over and dragged Monica from beneath the truck.

"Somebody call an ambulance," the principal yelled, "Monica's hurt."

A dozen cell phones snapped open.

"Christie?" I heard Monica call weakly.

"I'm coming!" I ran to her side.

"Help me, Tater," Will called to his friend, who'd been thrown back by the carriage lurching forward.

Tater helped Will lift the bleeding Monica onto the tailgate of the pickup truck, which someone had let down.

"Christie," Monica grabbed my hand. I was relieved that her grip was strong, but there seemed to be an awful lot of blood. "You didn't have to go to this much trouble to win a crown."

"Oh, hush." I tried to hold back tears of panic. Reaching down, I grabbed the hem of my gown and tore off a strip a yard wide. I wrapped Monica's arm with a fat swath of cloth just as her mother and Aunt LuLynn rushed up.

"Are you okay?" her mother cried. "Monica, you're bleeding!"

"Look at your dress!" LuLynn said. "Oh my! Oh my!"

"Me?" Monica managed to say through the sobs wracking her slender body. "Look at Christie! Christie, you ruined your dress! For me!"

"Shut up!" Tears ran down my face as I gave way to her mother and Aunt. "Who cares about a silly old dress?"

I could hear the ambulance siren coming closer. I had no idea how badly Monica was injured, but one of the bones in her arm was poking through the skin. It wouldn't be long before the blood soaked through the satin. "Hold your arm as tight as you can to help stop the bleeding."

Monica was trying hard not to cry, but tears were streaming down her cheeks. "Christie . . . Mama . . . Aunt LuLynn . . ."

"Shhh," LuLynn said. "Don't talk. The EMTs are almost here."

"I have to," Monica insisted. "Christie, listen! I don't want anyone to blame you."

"Why would anyone blame me?"

"Because of the crown, you know."

I glanced over as the ambulance screeched to a halt. Everyone in the parking lot had parted like the Red Sea to let it through.

"Monica, be still," I told her. "I'm not interested in any crown. The emergency guys are here. Hang in there!"

But Monica didn't answer. I peered between her mother and aunt's arms at my best friend. She'd passed out.

After that, everything was a blur. Even though I tried to insist on following the ambulance to the hospital, everyone insisted that I stay. Will was the one who convinced me.

"I want to go with her, too, but we can't do anything for her right now," he said. "We'd just be in the waiting room for no telling how long. Might as well give the folks here their Homecoming show. I promise I'll take you to the hospital as soon as the game is over and I can change."

He was right, I knew. Monica's mother and aunt were with her. They wouldn't let me back into the room with her, so I couldn't do anything.

"I'm sure they'll call as soon as they know something," Will added.

I took a deep breath. "You're right. Okay, let's do Homecoming."

Three hours later, I got a call from LuLynn. Monica was okay. It was just a broken arm, but they were keeping her overnight because she'd bumped her head, too, and they wanted to make sure she was okay. She would be in Room 257 in an hour.

I closed my phone with relief.

"Monica is okay," I told everyone around me. "She just has a broken arm."

They all cheered, still basking in the easy win over Harrington Academy. The game had ended twenty minutes earlier and I was waiting for Will to come out of the locker room. Ten minutes later, he came out.

"I heard about Monica. You ready to go see her?" he asked.

I nodded.

"Want to go home and change first?"

He had on the jeans he'd brought to change into after the game. I'd been planning to go home before going to post-game parties.

"No, please, let's go. I can't be certain until I lay eyes on her. Besides," I smiled. "We have a delivery to make."

He returned my smile and added a conspiratorial wink. "Let's go, then."

Tater stopped us at Will's car. "Did you say LuLynn's at the hospital?"

"Yes, why?"

"Oh, it's a secret." He waved as he walked away. "I'll see y'all there."

Arriving on the second floor of the hospital in Bigelow, we met Dr. Champion in the hall. "Christie, I'm glad you're here. Monica's been asking for you."

We followed him into Monica's room. She lay back against the pillows, her Homecoming Queen formal swapped for a hospital gown. Her face was ashen and her left arm was wrapped in a sling. Her obvious pain broke my heart.

I rushed to her side. "Oh, Monica, I'm so sorry this happened to you."

Monica's eyes opened slowly, glittering with tears. "*You're* sorry? Don't be. It's my fault. I'm such a failure."

I grabbed my best friend's good hand. "No! How can you say that?"

"I am. This is all my own fault." Monica's chin quivered and she turned her head, facing away from me. "I wanted that crown so bad for Aunt LuLynn. Too bad, maybe."

"So you don't know who won?" Will asked.

Monica shook her head. "Aunt LuLynn went home for some clothes, and Mom is downstairs getting something to eat. I haven't talked to anyone else. But I know you must've won, Christie. I hope you did."

"I won," Will said. "I was crowned Homecoming King at halftime. How about that?"

"And the Queen?" Monica asked him, since I wasn't telling her. "Don't tell me it was Ashley."

"No," I said. "Oh, we won the game. The

team looked great against Harr—"

"Tell me!" Monica demanded.

I looked at Will. "Should we?"

"Don't you think we should wait until her mother and aunt get back?"

"No!" Monica wailed. "Please!"

"Well . . ."

Suddenly tears welled up in Monica's eyes. "No, you're right. I deserve this. Christie, I'm sorry. I've been so mean to you lately."

"Mean? Well, our relationship has been a bit strained lately, but . . . we'll always be best friends. We won't let what happened to our mothers and aunts happen to us. Promise?"

"Aunt LuLynn can be so selfish sometimes. She should have dropped this crown thing a long time ago."

I laughed. "Aren't they silly? You'd think after twenty years, they'd get over themselves. It's not as if they can change anything."

A commotion arose in the hallway. I looked at Will and Monica, who shrugged. Before anybody could stop them, three women strode in: Monica's mother and aunt, and my mother.

"Monica, are you all right?" Mom said, setting down a huge vase of flowers she'd no doubt purchased at the hospital flower shop. "I'm so sorry. We saw everything, you poor dear."

"I'm all right, Mrs. Ridgeway. Just a broken arm."

Just then I noticed that LuLynn was wearing a crown on her head. "Monica, look at that!"

Monica nearly leaped out of bed with joy. "I won? Give me my crown." The cast caught on the bed rail and twisted her arm as she tried to rise. "Ow!"

"Not so fast, Monica." LuLynn smiled broadly. "Be careful. Don't worry about this old crown. We want to make sure that cast is set all right."

"Right, Monica." My Mom slid her arm around Monica's shoulders. "You don't understand. That's your aunt's crown!"

"Hers? How? What?" Monica and I chorused, stunned.

LuLynn nodded enthusiastically. "Apparently Tater and some of the other boys had been tossing mud clods around on the new field yesterday afternoon. Well, he dropped it onto the concrete sidewalk outside the stadium and it broke. When it did, a piece of metal was exposed."

Monica's mother took up the story. "He threw it in the back of his car, intending to take it home and wash it off, but didn't remember to do that until today, just before the game."

"He scrubbed it, is more like it," LuLynn said

"Well, he *had* to scrub it. Vigorously, I might add." Mom chuckled. "Imagine him in his mama's kitchen trying to clean up a crown. Well, he did the best he could and then went to find Sandy Crane."

"Sandy about slugged him." LuLynn laughed. "She knows home economics as well as police work. She grabbed the crown, scrubbed it with a toothbrush and Ajax and got it sparkling clean. Then just before half-time, Sandy found out about the accident and you being in the hospital. She started plotting."

"You know Sandy," Mom said, talking about her good friend Sandy Crane, officer and dispatcher for the Mossy Creek Police Department. "She swung into action. Found LuLynn at your house, grabbed her and took her to the party at Mayor Walker's house. Since you girls weren't there, Ida crowned LuLynn. Everybody just went wild."

I glanced from my mother to Monica's mother to LuLynn. "So, you guys are all friends again? Finally?"

LuLynn looked a little abashed. "Yes. I've been so stupid. All over something that was really nobody's fault. I thought all these years that Abby — my very best friend in all the world — had been so jealous, she stole my crown. When all the time, it had gotten trampled and then buried in the Mossy Creek Football field."

"So, if that's your crown," Monica said. "Who won tonight?"

LuLynn gasped. "My dear, darling girl, you don't know?"

"No!"

LuLynn looked at Will and me.

I grinned. "We were just about to tell her when y'all came in. Will?"

Will reached into his backpack and drew out a crown. He placed it on his head. "I'm King, you know."

Then he pulled out another one. "A king who has to crown his queen. A little drum roll please."

The two mothers banged their fingers on the rollaway table beside the bed.

Will started toward me, winked, then turned, walked over to the bed and gently placed the crown on Monica's head. "It is my honor to crown this year's Mossy Creek High School Homecoming Queen."

Her eyes were wide and round. "Me?"

"All hail Queen Monica!" I shouted.

Then Will took the crown off of Monica's head and placed it on mine.

"All hail Queen Christie!" he called.

Monica placed her good hand on her hip. "What's going on? Is Christie Homecoming Queen or am I?"

LuLynn looked at me, then Monica, her eyes sparkling with fun. "The most wonderful thing happened. You both won. First time in Mossy Creek history there was a tie."

Mom took up the story. "For now, only one of you gets a crown. The other will have to come later."

"Not so, my dear friend," LuLynn said. "Tomorrow night, when you girls take the stage at the dance as the reigning Mossy Creek Homecoming Queens, you'll both have crowns. Christie, that one's yours, because it was placed on your head at the halftime ceremony." LuLynn turned to her niece. "And, this one's yours." She removed her own crown, gazed at it with tears in her eyes for a moment and then placed it on Monica's head. "Because, no queen should have to go without a crown. Not even for a day."

PART NINE:
THE GREAT
TIME CAPSULE CAPER

Louise & Peggy, Saturday afternoon

Peggy and I managed to horse the filthy time capsule into the back of the SUV, turned the air conditioner on full blast to cover our odor, and drove to the rear of the police station. I called both Ida and Amos's cell phones from the parking lot. Still no answer. It was now full dark and less than an hour before the dance started.

"Now what?" I asked.

"The heck with what Amos says. We'll hand it over to Mutt."

"We will not. Amos was very specific." I checked my watch. "We are going to take it to the dance. Amos and Ida must already be there doing last minute checks."

"Then why aren't they answering?"

"I have no idea. Maybe there's a cell tower out or something." I turned on the ignition and backed the car out of the lot. As I did, my headlights revealed Mutt just coming out the back door.

He hollered at me, "Miz Louise? Y'all need something?"

I ignored him and kept driving.

Mossy Creek Gazette

Volume VIII, No. Five   Mossy Creek, Georgia

"MOON" OVER MOSSY CREEK
by Katie Bell

YONDER — It was "full moon time" last Saturday night after a Greyhound Bus took evasive maneuvers to avoid a pickup truck in its path.

According to Officer Mutt Bottoms, the bus driver reported that he blew the bus horn and hit the brakes to avoid hitting what witnesses said was a black Dodge Ram pickup, late model.

The incident happened at 10:57 p.m. Saturday on that nasty curve just as you approach Colchik Mountain, just past Bailey Mill. The bus was on its usual route, destination Atlanta.

The pickup briefly disappeared from the bus occupants' view as they passed. Two minutes later it was seen again coming back around the curve. Four young men in the back of the pickup dropped their pants and mooned the travelers as they passed the bus.

When asked how she knew the men were young, Mimsy Allen of Mossy Creek replied, "Bless me, Katie Bell! I've got three sons and eight grandsons. With all that male booty running around my house most holidays, don't you think I'd recognize young booty when I see it?"

Mimsy was on her way home from visiting her son Charles, who lives in Woodstock, GA with three of the said grandsons.

Officer Sandy Crane told this reporter that the Mossy Creek Police Department is on top of the case and will quickly bring the bare-bottomed perpetrators to justice.

Parade Route Set

The Mossy Creek Homecoming Parade begins 10 a.m. sharp on Saturday and events run until noon.

The parade route is approximately one mile and will travel at walking speed. The parade will be forward moving and there will be a designated performance area on the North end of Town Square. The parade will end at the newly cleared site for the Mossy Creek High School Stadium.

A parade contest will judge Best Float, Golf Cart, Vehicle and Walking Unit. Each group will be judged throughout the duration of the parade. Winners will receive a plaque and recognition during the Homecoming Dance on Saturday night.

TAG TAKES OVER

When I went to Catholic high school in
Philadelphia, we just had one coach for
football and basketball. He took all of us
who turned out and had us run through a
forest. The ones who ran into the trees
were on the football team.
                                    — George Raveling

Tag Garner, Wednesday
Two things have happened to me that I
never expected to happen. First of all, I've
become an assistant football coach and
substitute teacher at Mossy Creek High
School. And the second — more earth shat-
tering than anything else that's ever happened to me — is I'm about to become a
father . . . for the first time.

Maggie Hart, the best thing that ever happened to me, is pregnant. And before you
ask, no, we're not married. Yet.

I'm Tag Garner and I met the woman I

love more than life itself when her mother stole a tiara from my shop. When I caught Millicent shoplifting, she bit me and slugged me. It was worse than being attacked by a ferocious dog. Millicent Hart, now Lavender, is a little old blue-haired lady. Who'd ever think she'd launch herself into an attack and bite me?

I've asked Maggie to marry me. She keeps refusing. Not because she doesn't love me, but on general principle. I don't understand it. As far as I know, getting married is every girl's dream. Not Maggie's. That woman has a mind of her own. She's fifty years old and, before you say it, yeah, she's getting too old to be pregnant. That worries me a lot, but it happened. One of those accident kind of things.

But man, if you could have seen the look on her face the day she found out she was pregnant. I've never seen her happier. She runs a shop here in Mossy Creek. Moonheart's Natural Living is the name of the place. She makes potpourri, soaps, lotions and all kinds of natural products, all popular with Creekites and tourists alike. Right after she got pregnant, she started a line of baby products that took off like crazy. She's even got a contract with one of those big baby chains to carry some of her baby products, so she's busier than ever. She set up a little production plant in the outskirts of Mossy Creek to handle the increased sales of those items. Funny thing, she's been in business for years and it took getting pregnant to really make her successful. After the baby's born, she's going to open a couple more shops, one in Bigelow and one up in Clayton.

So now you know about the loves of my life, Magster and the babies. We don't know what they are yet. We just want them to be healthy. Oh, did I say we're having twins? That's another problem to worry about. To say that I'm worried is an understatement. I love the idea of having a baby (or babies) but Mags is my life. I can't even think about life without her. You think it was bad when I got the news that I couldn't ever play football again? I thought my life was over. But if I were to lose Mags . . . well, let's just say you might as well bury me with her.

Oops. Gotta run. The bell just rang for class. Don't tell anybody how much I enjoy teaching art at the brand new Mossy Creek High School. If you'd told me I'd end up teaching school, I'd have laughed you out of town. But I have to admit, I love it.

Willard Overbrook puzzled the hell out of

me. Why was he lying in wait for Fred in the high school parking lot after practice? He'd obviously waited for the coach to come out of the locker room, and that worried me.

You couldn't find a bigger Georgia fan than Willard in these mountains. So you'd think he'd have been excited when I suggested Fred Mabry for head football coach for the Rams . . . the Mossy Creek Rams, that is. I was stunned when Willard started a campaign against him. And he never could look me in the eye and give me a straight answer for it. The principal had interviewed a former offensive coach from 'Bama, but he wasn't nearly as qualified as Fred.

It took a hell of a lot of persuading to get Fred hired, not to mention Fred's own doubts about it. He'd retired from Georgia when Vince Dooley did and was enjoying his freedom. But when I mentioned the ruckus that got raised over his name being mentioned as the first Mossy Creek High coach in twenty years, Fred changed his mind and fought like a real Georgia Dawg for the job. Go figure.

Anyway, everybody seemed to settle down when we started winning games. Everybody except Willard. His open hostility just didn't make sense. And to make matters worse, he refused to discuss it with anybody. Not even me.

So what was he doing, waiting on Fred in the parking lot?

I watched them surreptitiously, pretending fascination in the bag of vegetables Ida had dropped into the passenger seat of my Spyder. They didn't seem to be antagonistic. In fact, Willard seemed exactly the opposite. It was almost like he was apologizing.

I knew I couldn't pretend to be fascinated by vegetables forever. I needed to run home and tell Mags that Fred was coming for dinner. I wanted to brief her on his revelation about what he did to that kid at Georgia so many years ago. Man, of all the things Fred could have told me, that was the most astonishing. He was being too hard on himself. I'm not excusing what he did. It was wrong, but he didn't kill the kid. If anybody was responsible, it was the boys who beat the kid after Fred knocked him down.

Just then Fred called, "We're fine. Go on home to Maggie."

"You sure?" I studied Willard, trying to gauge his level of potential violence.

Fred waved me away. "I'll be along directly."

Willard didn't look particularly combative,

so I put the bag back into the seat, walked around the car and climbed in.

Whenever I turned the key in the ignition and the high performance Spyder engine roared to life, it was like I was a teenager all over again. When I sold my 'Vette, Mags thought I was through with fast sports cars, but I'm not the mini-van or even the SUV type. I smiled as I snarled out of the parking lot like an uncaged beast. My hair wasn't as long as it once was, but I still enjoyed the wind blowing through it.

As I got closer to the town square, a car flashed its lights at me. It was Willie Bigelow, our quarterback. I threw up my hand in greeting and gratitude and slowed down. His flash no doubt meant that Mutt Bottoms was sitting in his squad car just over the hill — waiting.

I slowed to a funereal pace and, as I drove by Mutt, I waved and hollered. I could see by the expression on his face that he wasn't happy. Mutt's not stupid. He'd probably figured out what happened. Nothing he could do about it though.

I drove around the square and headed toward home. I'd moved in with Mags right after her mama moved into the Magnolia Manor Nursing Home. Millicent tried to tell us she was doing it so we'd have more privacy. Fact is, she was foolin' around with Tyrone Lavender, Anna Rose's father. Now they're married and still living at the Magnolia Home. They love it. They play bridge and bingo and make all kinds of crap . . . er, craft projects.

There were no cars parked in front of the Antebellum home of Moonheart's Natural Gifts, so I slid into the driveway, shut off the ignition and bounded out of the car. I couldn't wait to see my gal.

Bells jingled as I opened the front door. It was almost closing time, but I didn't lock the door behind me. Mags would have a fit if I locked it a minute early. "Hey, Magster! Babe! I'm home."

"In the workroom, sugar," came her sweet voice from down the stairs.

Before I could reply, Giselle came gamboling up the stairs and nearly knocked me down. I squatted down and hugged her. She may weigh over a hundred pounds, but she thinks she's a lap dog. She's a Briard, most beautiful dog in the world. "Calm down, girl."

I stood up and headed down the stairs. "Mags? I thought you weren't going to work down there until after Ren and Stimpy were born."

"Don't call them that!" She reached the

top of the stairs and stretched up to kiss me. "First it was Fred and Barney, then it was Abbott and Costello. What next? What if they're girls? Or a boy and girl."

I dropped into a wicker chair with soft floral padding and pulled Maggie into my lap. I rubbed my hand across her stomach and grinned. "I don't care what you call them as long as they're healthy. And as for what they are, Mags, do you think we should have found out?"

She sighed and laid her head on my shoulder. "I don't know, sugar. Sometimes I can't stand not knowing. Sometimes, I'm glad I don't."

"You look tired. Are you sure you're not doing too much?"

"You're right. I am tired. I need to spend the evening relaxing. We're only a week away from delivery."

The door chime sounded and she automatically glanced at the clock. "A late customer, I guess."

Giselle bounded to the door and spun in place, barking joyfully.

"No, I'll bet it's Fred." I helped Maggie to her feet and then rose. "I invited him for dinner."

She walked into the shop in time to see Fred come through the glass door. "Oh, hey,

Fred! I'm glad to see you."

He walked toward her smiling. "And I'm glad to see you. You look beautiful as ever."

"Beautiful? I feel like I swallowed something the size of a number ten washtub, and it's stuck in my belly." Maggie hugged him and laughed as she rubbed her protruding stomach. "So how's the team? We gonna win Friday night?"

"We'd better. Last week was a disaster, but I'm kinda glad it happened like it did. The boys got a taste of losing and they didn't like it one bit." Fred nodded at me. "This guy's really inspired them."

I shook my head. "Inspiration can only go so far. It's the quality of the coach that makes the difference. And you're the best."

"Hope you like country suppers, Fred," Maggie said. " 'Cause that's what we're having — creamed corn, butter beans, green beans, cornbread, sliced tomatoes from the garden and Vidalia onions."

"You don't know how good that sounds, Maggie. My favorite foods."

"I've got plenty." She started toward the kitchen. "Give me a few minutes to set the table and get organized. Everything's ready."

I watched my wife walk out of the room. Her assessment of her size was exaggerated, even with the twins. That's one of the things that had me so concerned. She should've put on more weight.

As we sat down to supper, Fred glanced at me and then at Maggie. "Maggie, I want to tell you what I told Tag this afternoon. I need to come clean about this."

Before Mags took the apple pie out of the oven, she'd heard the story. I could see that I'd been right about her reaction. After echoing what I'd told him, she got up and hugged Fred. Then she went into the kitchen to get the pie and ice cream.

"Okay, Fred," she said as she returned. "Fresh baked apple pie and ice cream. Your choice. Vanilla or chocolate."

I chimed in, "You go for the vanilla, Fred. I'm having the chocolate."

We all laughed. Over that delicious pie, Fred related the tale of what Willard had said. I was stunned. "Fred, nobody would ever have thought that was the reason for Willard's opposition. He kept talking about fresh, new faces and young coaches for a young school. He hinted that you might be over-the-hill. That's a laugh."

Fred did laugh, but then shook his head. "Well, I was beginning to think of myself that way. But these boys, Tag . . . and Maggie, these boys gave me a new lease on life."

When we left the table, Fred excused

himself. "I need to get on home. I've got to stop by the store and pick up something for the heartburn."

I watched him pull out of the driveway, then turned back to Maggie. "Sorry about that. I should have called when I left school, but I was kinda worried about Fred. I left him talking to Willard and you know Willard's got a temper."

"Why did you leave him then?"

I took her hand and we walked toward the kitchen. It was immaculate. Mags is one of those cooks who can prepare a fabulous meal and you'd never know it if you looked in the kitchen. She surveyed the counters and nodded. "Let's go upstairs. I'm pretty tired."

I held her back. "Are you all right? Do I need to call the doctor?"

"No," she said, laughing. She put her arms around me, kissing me lightly. "I love you, Tag Garner."

That's it. That's all she had to say. At that point, I would have done anything for her. "And I love you, Maggie."

Giselle came bounding up and wriggled between us. Maggie laughed. "This girl's jealous!"

"I don't think she's jealous. I believe she sees this as an opportunity to get both of us loving on her at the same time." I knelt down and hugged the big furry beast. "Yeah, that's right, isn't it, girl?"

"Now I'm jealous!"

"I can't win. I love you both."

"And we love you." She was absently scratching a spot behind Giselle's ear. "I hope she's not jealous of the babies."

"Are you kidding? She's a working dog, you know. Briards are excellent babysitters."

"Yes, but can she change diapers?" Maggie said and raised her eyebrows thoughtfully.

"I suspect we'll all be changing a lot of diapers in the very near future," I replied.

I didn't have to teach the next morning, so I went to my shop. Maggie was too busy to spend much time with me since she had so few productive days left before the babies were due. And I have to admit, I was too antsy to sit at home and watch her work, no matter how much I enjoyed it. The Homecoming game was too close. And even more important, the Bigelow game was in two weeks. That would determine whether Fred and I were heroes or pig slop.

I nodded at my assistant as I entered and hurried into my studio to work. I'd just slid into my chair when the front door chime caught my attention. My almost mother-in-law, Millicent Lavender was striding purposefully toward me. I rose and started toward my door, but she beat me to it.

"What are you doing?" she demanded, her tone imperious. No — threatening. "Do you know what Maggie's doing? You're supposed to be taking care of her. What's the matter with you?"

By now, I was used to her abrupt manner when it came to her daughter's welfare. "Good morning, Millicent." I leaned down and planted a kiss on her cheek.

"Don't try to sweet talk me. I want you to take yourself home and demand that she sit down until those babies are born." She pushed me back, crossed her arms and glared at me.

"You're not gonna slug me or bite me, are you?"

"I make no guarantees. What are you doing here? Why aren't you with her?"

"Millicent, I just left there thirty minutes ago. She's trying to get everything ready for —"

"Shut up and listen or I will slug you! You go home and make her stop."

I looked at the small woman leaning threateningly across my desk, pounding on it. However, her ideas of what Maggie should be doing and Maggie's ideas were entirely different. And I had to live with Maggie, who was a formidable force in her own right. "Okay, Millicent, let's go. We'll confront the lioness in her den."

"Me?" She stepped back and shielded herself by crossing her arms over her chest again. "Why should I go? You tell her what I said."

I rounded my worktable and took her arm. "No, I think this will take both of us."

I herded her out of the office, her sputtering excuses all the way. Chuckling, I realized what she was up to. She wanted me to take the brunt of Maggie's anger. "Maybe we'll take her a sweet roll from the Naked Bean," I said.

After purchasing said sweet roll, we arrived at home and found Maggie on the floor, arranging a display of bags of potpourri. "Tag? What . . . Mom? What are you doing here?"

Maggie tried to get up. I rushed over to help her. "Why are you on the floor? Don't you have help for this kind of thing?"

Millicent reached over and hugged Mags. "Tag has something important to tell you."

"Me? No, this is your show, Millicent. Go for it."

For a second, Millicent chewed on her

lower lip. "Maggie, Tag believes you're working too hard. He's enlisted me to insist that you stop at once and rest until after the babies are born."

"Aw, Magster, you know . . ."

Maggie burst into laughter. "Yes, I know dear." She turned to her mother. "It won't work, Mom. I know you put Tag up to this. If it will make you feel better, why don't you stay and talk?"

"Nope! Can't stay. Too much to do." Millicent glared at me and stalked back out the front door.

I watched her leave. "I know that look. Mags, she's up to something."

"I think you're right." Maggie watched as Millicent marched down the front steps. "God only knows what." She turned to go back to work and then stopped. "Tag, you don't think . . ."

"Don't look at me. She's your mother."

"Maybe I should follow her." Maggie turned toward the workroom. "Hey, Anna Rose, I'm going to be out for a few."

"Where are you going?" I asked.

"Hamilton's Department Store."

I watched as she strode down the steps. As she scooted through the gate, she put her hand on the small of her back. She'd been doing that a lot lately. I imagine carrying twins isn't easy at any age, especially fifty.

I glanced into the workroom. "Hey, Anna Rose, what's up? You and Beau doing okay?"

"We're fine. I just stopped in to help Maggie for a while. I'll get busy while she's gone."

Anna Rose Lavender Belmont was Maggie's best friend and, technically, her stepsister since Millicent and Tyrone had married. Her movie star husband, Beau, was my best friend. We'd all been shocked when Beau sneaked into town and hid out with Maggie so he could surprise Anna Rose. I was more than a little jealous when I found out a movie star was sleeping in the house with my girlfriend — unchaperoned. That was when I made the decision to move in with Mags. I realized that if I didn't want some other guy sweeping her off her feet, then I needed to be standing right beside her. I've been here ever since.

"Where's Giselle?" Anna Rose asked. "She usually comes loping up the stairs when I come in."

"Mia took her for a run."

"So how's Mia?" Hermia Lavender Belmont was Anna Rose and Beau's daughter — the drama teacher at Mossy Creek High School. "Has she recovered from that gawdawful play she put on last spring?"

Anna Rose chuckled. "What a flop. What was she thinking? If Beau and I hadn't been away, I'd have been here to support her, but we had to be in Hollywood when he got his star."

"Yeah, Mags and I would have been there, but Maggie was in the first throes of morning sickness. In her first trimester, she got 'morning' sickness in the evening."

"That was probably for the best. Mia needed to learn that Mossy Creek isn't ready for ultra modern plays. We're old-fashioned." Anna Rose smiled proudly. "She's one of a kind. This week, as a fund-raiser they're doing a 'modernized' version of *Romeo and Juliet.*"

"That should be interesting. We'll probably go to that one."

"I hope she gets a good crowd. I saw a poster that made it look interesting."

I nodded in agreement. "Yeah, I told her to put one in my window. Oh, and I actually saw one of the posters in Bigelow yesterday. I've gotta run. I've got football practice."

"Go Rams!"

As I walked to the car, I decided to check on Maggie and Millicent, and so drove over to Hamilton's.

As I entered the department store, I heard the first sign of a problem and grimaced. This couldn't be good. Then I saw her. Millicent was standing just inside the door with one of those baby strollers made for twins. One of the store clerks was gripping one handle and Millicent the other.

"Crap!" I said as I opened the door. "Millicent, what's the problem?"

Maggie was nowhere in sight. Wondering what happened to her, I glared at my mother-in-law to be. Okay, *technically,* she wasn't my mother-in-law. But she would be if Maggie would relent and marry me, which, at this point, seemed doubtful. She was a stubborn woman.

Millicent looked up at me, teary-eyed and fragile. "This . . . this person practically attacked me. I was . . . I was just coming to see if this was the kind you asked me to buy."

Ah, now I understood. The clerk, obviously a new one, had caught her stealing the stroller. I should let them call Amos, but with Maggie in her "delicate" condition, I didn't want to risk putting her into early labor. "Exactly the one. How much?"

Millicent's crocodile tears subsided, and she beamed at me. "Why, Tag, I didn't even look. I just thought it would be perfect, so I didn't care how much it cost."

"I'll buy it, Millicent," I said to smooth things over. "You can take it on home. It won't fit in the Spyder."

I ripped the tag off as Millicent headed out the door, humming as she pushed the stroller. The clerk glared at me, obviously not believing the story. "Sorry about the confusion. My mother-in-law," I said, avoiding a long explanation, "has a touch of dementia."

"Right," she said, still eyeing me warily.

"I'm Tag Garner, by the way. I guess you're new in town."

"No, I guess we've just never met. Tater is my son."

"Tater? No kidding. I'm assistant coach on the Mossy Creek High Football team."

"Oh, Mr. Garner. Tater talks about you all the time." She peered past me and I glanced over my shoulder to watch Millicent sauntering down the sidewalk. "I'm sorry about . . . I mean, it seemed like . . . that woman —"

"Tag, I can't find —"

I slid my arm around Maggie. "Millicent just left with the stroller. I guess she couldn't find you to show it to you. She was coming out to show it to me when Mrs. —"

"Oh, just call me Gilda."

"Right. When Gilda stopped her." I laughed and winked at Maggie, who looked astonished. "She thought Millicent was stealing it."

Maggie almost choked. I clapped her on the back and she finally righted herself.

"Well, Gilda, put it on my bill," I said and ushered Maggie toward the door. "Thanks a lot. Sorry for the misunderstanding."

By the time Maggie and I reached the car, we'd erupted into gales of laughter. "Tag, how could you?"

"I didn't want to be trying to bail her out of jail when you go into labor."

"All I know is, we've got to make sure Tyrone knows she's at it again. He'll keep her closer to home if he knows about it." I opened the passenger door of the Spyder.

Maggie shook her head. "I'll walk. Thank goodness for Tyrone. Most everybody knows Mom's a kleptomaniac, but Gilda obviously didn't. If Tyrone can't keep her at home, she'll be the talk of Mossy Creek again."

"I'll go tell Tyrone what's going on." I climbed over the door and started the engine. "See you in a while. I've got football practice."

Game day finally arrived. I can't remember ever being so nervous about a game. Not the bowl games when I was at Georgia. Not even the playoff games when I was a Falcon. I guess the difference was that I didn't have as much control over the outcome of the game as I had when I was actually playing.

Fred and I followed the boys as they dashed out on the field and burst through the big paper sign proclaiming Mossy Creek as the future state champions. The stadium was full to the brim and the fans were on their feet screaming and cheering louder than they ever had.

Fred looked sort of green around the gills, as my granny would have said, meaning he didn't look well. I was beginning to think it was more than a case of heartburn. We stood, side-by-side, on the sidelines watching the coin toss. He grimaced, but managed to congratulate Willie for winning the coin toss. We opted to receive.

Harrington kicked off. Tater plowed his way up field, not with Luke's finesse, but he managed to get the ball to the forty yard line. Cheers erupted again. The specialty team ran off the field and our offense hurried out to replace them. Willie called the play in the huddle. That's the good thing about Fred. He trusts his quarterback to do his job.

On the first play, Willie threw the ball

long. The receiver missed and got tackled.

Two plays later, we scored. I was certain the few folks left back in Mossy Creek could hear the roar. We kicked off. Harrington took over. On a lucky play, their player nearly fell, but managed to retain his balance and, because of that near fall, got past our defender. He zigzagged down the field and scored. Inside the first five minutes of the game, both teams had scored.

After that, we pushed against them and they pushed against us. Three minutes from the end of the first quarter, we scored a field goal, making the score ten to seven in our favor.

Fred grunted and I looked at him. His face was pasty white and he clutched his left arm. "Fred, what's wrong?"

I grabbed him and led him to the bench.

He sat down.

"Greg, go get the EMTs." I turned back to Fred and knelt beside him. "Just take it easy."

"Naw, I'll be all right. Let me get back to the game. I'll take another Tums and everything will be fine."

"Fred, that's not gonna happen, my friend." I saw Greg dashing across the field with the EMTs right behind him. As they arrived, I rose and let them in.

"Tag, you gotta take over, man," Fred said, groaning with pain.

The game. My best friend was probably having a heart attack, and I couldn't stay with him. All I could do was make him feel better by doing what he asked. "Okay. Don't worry about anything. We got it covered."

The EMTs loaded him onto a gurney. "Don't worry about anything, Fred. You'll be fine. I'll be at the hospital as soon as the game is over."

I headed back to the sidelines. If I hadn't insisted that he come to Mossy Creek, he might be fine. As things stood, he might be dead within the hour.

Plays continued. Players dashed onto the field and off. Whistles blew. We scored again. By now, the team knew Fred was having a heart attack.

I tried hard to be cheerful, but I even sounded hollow to myself. Greg looked like he was about to burst into tears. I put my arm around him. "Hey, man," I said. "Get ready for half-time. Coach'll be fine."

Greg nodded uncertainly and hurried toward the locker room. I watched the doors to the ambulance close and returned my attention to the game. It was the least I could do.

I saw Maggie rise, as if she was coming

down to see what was going on. I shook my head and made a sign that everything was okay for now. She sat back down with Anna Rose and Beau.

Two minutes until half-time. The score was still ten to seven. Along the sidelines, the horses and harness carts were lining up, ready for the Homecoming celebration. What a night this was turning out to be.

Finally, the clock ticked down and the team ran off the field. As I walked in behind the team, I spotted Hayden "HayDay" Carlisle in the stands.

Sandy Crane stood guard by the entrance to the locker room area, and I pulled her aside and asked her to fetch him for me.

He caught up with me just as I was entering the locker room, a puzzled look on his face.

"Hayden, thank goodness! I need your help. Fred's having a heart attack, and I need you to help me on the field for the second half."

A look of astonished horror replaced the puzzlement. "Tag, you know I haven't thought about football in years. You'll have to get somebody else."

I watched him start to turn away. I knew what happened to him back on that awful day when the school burned and his football career was ruined.

"HayDay, wait," I grabbed his arm. "Look, these boys just lost a coach they love and respect. You can't let them down because of what happened to you."

He looked undecided for a moment, but shook his head. "You got the wrong man, Tag. Sorry."

"Can't you put your old feelings aside for the good of these boys? They need a leader."

"They've got you," he said.

For just a moment, I wanted to slug him. "Sure. They've got me. But they need you, too." I shook my head and stared straight into his eyes. "Do you think it was easy for me to step on that field again? Don't you think I wonder every day if I'd have made it into the Hall of Fame if that linebacker hadn't crushed my knee?" I searched my mind for something else to say, anything that might persuade him. At this point, my concern was as much for him as for the boys. "You owe it to them. They're just starting out and need somebody who can help them through the good times . . . and the bad times. And you know what, Hay-Day? I think you need them, too."

He shuffled away from me, turning his back. "You got the wrong guy, Tag."

I watched helplessly as he shrugged and

walked away. I'd honestly believed I could talk him into coaching, but right then I had to concentrate on the team. They needed a talk from a coach and I was the only one around.

The boys were sitting around, their helmets on their knees, just staring. They needed a pep talk and they needed it bad.

"Okay, men," I started and looked from one earnest face to the next. "We've been dealt a blow, but we can overcome this. After the game, we'll all go to the hospital and check on Coach. For now, we need to concentrate on winning this game for him. He'd . . ." My voice trailed off. Their attention had gradually shifted. I turned and saw Hayden standing in the doorway.

"He's right, you know. You boys . . . you *men* are strong. You can't let something like this get you down." Hayden walked farther into the room. "Adversity makes us stronger. Look at Tag. Heck, look at me. Both of us were dealt blows that might have turned us into . . . well, we coulda hit the bottle and never put it down.

"Football isn't just a game. It teaches you how to live your life. Coach Mabry has been here every day for you, knowing he had something bad wrong. He put his life on the line for you. How are you gonna repay that? By sitting around whining? Or are you gonna get out there and whup some butt?"

Willie Bigelow walked into the locker room, carrying a crown in his hand. I guessed he just became King and vaguely wondered who the Queen was.

"Hey, guys, we gonna do this or what?" he said with a grin. He pulled on his helmet and balanced the crown on top. "Think I can go through this half without getting the crown knocked off?"

That broke the tension. The boys started to laugh. I looked over at HayDay and nodded. "Okay, boys. Let's hit the field. We're gonna win this for Coach Mabry and win it big!"

They almost trampled me getting out the door. Thank goodness the horses and carriages were out of the way. I glanced at the area set aside for the Homecoming Court. There were two empty seats. Interesting, I thought and ran after my players.

I looked for Maggie, wanting to see her wave with encouragement. This was tough for me as well as the boys. She wasn't in her seat. Neither was Anna Rose. Beau had walked down to the sidelines.

During the mayhem of getting the second half started, I ran over to see what was going on. "Hey, man, where are the girls?"

He grinned. "You're about to become a papa."

"What? Now?" I gasped and looked over my shoulder. The boys were lining up for the kickoff. "How am . . . Beau! What am I going to do?"

"Maggie said to tell you to march your butt back out there and finish this game. It's going to be a long time before the babies come." He clapped me on the shoulder. "I'll take you to the hospital when it's over."

"I've got to go *now.* I can't let Maggie do this by herself."

"Chill out, man. Everything's under control." He nodded toward the field. "Those boys need you more right now. Their coach just had a heart attack. This is their biggest game this year . . . so far. You gotta be there for them, man."

"Beau, Maggie's . . . well, she's fifty. Anything can happen. I've got to be there."

"Yeah, she said you'd say that."

"Well, it's true."

"Yep. It's true. But if you really want to make that woman madder than she's going to be when those labor pains start in earnest, you just go ahead and abandon these boys."

"Madder?"

"Well, my understanding is that women

get pretty mad at their husbands. Or in your case, the fathers of their babies, while they're suffering that excruciating labor pain."

"Crap. What am I going to do?"

"It's less than an hour, Tag. You'll be there." He nodded toward the field as the football flew into the air in the most perfect kick a Mossy Creek kicker ever kicked. "You're not going to let them down."

Defeated, I turned and trudged toward HayDay.

He looked at me with a question on his face. "What's up?"

I inhaled deeply, trying to dispel the light-headedness that seemed to consume me. Maggie in labor. Without me. We'd practiced together. She depended on me. "Maggie's in labor."

"Hey, congratulations. Are you leaving now?"

I glanced at him and then downfield. The Harrington player caught the ball and got slammed for his trouble. The ball popped loose and Tater caught it. He raced for the end zone and scored. I steadied my breath and tried to calm down. Less than an hour. I had to keep that in mind.

"I'm staying. These boys are counting on me." I turned back to him and tried a half-baked smile. I clapped his back and nodded toward the activity on the field. "They're counting on *us*."

The team played like they were the Dawgs on their best day. Those kids could do no wrong. They caught pass after pass. They rushed for big yardage. Our linebackers kept Harrington from getting a single first down. We intercepted two passes and created three fumbles.

Greg was on the sidelines going crazy. That kid was there every time a player came off the field, handing them towels and Gatorade. Then he'd be on the sideline, calling encouragement and whooping it up when they did something good.

Toward the end of the fourth quarter, we were so far ahead I sent in the second string players. By the time the game was over, every single player had spent some time on the field. Everybody would be able to say they had a hand in this win.

The horn blasted announcing the end of the game and the Mossy Creek players mobbed each other, then HayDay and me in celebration. Then, like the true gentlemen they were, they lined up on the fifty yard line and marched across the field to shake hands with the players and coaches of Harrington High. As they rushed back across the field, their joy was obvious. This game meant more than just a regular football game, more even than a Homecoming game. These boys had played for pride, for being the first Mossy Creek High School team in twenty years. And for a coach whom they'd grown to love and respect, who now lay in a hospital bed fighting for his life.

"Okay, boys. Let's get showered." I looked from face to expectant face. "We've got to report our win to the coach."

"Hey, Coach Garner," Willie said. "I just got a call from Christie. She said Monica is okay and that your wife's at the hospital, too."

I couldn't help grinning. "Yep, she is. Looks like this is gonna be a big night for Mossy Creek. We won the Homecoming game in a big way. And I'm about to become the daddy of twins."

"Hey, Coach," called Tater. "I got a couple a names for you. I think you need to call 'em Tater and Willie, after the heroes of this game."

I laughed in spite of everything that had happened. "Yeah, right. And a few years from now, when my daughters are running for Homecoming Queen, who's going to date girls named Willie and Tater?"

Tater blushed. "They're girls?"

"I honestly don't know." I gazed at the guys. "I'm hoping for at least one football player."

"Hey," Willie said, "Maybe you'll get a boy and a girl. A football player and a Homecoming queen."

The boys showered in record time, and we were on the way to the hospital. I dashed into the maternity area and breathlessly demanded to be taken to see Maggie. The nurse smiled. "Yes, sir. We've been expecting you."

She led me through a couple of sets of double doors that slowly swung open and we were in the labor suite. There was Maggie with Anna Rose.

"Well, Coach, did we win?" Maggie asked, looking more beautiful than I'd ever seen her.

"Yep." I leaned over and kissed her and then nodded to Anna Rose. "Tater says we need to name them Tater and Willie in honor of the heroes of this game."

"Tell Tater to keep his names to himself." Maggie laughed, a sweet musical laugh that never failed to entrance me.

"That's pretty much what I told him." I glanced at Anna Rose. "Any word on Fred?"

She shook her head, and Maggie caught my arm. "Go see about him. I'm fine for now. Only five centimeters. It's going to be awhile."

"No, I'll just hang out with you. I need to be here in case . . ."

"In case what? In case I need somebody to yell at?"

I tried hard not to look sheepish. "I'm sorry about this, Maggie. I mean . . . I hate . . . You know I can't stand . . ."

"Stop stammering and go see Fred. He needs you worse than I do right now." Her voice softened and she smiled. "He doesn't have anybody. Anna Rose can sit with me until you get back."

"Well, maybe for a minute." I gazed at Anna Rose. "Call me the minute anything happens."

She nodded, and I left. I asked the same nurse who'd led me to Maggie's bedside for directions to the cardiac unit.

After only two wrong turns, I ended up at the desk in Cardiac ICU. "Fred Mabry, please."

A nurse who looked like any harpy you can imagine in a horror film looked up at me. Her teeth were yellowed with age and her jet black hair had to be out of a bottle. Maybe it was shoe polish. She had that look about her that reminded me of Nurse Ratched from *One Flew Over the Cuckoo's*

Nest. I started to ask her how much she'd charge to haunt a house. After all, Halloween was getting close.

"Are you family?" she asked in a voice husky from cigarette and alcohol use. "Only family members are allowed to visit. For ten minutes only."

I started to say no, but stopped and inhaled. "Son. I'm his son."

She glared at me a moment and then shook her head. "Your brother is here already."

"My . . . brother?"

"Yeah. Baldish guy. A lot older." She peered at me over her reading glasses. "You *do* have a brother, don't you?"

Was she testing me or telling the truth. I didn't know. I finally decided to tell another lie. "Yeah. Half-brother."

She just shrugged. Thank goodness she didn't recognize me. I followed her through the hallway and into the unit. Over her shoulder, I could see Fred, hooked up to a bunch of beeping machines and IV drips. The nurse said, "Mr. Mabry, your other son is here."

Fred's eyes slowly opened. "My other son?"

Before he could say he didn't have a son, I jumped in. "Hey, Dad, just got in. We won the game." Then I noticed Willard Over-brook standing there. "Hey there . . . brother. I didn't expect to see you here. Um . . . yet."

The nurse eyed me suspiciously for a moment. Fred focused on me. "Oh, yeah . . . Hey, son. Glad we won."

Willard nodded. "Sorry I missed the game. I felt like *Dad* needed somebody here."

With that, the nurse stalked away, obviously not believing either one of us for a minute. I shook Willard's hand and moved closer to Fred's bed. "So what's the game plan?"

"Heart attack. They've isolated it to an artery and will probably put in a stent later on. Seems like most of the doctors in town were at the game."

I chuckled. "Well, they caught a good game then."

"How's Maggie?"

"You're about to have a stent put in and are asking about Mags?"

"Yep. You gotta make an honest woman of her, son."

"I'd do it in a heartbeat . . . Dad." I kept up the ruse in case the old bat was still listening outside the room. "She's holding out on me."

He tried to chuckle and coughed instead.

Willard leapt forward as if there was something he could do. "You all right?"

Fred nodded and looked at me. "What the hell are you doing here? I heard she's here having your baby." His eyes narrowed and his forehead wrinkled. "I raised you better than that. Just take yourself back to her. I'll be fine here." He angled his head toward Willard. "I got your brother Willard here. He'll come after you if I need you."

"You always did love him best," I teased, and Willard laughed.

Fred growled, "Get out of here and take care of your woman. She needs you."

I was beginning to feel useless. I told "Dad" and "Brother Willard" I'd see them when I could and left. Fred must be feeling better. His sense of humor was returning.

In the waiting room, I was mobbed by the team. They were all waiting for word on Coach. "Okay, guys, looks like he's going to be fine. They've got him stabilized and they're going to put in a stent later."

I answered a bevy of questions and they stepped toward the door. "I'm going to check on Maggie. I'll be back when I can."

I hurried down to the labor and delivery area. I heard a shriek and dashed into the birthing room. "Maggie! Was that you?"

"Yes!" She released a stream of expletives as she gripped the bed railings, her knuckles turning white. Gradually she began to relax. Finally, she asked. "How's Fred?"

I related the story of my newly discovered "brother" and the details of Fred's condition. She relaxed as I was talking. I sat down on the edge of the bed and leaned back, pulling her into the circle of my arms. "Just relax, honey. Everything's going to be fine."

Even though I'm not much of a praying man, I closed my eyes and offered a silent prayer for the health and well-being of Mags and my babies. Hours passed that seemed like days. Maggie grunted and screamed and puffed and inhaled and exhaled and screamed some more.

I cried. Honest to God, I cried. I never felt so helpless in my life. I'd have given anything to take that pain from her. Finally, the first baby's head poked out. It was the tiniest human I'd ever seen. My daughter weighed in at three pounds and eight ounces. I watched, mesmerized as they cleaned her up and whisked her away in the neo-natal incubator that would be her home for the next few days at least.

And then came my son. He was a bit larger at four pounds, two ounces. They both had all ten fingers and toes. They both were breathing. Even though they'd have to stay here for a few extra days, they were going to be fine.

Maggie was fine. We decided it would be okay to roll her down to see Fred. My "brother" Willard was there. Nurse Ratched was nowhere to be found, so we sneaked in.

"Hey, Fred, Willard," I said in a low voice. They greeted Mags and me enthusiastically. Fred's procedure had been done and his color was much better. "Well?" he said, a question in his voice. "Are you going to tell us what the babies are?"

Mags beamed. "We have a girl and a boy."

"So much for Tater and Willie," I commented dryly. We're going to have to be more creative than that."

Maggie shook her head. "We're not naming them after anybody we know. I'm thinking of Magnolia and Milford."

I gaped at her in astonishment. "Maggie! You're not!"

She laughed. "Okay. Just teasing."

Trying to appear nonchalant, I nodded. "I was thinking of something like Dooley for our son."

"Dooley . . . as in Vince Dooley?"

"Do you hate it?"

"No, actually I sort of like it." She reached

out and gripped my hand. "It's different and it means something."

I was thrilled she liked the name. Vince Dooley meant a lot to me. It was kind of my personal tribute to him, I guess. "Okay. So what's our daughter's name?"

"Hmm . . . How about Dayna?"

"Dooley and Dayna. Works for me. But what does the name Dayna stand for?"

"Nothing in particular. It was the name of a character in a book once and I liked it."

"Perfect."

Fred opened his eyes and nodded. "And when do I get to see these babies?"

"As soon as they gain enough weight to be released from the neo-natal unit."

Willard stayed a moment longer, congratulated us and then left. He left so abruptly that I glanced at Fred. "What's up with him? He's been here like glue and now he dashes like his pants are on fire."

"I asked him to do something for me."

Though I asked, Fred refused to say anything else. Nurse Ratched came in. "Time for you folks to go. We're moving your 'father' to a regular room."

Maggie and I left with a promise to come back when he got settled. As I pushed her back up the hall, she looked a little sentimental. "What's up, Magster?"

"Oh, I don't know. I was just thinking."

"Always a dangerous thing," I teased.

"No, seriously." She looked back at me. "Do you still want to get married?"

I stopped, spun the wheel chair around and knelt beside her. "Of course, I do. Do you even have to ask? What's changed your mind?"

"The twins. I was thinking I would like to have the same last name they have. I mean," she fought for words to explain. "It would just be much simpler."

Knowing Mags, that had little to do with her change of heart. I kissed her and pulled her close. "Sure it would. I love you. We'll marry as soon as we can arrange it."

Feeling very light all of a sudden, I took her back to her room and tucked her back into bed. She was dozing when my phone rang. I grabbed it as fast as I could, but her eyes fluttered open. It was Fred.

"Why didn't somebody take your cell phone away?" I asked. "Aren't you supposed to be resting?"

He laughed. "I got things to do. You and Mags come back down here. I got a problem I need to talk to you about."

"Oh. Okay." I clicked off and turned to Mags. "You okay? Fred needs us to come back down there for something."

"I'm fine. Let me slip on my pretty robe and fix my face. I must look awful."

"Never. But go ahead." In moments we were ready to go. I rolled her down the hall, into the elevator and up two floors. When we got to Fred's room, it was full of people. It looked like they were having a party.

He spotted us. "Hey, come on in."

I was a little puzzled. There were too many people in the room of a man who'd just had heart surgery. When we walked into the crowd, I realized the entire football team was there along with the Homecoming court, all dressed in their finery from the previous night. I noticed Willard was back, too. And with Preacher Hickman of Mt. Gilead United Methodist Church. He congratulated us enthusiastically and smiled back at Fred.

"Oh. Okay." Fred shifted in the bed and cleared his throat. "Okay, Maggie and Tag. Preacher Hickman is here to marry you two."

"What?" I said, gaping in astonishment. "Really, Fred, we don't have a license and —"

"Fine." Maggie said and smiled up at me. "Let's do it, Honey. We can take care of the details later."

"Wait, here we are!" Nurse Ratched entered trailed by two nurses from Neo-Natal and our two babies in their incubators. "These precious babies need to be here for their parents' wedding." She parked Dayna beside Maggie and Dooley beside me. "Okay. Now we have a maid of honor and a best man." She grinned and backed up.

There, in front of everybody, Maggie and I said our vows. When Preacher Hickman pronounced us man and wife, a cheer resounded through the entire hallway. Even though we hadn't been expecting this, it seemed to work out perfectly.

We had our fairy tale ending . . . even though it had its own twist.

PART TEN:
THE GREAT
TIME CAPSULE CAPER

Louise & Peggy, Saturday evening

There was already a crowd of cars parked in the lot in front of the high school, but I didn't see either Ida's SUV or Amos's cruiser. Where on earth could they be?

"Peggy, go in there, find 'em and bring Amos out here," I said.

"I'm filthy and I smell. You go."

"No way."

"Well, we can't simply sit here in hopes that one or the other of them will stick a head out the door," she said. "We'll both go."

I groaned. Charlie wasn't supposed to attend, but I knew my daughter Margaret and her husband Bud would be here. She'd never let me forget showing up looking like a bag lady, especially if there was something in that box that compromised her.

Still, what choice did we have? "We could forget the whole thing," I said. "Let them think we didn't find the box."

"Louise, don't be ridiculous. We sweated bullets to get it to Amos, then he and Ida simply defected. We're going to open that box and be there when every one of those things is taken out, even if there's evidence that the captain of the football team shot Jimmy Hoffa."

"We don't have a key."

"You have a tire iron. Bring it along." She climbed out of the car.

And I thought Ida was dictatorial.

Together we humped the box back onto the two wheeler and rolled it up the ramp and down the hall to the gym. We must have looked a sight. At first everybody gawked, then somebody — I think it was John Mc-Clure — recognized the box.

Suddenly we were surrounded. Everybody was laughing and hooting and banging on the top of the thing yelling "open it, open it." I did notice a few worried faces, but that was Amos's fault, not mine. Peggy and I had done our duty.

"We found it, we get to open it," Peggy said. "You," she pointed at LuLynn, "Go get a roll of paper towels from the girls' rest-room so we can clean it off."

Lulynn gave a high-pitched little squeak, but she ran, high heels, fancy dress and all.

Mossy Creek Gazette

Volume VIII, No. Six · Mossy Creek, Georgia

Homecoming History —
CLASS OF 1940 ELECTS UNUSUAL QUEEN
by Katie Bell

Homecoming in Mossy Creek has always had its festive traditions, from harmless pranks to crowning a queen to playing a football game in front of an entire community.

But the celebration isn't always predictable.

Her name was Susie Belle, and for one weekend in 1939, she was the most popular girl at Mossy Creek High School.

Nominated for Homecoming Queen by the school's newly formed FFA, Susie Belle benefited from disqualified candidates and an overall strange election process to be named Mossy Creek's Queen that year.

The hitch? Susie Belle was a pig.

Yes, Mossy Creek's distinguished list

of royalty includes the only porker ever elected Homecoming queen — anywhere.

According to the school records, more than 130 votes were cast for Homecoming Queen that year despite an enrollment of only 93 students. Members of the election committee were unable to unravel the mess and were forced to declare Susie Belle the winner.

As queens usually are, Susie Belle the Sow was the centerpiece of Mossy Creek's Homecoming parade that year. However, her fun ended there. As the student newspaper *Voice of the Mountain* later reported, "Eventually Susie Belle was barred from attending the dance because of her large size. Instead of foxtrotting with the boys, Susie Belle spent that night in her pen."

According to the records, Susie Belle beat out human candidate Eleanor Hamilton Abercrombie, the only other candidate not disqualified.

When asked about her ignominious defeat, Eleanor quipped, "I'm planning for my epitaph to read, 'But for Susie Belle, here lies a queen.' "

That's Mossy Creek for you! Never a dull moment!

SISTER KNOWS BEST

Where we love is home — home that our feet may leave, but not our hearts.
— Oliver Wendell Holmes

Pearl Quinlan, Tuesday

Change scented the air as I headed back from Bigelow on Tuesday before Homecoming only to find my sister Spiva waiting next to the pumpkins and colorful potted mums outside my bookstore. She was holding two cups embossed with the Naked Bean logo. My pulse sped like the brisk breeze scuttling autumn leaves around the square — and not because I was thrilled at the prospect of coffee.

"Hey, Pearl," she said. "Where've you been?"

Sure, to the casual observer it was a normal conversation starter. But guilt slammed me to the leaf-strewn sidewalk like a champion wrestler.

"Nowhere. I mean, I was *somewhere.* Running errands." Careful not to look her in the eye, I focused on turning the key in the lock. Was my voice pitched higher? Did I sound defensive? Did she know I'd been looking at a condo? I'd begged Julie Honeycut, my real estate agent, to keep the hunt quiet. I wasn't sure when or how, but I would spill the beans — eventually.

Spiva and I shared the small three-bedroom, one-bath home where we grew up — and where her toiletries and bossiness encroached on my physical and mental space on a daily basis. The condo I looked at had a master bath, where I wouldn't share shelving with anyone. It even boasted a close-up mirror with an arm that retracted back to the wall when you didn't need it for tweezing and other purposes women of a certain age require.

Seemed like a no brainer, leaving a situation where Spiva did things like *accidentally* open my mail, but she'd been my buddy and champion when she wasn't aggravating me. If I moved, our relationship would change, and maybe not for the better. I didn't know if I could live without my sister. I never had.

The bells jangled as she followed me in, and I flipped the sign hanging from the glass door to "Open." I glanced at the community bulletin board full of fliers that had long since served their purpose and checked the clock on the wall behind the register. If I had time today, I needed to pull the cork.

"What brings you by?" I asked, trying to sound nonchalant.

"Do I have to have a reason to come by and visit?" Grinning, she set a large cup of coffee on the counter in front of me.

"Thanks. But aren't you usually working at this time of day?"

Spiva ran the children's clothing section of Hamilton's Department store. She liked to say that she could put up with the occasional ill-mannered child at her job because children like that rarely shopped at Hamilton's *and* because she didn't have any to deal with when she came home at night.

Waking my computer out of sleep mode, I eyed the offering in the cup dubiously, certain it was a caramel macchiato with extra whipped cream and wondering about the caloric content. This brew had to be yet another attempt at sabotage, like the pizza my unrepentant older sister ate in front of me the other night while I feasted on rabbit food. I wasn't falling for it, no matter how much that one hundred percent Columbian roast beckoned.

She pushed the cup closer to me. "Rob's got me on split shift today because one of the other department managers had a doctor's appointment."

I nudged the drink back towards her. "I shouldn't."

"For goodness sake," her mountain twang raised in irritation. "It's a non-fat, skinny hazelnut latte. No sugar, no fat."

Prepared for a mistake, I took the tiniest of sips as my email loaded. The slight aftertaste of artificial sweetener and lack of creamy smoothness attested to the truth of her words. I recalled the days of full fat latte coffee breaks with bear claws from Beechum's Bakery. Those days were long gone, as was Beechum's Bakery, which had recently been absorbed into the Naked Bean. "Why are you being nice?"

Spiva pouted. "Why do you think I want something if I'm being nice?"

"Because your past behavior would indicate I'm right." I took another sip and opened the tracking link for UPS. Argie's DVDs would be in tomorrow's delivery as well as the parenting books for Maggie and Tag. I was so happy for Maggie. I'd been there when Allen Singleton dumped her in front of everyone and proposed to Bonnie Hamilton at a high school pep rally. I'd watched her open Moonheart's and fall in love with Tag. Sure, having a baby at fifty was unconventional, but that was Maggie through and through.

Spiva walked over to the new paperback table. She picked up a mystery and checked the back cover copy. "Since I'm here and all, I was wondering if I could borrow some of your jewelry for the Halloween Party at O'Day's."

"Sure." The custom closet in the condo had special drawers for jewelry, built-in shoe racks and lighting way beyond the bare bulb in my over-crowded cubby hole at home.

"So anyhoo . . ." Spiva said. "I ran into someone at The Naked Bean."

Nothing good could have happened at a spot known for both terrific coffee and the latest gossip. "Oh, really." I tried to appear indifferent when all the while I prayed she didn't say Russ Green, my real estate agent's fiancé, who probably knew everything about where I'd been. "Who?"

"Mal Purla Rhett. She's in charge of the Mossy Creek High Booster Club now. You'd think she was busy enough, what with being the church treasurer and the president of the Welcome Club *and* assisting Swee at Purla Interiors."

"You'd think," I agreed. "But why does

347

this concern you?"

"She's running the Booster Club Snack Bar during the big Homecoming game against Harrington Academy, and she doesn't have enough volunteers."

My heart sank. "You didn't."

"It's an opportunity to serve our friends and neighbors." Spiva placed her hands on her ample hips. "You told me you could still be a cherub without being chubby."

"I'd rather not spend hours serving foods I can't eat."

Spiva rolled her eyes. "One little hotdog isn't going to kill you."

"But it's not just hotdogs. Hamburgers, fries, soft pretzels, candy bars are all huge temptations for me. I don't want a setback."

"If you can overcome the temptation, you're in it to win it," Spiva said.

Amazed, I blinked repeatedly. "And if I succumb?"

"I guess you'll have to walk a couple extra miles next week." She shrugged. "No biggee."

"It's wrong to volunteer me without asking," I pointed out. This was yet another reason moving out would be a good thing.

"Fine," Spiva said. "I told Mal yes because she was desperate. In the spirit of Homecoming, Rosie Montgomery's donating chocolate meringue pies which will double the normal traffic at the snack bar."

"No." Just what I needed — my all-time favorite pie from Mama's All You Can Eat Café added to the offerings I could salivate over but not ingest.

Spiva narrowed her gaze. "Are you admitting that you can't turn aside a little temptation?"

"Those pies are a *huge* temptation." They were Mama's claim to fame, next to the chicken-fried steak with sawmill gravy. My stomach growled.

"Surely, you're not going to let this little speed bump get in the way of your diet success, Pearl. Besides, all the money minus expenses goes to rebuild Mossy Creek stadium. If you want to back out, just call Mal. I'm sure she'll understand when you tell her you can't handle it."

If I backed out, I'd commit to something far worse. It was just like Spiva to put me into a no-win situation. "I didn't say I couldn't handle it."

"Sounds to me like you said you couldn't or wouldn't. Pick your verb."

"Oh, all right. But don't you dare volunteer me to do anything else."

"Or what?" Spiva asked, a gleam of mischief in her dark eyes. "You'll short-sheet me? You'll unfriend me on Facebook? Ooh, I'm scared."

"Leave. Now."

"I will. And next time —" She paused with the door open to the crisp fall air. "Why don't you eat something while you're running errands? You're the biggest grump this side of Colchik Mountain when your blood sugar's low."

With that pronouncement, she left. I pulled out Julie's Mossy Creek Mountain Real Estate business card that listed all the ways to reach her. Spiva was tilting the scale for sure. I punched the numbers for Julie's cell, but couldn't push send. There it was, my tendency to hesitate rearing its ugly head.

This condo would change my address from Mossy Creek to Bigelow, which might not seem like a problem to anyone raised outside Bigelow County. But I'd been a Creekite my whole life and as such had nurtured my prejudice against dreaded Bigelowans. I wasn't sure I could handle becoming one — even for a built-in hutch that could display my grandmother's china to perfection.

Making such a big life decision under a cloud of anger could lead to regret. I had to be one hundred percent sure this move was what I wanted.

"What, I'd like to know, is *this?*" Spiva stood before me, still in her pantsuit from work. A large hoop earring dangled from one ear. She'd tied a colorful scarf on her head like a 'do rag and held up a small object.

Not sure if the costume was pirate or gypsy, I squinted and still couldn't make out what was being held in front of me like the missing piece of evidence in a murder. *Progressive lenses, here I come.* "Come closer. No. There. Stop."

She did, all the while looking at me with disgust. Part of the character she was taking on, I assumed.

I glanced down at the offending piece of plastic my pet ferret Twinkie would probably like to play with and hide. "Looks like a guitar pick."

"May I point out that *you've* never played the guitar. And *this* isn't just any pick." Spiva paced like a special prosecutor cross-examining a defendant. She faced me and pointed an accusatory finger. "Why did you steal it?"

I examined the pick, noting the shades of gray and pearl, the initials "A.S." scratched into its surface, and recalled the thrill this little rounded-corner triangle brought me when I was in high school. Everybody, and I mean everybody, had been in love with Allen Singleton, lead singer of the Chinaberry Charmers. He was dating one of my best friends, Maggie Hart. After the pep rally where he announced to everyone that he loved Bonnie Hamilton and proposed, the Charmers played a concert at the Moose Lodge. The shockwaves following Maggie's public humiliation led her to interrupt his set and rip him a new one.

In the hullabaloo that ensued, I removed the pick from Allen's guitar neck and apparently hid it in my jewelry box. Over the years, I'd forgotten about both the guitar pick and where I'd put it.

"So are you going to return it?" Spiva asked.

"I'm sure Allen didn't miss it. It's a guitar pick, for goodness sake." I pocketed it and headed toward the kitchen to make my low-cal dinner.

Spiva followed me. "No sister of mine is a thief. You'd best return it."

"You're being ridiculous." I removed the boneless skinless chicken breasts from the refrigerator. "You want what I'm having?"

"Stop trying to change the subject. If you

don't return the guitar pick to its rightful owner with an apology, you will force me to turn you into Amos or Sandy. Quinlans aren't thieves, especially those of the short-nosed variety."

"Do you think they can also arrest you for rifling through my stuff without asking?"

"You gave me permission to borrow your jewelry."

"But I didn't say you could snoop, which you did." Something that couldn't happen if I moved out.

"You're missing the point."

"Really? Because I think you're missing *my* point." I lifted one piece of chicken out of the package, then seasoned it with a poultry spice blend. I gave my nonstick pan a quick squirt of canola oil spray and settled the meat on its hot surface. As I opened the refrigerator to gather salad fixings and the leftover whole wheat pasta from last night, I added, "I doubt anyone in Mossy Creek, including Allen, has even thought about that pick in years."

"And that —" She shook her finger at me. Her hoop earring swung. "Would be mistake number two. I have it on good authority that pick was invested with the Chinaberry Charmers' mojo."

I carefully measured a half cup of pasta.

"If you're so concerned, Spiva, give it back yourself."

She pulled the scarf off her ultra short coif and shook her head sadly. "Nope. No can do. I can't *always* fix everything for you."

I couldn't help but roll my eyes.

"There's no time like the present to set things right," she urged, then stuck her nose in the pasta and sniffed. "Do you have any sauce for this?"

"It doesn't need sauce. It has basil, tomato and olive oil."

Spiva shuddered. "The only way I'm gonna be able to swallow that cardboard is if you put some Alfredo on it."

Even though Spiva had committed to doing the same diet and exercise program after our tiff in mid-January and had repaired her slower than slow treadmill, she'd fallen off the low-fat wagon.

"You can always make your own food," I said, ready to blow my top, ready to call Julie. One more dig was all it would take.

I noticed her peering at my face. My chin, actually. "What?"

"I've been meaning to tell you. You've got a hair."

I felt around the skin and located the offending reminder of aging. "How long has it been there without you telling me?"

Spiva shrugged. "About a week."

What was the point of living with your sister if she wouldn't even tell you when you had a wiry chin hair? The condo had a bathroom with great lighting and a close-up mirror, making a sister obsolete.

"My bad," she said as she placed an entire cup of jarred Alfredo sauce in the microwave to make my cooking palatable.

I didn't need her and her aggravating ways. "Watch the chicken for me."

I went to my bedroom, locked the door and called Julie Honeycut, whose voicemail came on. "I'm ready. Let's make an offer."

I opened the door and practically bumped into Spiva. People think big brother is bad, try big sister.

"An offer on what?" she asked.

The chicken took on an acrid burnt odor. I ran into the kitchen.

"You never listen to me, except when you're eavesdropping!" I yanked the skillet off the eye.

"Who cares about the chicken? Call it blackened and throw some of my Alfredo sauce on it. Who were you talking to?"

"If you must know, Julie Honeycut."

"She's a real estate agent."

"Yup."

Spiva stood there, dumbfounded. "You're

moving out?"

"Yes. I'm sorry, but I need my space," I said as she blinked away what looked like tears.

"Right," she said. Her voice grew smaller and tighter. "And when were you planning on telling me?"

"I've been looking for the right time, but there never seems to be one. It's a condo in . . . Bigelow."

"Bigelow?" she said, pulling herself together. She lifted one pencil-drawn eyebrow. "No Quinlan, short- or long-nosed, has *ever* lived in Bigelow. You know what? I don't think you'll actually do it."

"Really? Just watch me."

I had run out of buttons to push.

"I *said* four bow-wows, dress 'em in red and yellow and add fries!" Spiva yelled as I hurried to follow her orders. Since my call to Julie, our interactions had been frosty at best.

"Mention the pie!" Mal, uptight as ever, yelled back from slicing the deliciously decadent chocolate meringues Rosie had delivered.

Spiva asked, then yelled back to me, like I was her lackey, "Four slices!"

The fry basket started beeping as I slid

the tray loaded with everything I wanted but couldn't eat to the family Spiva was serving.

"The drinks?" the man urged.

"Shoot!" I whispered under my breath, earning the evil eye from Mal, who'd given us a speech about what she demanded during our service at the snack bar. One thing she didn't want any of was cursing, not that shoot was an actual curse word, but I guess it was too close for comfort in her mind.

I put ice into four cups, then pressed the nozzle for cola. As the first cup slowly filled, I thought about my other dilemma. The condo owners had countered my offer. I had until midnight tonight to respond.

"Can you put some *grease* in it?" Spiva yelled back to me, as several other workers followed the orders of Queen Bee Mal and delivered candy bars, chips, hamburgers and fries to the waiting customers.

I would have liked to have said, *"No, I can't because I have one nozzle,"* but I'd stopped speaking to Spiva since her prediction I wouldn't move out. Unfortunately, my silent treatment didn't stop her from talking to me.

Mal, who was standing next to Rosie, looked over at me and sighed. "This is why we need to raise enough money for state-of-the-art equipment. If we only had a machine like the one you have in *Mama's,* we could have filled twenty drinks in the time it's taking Pearl to fill four measly cups."

Way to give a woman donating tons o' pie a guilt trip.

If I were Rosie, I would have called Mal on it, but Rosie only nodded.

I finished pouring the four drinks and handed them off to the man, his wife and two kids. "Sorry for the wait."

A massive cheer went up from the stands, most likely Mossy Creekites because Harrington Academy wasn't exactly a contender. The band played their first down song, and the crowd at the snack bar dispersed to watch the game.

"You should start filling the drink cups now that we have a break, so we don't get bogged down again," Spiva ordered me in the lull that followed.

I did it, not because she told me to, but because I didn't like the stress of everyone waiting on me. Besides the soft drink station was relatively safe. I wasn't tempted to snack on anything here.

Mal shook her head of beautifully highlighted and cut hair, then pulled her smart phone out of her giant designer suede organizer bag. "I'm off to check on the booster club raffle sales. I'll be back."

As she left the snack bar, her small hiney, covered in what most likely was two-hundred-dollar jeans, indicated to one and all that she rarely indulged in any high fat treats or, worse yet, she'd been gifted with a high metabolism. I hated people like her. I sighed loudly.

Rosie looked up from dumping more fries under the warming lights. "What's wrong?"

"Events like this are hard for people like me. Everywhere I look there's some other food item that would blow my whole week's worth of hard work."

Rosie cocked her head to the side. "So why tempt yourself?"

"Why, indeed?" I said and glared at my sister, who suddenly found something she needed to wipe off the counter in front of her.

Another roar erupted from the Mossy Creek side of the stadium.

Orville Gene Simple, decked out in his Mossy Creek green and gold flannel shirt and his signature John Deere gimmee cap stopped at the counter. "Ladies, our team is about to score, and I'd like two slices of pie in celebration."

Rosie quickly plated them. "Gotta date?"

Who, but for divine intervention, would

go out with a man who would've lost a battle of wits with a toad? Then again, maybe I shouldn't be so critical. Bigelow County wasn't exactly teeming with middle-aged single men interested in mature, literate, chubby women in their forties.

"Nah, they're both for me," he said. "That pie's so good you can't stop at one slice. You gotta have two."

Picturing two glistening slices of pie, I turned away and tried to focus on my task of filling cups with ice and soda before the next rush. I recalled how silky the chocolate filling had felt against my tongue, how sweetly the meringue had melted, the buttery flakiness of the crust.

Spiva's voice carried, louder than usual, "Yeah, I remember you, *Allen.* How's Bonnie?"

Guilt about the stupid guitar pick washed over me. Tonight was setting up to be sheer torture. *Please,* I prayed, *for once, be prudent, Spiva.*

Trying to be inconspicuous, I turned to see if Allen Singleton could still make my heart flutter with something besides guilt. I wasn't listening to what he was saying to my sister. Who cared about Bonnie? I'd never truly forgiven her for snaking on my friend's man — even if it happened a heck of a long time ago, and even if I'd had a secret crush on him myself.

I'm not going to lie. He looked good. A little gray, a little wrinkled, a little heavier, but still those warm brown eyes that caused me to swoon in high school made me a bit lightheaded now.

Spiva shouted back to me. "You hear that, Pearl?" She wiggled her penciled-in eyebrows. "He's divorced."

"Sorry to hear that," I mumbled, even though I wasn't anything close to sorry, terrible as that sounds. Was it the universe's way of paying him back for treating Maggie badly? If so, karma had taken its time. I faced my task once more as he ordered a hamburger, fries and drink combo. For one, I noted.

What if Spiva brought up the guitar pick? Maybe that'd be a good thing. He'd probably say, what are you talking about? And Spiva would see how silly she'd been — thinking I had committed some horrible crime.

"How about a slice of chocolate meringue pie with that?" Rosie asked.

Allen patted his sweater around what some people, not me, would call his belly. "Can't. The fries are bad enough."

Rosie walked over to the drink station and

grabbed a cup. "Don't you think that's enough?"

"What?" I glanced down at the rows of soft drinks covering the table's surface in front of me. "Yeah, sorry, I got distracted."

Mal came back from her raffle check and hugged Allen. "So sorry to hear about you and Bonnie. You know my sister Swee's still single if you're looking."

He laughed but didn't latch onto the hook she was dangling. Spiva had her trademark peeved expression on her face. She was about to blurt out something. *Please, Spiva, don't tell him I'm single, too.*

She didn't. She did something far worse. "You know, Allen, I always thought the Chinaberry Charmers would have made it big."

My heart sped like one of those high-speed trains they have in Europe.

"Not everyone does make it," he said. "I think our luck turned for the worse when my favorite guitar pick went missing."

My breath left me. I *had* stolen their mojo. I single-handedly destroyed the dreams of the Chinaberry Charmers. Not only was I a thief, I was wrong about the guitar pick being unimportant. And what was worse, Spiva was right. How she would lord it over me.

I looked at the delicious layers of meringue and rich chocolate filling trying to seduce me a table away. I'd drown my guilt in pie. No, I'd take a thin, thin sliver. I'd only have two bites, then I'd toss it. I put a buck fifty in the till and grabbed an extra large slice. As my former idol and my evil older sister chatted about high school and other things, I tuned out.

The first bite was sheer heaven. I moaned in ecstasy. I took another and another and another bite.

"On second thought," Allen said. "Maybe I will have a slice. Pearl seems to like it — a lot."

Mortified, I stood there with a mouthful of pie, unable to swallow.

Spiva got that look in her eye. I wanted to shout "no" but couldn't. "You know, Allen, Pearl will probably kill me for telling you this, but she mooned over you big time back when you were with the Charmers."

Actually I was beyond wanting to kill her. I wanted to take myself out. And I would. As soon as snack bar duty was over, I was calling Julie and countering the owner's counter offer.

Incapable of realizing that Allen wasn't the least bit interested in me, Spiva continued singing my praises. All the while, the poor man looked like the proverbial deer stuck in the headlights.

"Maybe you should come by after the game. You and Pearl could get re-acquainted."

And I could come clean about the stupid guitar pick. I felt like my eyes must be popping out of my head, as if I were in a cartoon, which probably made this chubby cherub oh-so-attractive to newly single Allen.

He glanced over at me, hemmed and hawed. "Well, maybe. I have —"

"Come on," Spiva encouraged. "How's having a coffee going to hurt? If you don't get along, no harm, no foul."

Allen took a sip of his soft drink. "Would you like to go to the Naked Bean after the game, Pearl?"

"You don't have to do this," I said as my sister pinched my forearm.

"Don't be silly, I want to. See you after the game."

With that, he walked off. He must know I stole the guitar pick, and he only agreed to go to confront me and lay all his disappointed dreams at my feet. But then why was he so reluctant? Because my pushy older sister forced him. He figured agreeing was the lesser of the evils.

I wanted the earth to swallow me whole.

Once he was out of earshot, I tapped Spiva on the shoulder.

She had the nerve to look surprised. "Is this going to be mime? 'Cause I wouldn't want you to spoil your not-talking-to-your-sister record."

"It's behavior like this that makes living with you intolerable. Once again, you are trying to orchestrate my life. You need to butt out."

Mal checked the time on her watch. "Leave it at the counter, ladies. It's half-time, and we're about to get slammed."

Rosie sent me a look of sympathy. Mal snapped her fingers at me as hungry teens crowded the counters.

I'd hoped Spiva would leave me be, but since when had Spiva ever let a scab form? She kept picking and picking.

I brought her three bags of potato chips and three cokes for the giggling girls she was serving.

Instead of thanks, she said, "You think you don't need me, but you do. Here's your big opportunity to come clean about you know what."

I walked back to my station to get drinks for Mal's customer's order.

Spiva passed me as she went to plate fries

and a hotdog. "I'm afraid if I wasn't around challenging you, you probably wouldn't have the bookstore *and* you would have failed at your diet and exercise plan."

"Excuse me?" I couldn't help but be dumbfounded. She might have encouraged me to open the bookstore, but she'd been the biggest diet saboteur I'd ever seen.

Spiva stuck her chin out. "Where would be the challenge in following your plan if our cabinets were full of healthy foods? Where would be the challenge in life if you didn't go for what you wanted — the bookstore, former crushes who are now single included, as well as fancy condos."

"You're attempting to justify your bad behavior."

"No, this is really how I feel. If a place of your own is what you want, Pearl, then I'm happy for you. Buy that condo in *Bigelow* with my blessing."

All the people standing in line at the counter grew quiet, their faces masks of shock and horror. Spiva paled as the repercussions of her big-mouthed blurting dawned on her.

Sorry," she whispered.

"How could you?" I asked but didn't receive an answer.

Rosie pressed her hand to her chest as if

I'd stabbed her in the heart. "You're moving to *Bigelow?*"

Before I could explain, Spiva jumped in. "She's made an offer, but I don't think that's what Pearl wants deep down. Who in their right mind would want to move from Mossy Creek to Bigelow?"

Her need to defend my actions only made my situation worse.

"Are you moving the bookstore, too?" Mal asked, blinking, then texting someone with the news. "Because Swee might want your spot on the square."

"I'm *not* moving Mossy Creek Books and Whatnots."

Who knew how this information would be distorted by morning. I'd probably be tarred, feathered and run out of town on a rail.

I, Pearl Quinlan, had been stood up. Not wanting to look at my wristwatch yet again, I wiped down the tables behind the counter. The game had ended twenty minutes ago with Mossy Creek triumphant. Allen Singleton had not come to the snack bar after the game as promised, and my prediction of this being one of the worst nights of my life had come true in more Technicolor glory than I could have imagined.

It's one thing to be stood up as a teenager or young adult. It's even more humiliating when you're past your prime and your sister strong-arms some guy into agreeing to take you for coffee after a high school football game.

I should have known. My first step down the path to spontaneity in January hadn't exactly reinforced the desire to do it again. Under the influence of high fat hors d'oeuvres and Asti Spumante at the annual New Year's Eve party, I stupidly blurted to the whole of Mossy Creek that I would lower my cholesterol by means of exercise and diet. I became a cause for the whole town of Mossy Creek, who wanted to see me succeed. My sister, in turn, upped the aggravation level close to unbearable. Not as unbearable as this, though.

"Pearl?" Spiva said, her voice timid and worried, nothing like her usual loud bossy tone.

I raised a hand. "I don't want to hear it. I'm heading over to the hospital to check on Maggie." Her water broke during half-time.

"But what if Allen comes by to get you?"

"He's not coming. So stop trying to make me think he will."

Spiva took a deep breath. "I'm sorry."

"For what?"

She shrugged. "Everything, I guess."

"Why don't you list it, so I know that *you know* what you've done wrong?"

Spiva screwed up her face like she'd taken a sip of something sour. I thought she was going to refuse.

"Okay," she said finally, then used her thumbs and fingers to count off her list. "I shouldn't be so bossy. I shouldn't twist attractive men's arms into asking you out. I shouldn't have gone snooping in your stuff."

"And?" I prompted. "You can't think that's all."

"I shouldn't have mentioned you were moving to Bigelow in front of everyone at halftime. I didn't mean to. It just came out. Even though I might have said I'm fine with you moving, I'm not. I had no idea everyone would grill you about your move."

I mentally listed all the people who gave me grief in the hour left of the game after Spiva's half-time disclosure. Ida, Ingrid, Jayne, Sandy, Katie Bell, Amos, Patty and Mac. The only friends who didn't call me out for being Mossy Creek's latest answer to Benedict Arnold were Maggie and Tag, who were understandably busy. On top of that, several contractors stopped by and offered to help us renovate the existing house.

And a complete stranger, who apparently flips houses for a living, handed me a flier for a duplex he was getting ready to put on the market.

"See you later." I grabbed my purse from under the counter.

"Do you forgive me?" she asked. "I don't know why I've become so obnoxious. I always saw myself as your protector, but now I've become a bully. I can't say that I like it."

"I don't like it either. Maybe space is what we need."

"Maybe," Spiva agreed. "I think I'm going to start wearing a rubber band on my wrist and snap myself every time I feel the urge to boss you. You know, you still haven't said you forgive me."

"I will in time. I usually do." I jangled my keys. "Don't wait up. I'm not sure how long I'll be."

I walked to the parking lot and slid behind the wheel of my sensible compact. As I drove toward the hospital, I could only imagine the conversations going on about me. Yes, Pearl Quinlan — the woman who once passed out Bibles to spectators watching authorities pull Billy Paul Stancil from a well — was going to the dark side.

At the hospital entrance, I turned left and

parked in the half full lot and wondered if Maggie was the kind of woman who hunkers down and gets her birthing done quickly. In the main lobby, I asked the lady at the information desk where I could locate labor and delivery. I followed her instructions and wound up in the fourth floor lounge.

Maggie's friend and theater owner Anna Lavender was already there flipping through a magazine. She looked up when she heard me walking down the waxed faux wood floor. The waiting area was done up in a warm and inviting mountain lodge theme, not my style, but nice.

Anna smiled and patted the cushion next to her on the couch. "Hey, how was the game?"

"Thirty-eight to seven, Mossy Creek." I sank into the high loft cushion. After the emotional upheaval, the rushing back and forth in the snack bar and a full day of work, I could fall asleep sitting right here. "How's Maggie doing?" I asked, closing my eyes.

"Pretty well. Tag's a little frazzled, but that's to be expected. So when were you going to tell everyone you're moving?"

My lids shot open. "You know, too?"

She lifted her cellular device. "We live in a modern age, Pearl. What's the deal?"

"The deal is that I've had enough of

Spiva. I found a beautiful condo. Unfortunately, it's in Bigelow. That's the only sticking point."

She sniffed.

"You think I'm making the wrong choice, too, don't you?"

"Have you thought about counseling?" Anna asked, as if I was divorcing my sister. I guess that's how it looked. Did Spiva feel that way, too?

I shook off the fleeting sympathy. "This visit isn't about me. I wanted to see if there was anything I could do for Maggie and Tag."

"They're good," Anna said. "I, on the other hand, would love some herbal tea, but I promised Tag I'd stay right here in case he needs me. He's afraid he's going to faint and Maggie will be without a coach."

"No problem."

I followed the signs until I reached the cafeteria deep in the bowels of the hospital. Quickly, I walked down the line, grabbed a cup, filled it with hot water, and selected an herbal tea. I paid the attendant and turned to find the man who stood me up sitting ten feet away.

Perhaps karma had taken the scenic route with me as well. The odds of running into a person I hadn't seen in over twenty years twice in one day led me to believe we had some unfinished business. But I was a chicken. I'd mail the stupid guitar pick to him and be done with it.

Two more steps and I'd be past eyeshot. Whew! My shoulders relaxed. It wasn't like he'd recognize me from behind.

"Pearl?" Allen called out, his melodious voice filled with confusion.

I faced him. "I'm not following you. I'm getting a friend some tea." I held up the Styrofoam cup and foil-covered tea bag.

"Is your friend okay?" he asked, which was pretty nice considering he probably still thought I was stalking him.

"She's fine. It's for Anna. Maggie's in labor."

"Oh, right. I heard." He shook his head. "I can't imagine having a baby at our age. Can you sit for a minute? I'd like to explain."

I debated, then took the empty plastic chair across from him.

"I would have shown up if I could have. My daughter Allison twisted her ankle at the game. My only thought was to carry her to the car and drive to the emergency room. Bonnie met us here."

"Did she break it?" I asked, hoping she didn't.

"Most likely it's a bad sprain. Bonnie was making me feel so guilty about letting it happen that I ducked out to get that cup of coffee that I never got. She's going to call me when the doctor comes back."

I summoned all my remaining courage. "So why weren't you so keen on Spiva's suggestion before your daughter hurt herself?"

He looked down at his cooling coffee. "I have, or should I say had, parent duty this weekend. That was my only hesitation."

How I wanted to believe him. Even though my outside wasn't as chubby, I still felt that men found me lacking because of my size. "Thanks." I lifted the cup of hot water that had cooled. "Looks like I need to replace this."

Allen followed me to the hot water urn.

"I'm sorry I didn't think to have someone tell you I wouldn't be able to make it after the game."

"Apology accepted." I turned to leave, but Allen blocked my path.

"Pearl, we grew up together. I dated one of your best friends. We both love chocolate meringue pie. You own a bookstore. I like to read. I'm curious about what else we have in common. Aren't you?"

The mother-of-pearl guitar pick came to

mind. My face heated like I was standing in the sweltering sun. I had to confess. I couldn't hide my mojo thievery from him any longer.

"I'm not so sure you'll still feel that way when I tell you something," I took a deep breath. *Just do it.* "I'm the person who stole your lucky guitar pick. I'm the reason the band never made it."

Allen laughed, and I wanted to slink away. But I didn't.

"I'm glad you find this so amusing."

"I'm not laughing at you," he said. "I'm laughing because the guitar pick became a convenient excuse for me over the years when people asked why the Charmers disbanded. The truth is we never made it because the times changed and the Charmers sound didn't change with it."

He touched my shoulder affectionately. "I don't want you thinking what you did jinxed the band. Promise me you won't."

"I won't." As much as I hated to admit it, Spiva was right. It felt good to get that guilt, short-lived as it was, off my chest.

"Good." Allen's phone beeped. "This is probably Bonnie." He glanced down at the screen. "Yup, I need to head back for the doctor's verdict. Listen, would you want to meet me for coffee at the Naked Bean later in the week? That coffee's a heckuva lot better than this stuff."

"Sure," I said, not quite believing what I was hearing.

"Is Thursday evening good?"

I quickly thought of what I had planned. Nothing. "Yes, that's fine."

"Great. See you then. I'm looking forward to finishing our conversation *and* to finding out what would make you want to move to Bigelow."

"How did you —"

"Nothing announced at a football game snack bar remains secret."

Happier than I thought possible considering the events of this evening, I brought the tea to Anna.

"Ooh, cinnamon vanilla. That looks good. Thanks."

"Can you call me in the morning to give me an update?" I asked, glancing up at the big contemporary clock.

Now that I had only an hour left to accept the counter offer, I wasn't certain the move was right for me. Instead of walking to work, I'd have to drive. I wouldn't run into friends like I did now when I strolled to the bank or post office. And would moving really change any of Spiva's domineering behaviors? Not unless I moved to Mars.

"Will do," Anna said.

"And tell Tag and Maggie the parenting books came in," I called out as I left. "I'll personally deliver them to the house once mama and babies are home."

Home. The word resonated with me. As nice as I imagined all my things would look in the condo and how Twinkie would love all the space, I couldn't picture myself there. The house where I'd grown up no longer gave me the happy home feeling either.

About fifteen minutes later, I pulled into the driveway. Spiva's light was on even though I'd told her not to wait up.

Decked out in her cherub flannel pajamas, she opened the door and ushered me inside and out of the chilly air. I took my usual spot on the couch.

"I've been doing a lot of thinking," Spiva said.

I checked the time on my watch. "Can this wait? I have to call Julie."

"What I have to say needs saying before you make that call. Just give me a couple minutes to plead my case."

"Okay."

Relieved, Spiva sat down at the other end of the couch. "What I said earlier at the snack bar, I meant. I am sorry. I don't want to drive you away."

"But I can't live like this anymore."

"I know. I think we should put the house up for sale and maybe get two houses next door to each other, or across the street from one another, or maybe even a block away. That way we can be close, but also have our space."

I remained noncommittal.

"I know you had your heart set on that fancy condo, and I'm not trying to bully you into doing what I want. Even though I do want you to agree." She gave me a slight, self-deprecating grin. "It'd be great. If we want to have dinner together we can, but we don't have to. If you still want to do movie night on non-football Fridays, we can. We can decorate our own places. I can go ultra modern without worrying about clashing with your traditional style."

I thought about the duplex flier in my purse.

"I won't be as tempted to meddle if we're not living under the same roof," she added. "You don't even have to give me a key to your new place. And you won't have to be tempted with my bad food, but if you want to borrow my treadmill at a moment's notice, you can. Plus, if we do this, you don't have to leave the town you love."

The truth was I didn't want to leave

Mossy Creek. And maybe I was crazy, but Spiva's announcement about my impending move may have proved to be a blessing. That stranger wouldn't have given me the flier if he hadn't heard about my potential move to Bigelow. When it came down to it, my friends' protests weren't necessary to convince me against the move. All I had to do was look deep in my heart to know where home for me would always be.

"You're awfully quiet, Pearl. Do you have any thoughts about my solution, which doesn't necessarily have to be the one you choose? I'm being too bossy again, huh?"

"Yes, you are. Nevertheless, your solution has possibilities."

Spiva's dark eyes lit. "It does?"

"I'm going to tweak it, though." I pulled the flier out of my purse. "What are your thoughts about a duplex?"

She ran a hand through her ultra short hair. "Well, that'd be less expensive than two properties, but I don't know. What do you think?"

I motioned for her to scoot closer. "I should have said luxury duplex. Look at all the amenities. Master suites on opposite sides of the building so we'd have privacy, garages. A cute courtyard. Porches."

"Ooh and fireplaces. And it says right

here, 'completely remodeled kitchens.' This is in Mossy Creek?" Spiva shook her head. "Doesn't that beat all. This place seems like it was built with us in mind."

Oddy enough, it did.

I took her plump hand in my own. "I don't want to cut you out of my life completely, Spiva, but I need to make my own decisions and mistakes. I need you to stop talking at me and listen. I need you to stop interfering. If you can promise to do those things while living next door to me, then yes, this place would be perfect for the both of us."

Spiva crossed her heart like when we were kids. "I promise."

I pictured Josie Rutherford helping us decorate the courtyard we'd never seen as I texted Julie.

Tell the owners "no" on the Bigelow condo. And let's make an appointment for you, me and Spiva to look at a duplex off Laurel Street.

WMOS
RADIO

"The Voice Of The Creek"

Just a reminder to all of y'all —

When all the Homecoming hullabaloo is over, y'all need to head on over to the Masonic Lodge's Annual Harvest Haunt. This year's Haunted House theme is *The Headless Ram,* in honor of Rammy the Ram — mascot of Mossy Creek High School. And yes, you'll see gory scenarios involving Rams, but I ain't saying any more on that subject. Some of your favorite grisly rooms are still there, but located in different spots, so you won't be expectin' them.

Joel Stanton is back from college again this year to head things up because he's just so fiendishly clever when it comes to spooky things and making y'all scream. I say "y'all" because I don't ever scream. Nosirree, not me.

(A snort is heard in the background)

Okay, okay, maybe a howl or two, but nothing girly like screaming.

But most of the Haunts this year are completely new, Joel says. He's been designing and engineering the Haunted House since he was in high school.

"He's just got such a knack," said Will Taylor, head honcho over at the Lodge. Will added that what they don't need to keep in the till for seed money on next year's Haunted House will be donated to the Stadium Fund this year, instead of to the Masonic Charity, which is usually the case.

So y'all go on out there and scream!

WILD GOOSE CHASE

We're fools whether we dance or not, so
we might as well dance.
                                    — Japanese Proverb

Amos Royden, Saturday
As yet another whispered phone message
offered a lead on the time capsule, I tried
not to draw parallels between the hunt for
the capsule and my ridiculous pursuit of
Ida. Both the capsule and Ida were proving
illusive. I had yet to get my hands on either.

Frustration, thy name is Amos. Truth be
told, I'd feel less frustrated if I knew Ida
was just as unsettled by the situation, but I
suspected she was delighted by the demands
of our lives. The interruptions to intimacy
gave her excuses to slow things down without having to actually ask me to go slower.

I suspect if she thought the relationship
was going to crash and burn, slowing down
would have been the last thing on her mind.

She'd have sped things up so she could put it behind her, efficiently dust her hands off and say, "Yeah, that didn't work. Told you. Moving on."

Ida liked tidy. I was anything but a tidy fit for her life.

Over the summer we'd progressed from a public kiss to a few bona fide dates interrupted by previously scheduled vacations, babysitting of Little Ida during Rob's second honeymoon, double shifts to cover Sandy during her pregnancy leave, a two-week mayor's conference and a three-week FBI course paid for by the town and for which I'd practically had to kill to make the short list of accepted participants. Cancelling hadn't been an option.

The minute I got back in town, the time capsule situation exploded. The first words I had hoped to hear from Ida weren't, "Oh good. You're back. We have a problem with Homecoming." But those were the words I heard.

Sometimes I wondered if my love life was some sort of cosmic joke. I live in a small town and had still managed to find myself in a long-distance relationship that struggled to find its rhythm every time one of us left and came home. If I'd wanted to communicate with my woman through email, I would have signed up for NetMates and filled out forty-seven screens of compatibility questions. If all I'd wanted was warm comfort on a cold night, I'd have registered at Matchups and filled in a short profile. I'm not sure if owning handcuffs is a plus or a minus in a profile, so it's just as well I didn't go the Matchups route.

Instead, I'm left sporadically pursuing an aggravatingly busy public figure now that the actual traveling is done. Unless I change the game. Yep. Time for a game change. I wasn't waiting for Capsule Frenzy and Homecoming Fever to die down. If the constant interruption and crisis of our lives made carving out time to be together difficult, then it was time to rely on some of the oldest wisdom I know: haunt the ones you love.

Tracking Ida down wasn't difficult. She was behind her desk in the Mayor's office, a spider in the middle of its web. Her dark hair was loose, shiny as a shampoo commercial and speared by a pencil perched on the top of her ear. She looked up and gave me a sudden, unguarded smile. I got those more frequently these days. Especially if it was just the two of us in a room. She waved me in and pointed to the phone. Then she made circles with her index finger, asking me to give her time to wind up the call.

I nodded. Fine with me. I shut the door, but couldn't lean against it. She had her dry cleaning hanging there. Or maybe not her cleaning, because there were black strappy heels — tall heels — in the bottom of the clear bag. Looked like the Mayor intended to change into a "little black dress" for what we hoped would be the unveiling of the time capsule tonight. I approved. I liked Ida in any little thing. That got me thinking and then thinking got me in trouble as soon as she hung up.

"What are you smiling about now?" she asked. "No! Don't answer. I don't want to know. I've got a lot of work. Just keeping people calm seems a full-time job today. I don't have time for whatever is behind that look on your face, too."

She looked serious, forgetting that I rarely take "No" for an answer to anything. Especially not now that I was home again and the calendar was clear of excuses to moving the relationship forward. I did my best to remove any hint of ulterior motive from my expression as I suggested, "Then maybe you'd have time to run out to the Harvest Haunt with me to retrieve the capsule."

Ida flew out of her chair. "You found it?"

"Not yet, but there is a reliable tip that someone dug it up a long time ago and reburied it in a root cellar under the barn the Boosters are using for the haunted house fundraiser. The folks who dug it up thought it was treasure and when they saw it was just, and I quote, 'Old junk,' they shoved the box in the root cellar of some barn out on the abandoned end of Pankie Road. That's where they'd gone to open their little treasure chest. We've got enough time to get out there and back if we hurry."

"There's only one barn out there."

"Yep. Makes perfect sense our teen thief would dump it there at the spot where his or her hopes for loot were dashed."

"That's where a lot of the teenagers go to make out. It makes more sense than some of the leads we've had."

"Yep. That's why I thought you'd like to go, too."

She snorted. "To make out?"

"Why? We can do that right here." I reached over and found the lock behind the cleaning bag. I flipped it to the horizontal position and waited for the reaction. She always had to find her balance with the relationship anytime we'd had a break. She trusted me. I just don't think she trusted herself. She recognized a kiss for the gateway drug it was and usually treated kisses with caution at first, warming up slowly. Fighting with herself over whether she was ready to "go there."

I expected skittish. I'd locked the door as a signal that I might be her Police Chief but I was far from tame. I wasn't prepared for the spark in her eyes and that had me reassessing my options. If Ida had skipped wary altogether and was anticipating our welcome home kiss, I wasn't going to waste that moment inside an office with paper thin walls and her assistant just outside the door.

Unlocking the door, I said, "But we really don't have time for what I'm thinking, so let's go maybe be the Heroes of Homecoming and find the capsule. Unless you want me to find it and go through it myself or find someone else to supervise me? There really should be two people making decisions about what's in that capsule."

"So, you're saying if I go, I get to be the boss of you?"

"You *are* the boss of me. You sign my paycheck."

The woman snorted, pulled a red jacket from the back of her chair and said, "Let's go. But leave Louise and Peggy on their hunt just in case we're wrong."

I let her walk out the door in front of me

before I grinned. I had no problem with Ida as an employer, but we really had yet to decide who was the boss in the relationship. That was going to be interesting.

On the way out to Pankie Road, Ida peppered me with questions. Had I checked with the Boosters to see if they'd taken anything out of the barn? Had they used anything they found in the exhibits? Did I have a key to get in?

Yes, I checked. No, they didn't use anything. Didn't need a key. They had a volunteer on site 24-7 because of the insurance policy.

She asked me about the FBI training course and then fell silent as she ran out of boss questions. She shifted nervously and then laid her head back against the head rest. "I'll just be glad when Homecoming is done."

"Tired?"

"I hope to shout."

"Running this town is a hard job. You've done it a long time, but you don't have to keep doing it. You can stop being Mayor, you know. It's not a life sentence. You could do something else."

"Really? What else would I do?"

"Focus on the vineyard."

I didn't turn my head to see her reaction. Memories of Jeb were mixed up in the vineyard plans, but that didn't trouble me. I squeezed her knee. "It's time you brought in a consultant if you're serious."

She straightened up. I didn't take my hand off her knee.

"Unless you know something I don't," she said very softly, and without the hint of a joke this time, "you are not the boss of me."

Before she could gingerly or not so gingerly remove my hand, I did it myself to shift the jeep. The turn for Pankie was just ahead. "I know that if you don't decide, the town's going to decide for you and use you up. You don't owe them every waking moment. They could get along fine without you if they had to."

She sucked in air so fast I had a brief flash of worry that she'd smack me while my attention was on making the turn. Instead she just loaded up a verbal double barrel. "Now that's a rotten thing to say. You make it sound like I meddle or poke my nose in when people don't need me. Worse, you make it sound like I'm too delicate to do my job and run a business. And to think I was glad you were home! Not anymore. No sir. Not if you're going to keep trying to run me out of office. Or insinuate that I'm a one-trick pony. First you set up Dwight and ambush him with Win Allen and now you're trying to move me out of my desk."

"Wait just a damn minute. We need to get one thing straight." I shot her my best pleading puppy dog eyes, "So . . . you *are* glad I'm home? You *did* miss me terribly?"

An odd strangled noise came out of Ida, and she cradled her head with her hands.

"Headache?"

She dropped her hands, drew herself up and looked at me. "No. The pain's actually much lower. In my gluteus maximus to be precise."

"I'm sorry to hear that." I pulled the jeep to a stop in the field that doubled as a makeshift parking lot for the Haunt. "Will it help if I rub it?"

"No, but you can kiss my —"

"Hello!" The shout from the waiting volunteer cut off whatever she was about to suggest.

We piled out of the car and walked toward Foxer Atlas and the sprawling barn. Both the man and the barn were well-weathered but sturdy. Foxer had once thrown me out of a softball game without blinking an eye. He took his umpire duties seriously. I take great pride in the fact that I did not follow him around town the next day looking for an excuse to give him a ticket.

He held out a hand to shake. "You're just in time. Lifesavers really! Dwight told me he'd send someone out before we opened tonight. But they're not here yet. Chicken-and-dumplings is on the menu at Mama's today, and they promised they'd put me some back. They always sell out. I need to get over there before they give away my portion." He moved as he talked. "I figure it's safe to leave if you're here for a bit. You all right? The other volunteer will probably be here in thirty."

"No problem," I said. "You go on. We're just going to —"

Ida leaned meaningfully into my hip to warn me off telling the truth of our visit.

"— to do a routine, random safety check," I finished. I pivoted as I said it to keep up with Foxer who'd blown past us and was on a missile trajectory for his car. Unnerved by his behavior, I scratched my head and told Ida, "I had no idea the dumplings were that good. I may have to do a taste test."

She dragged me back around and toward the barn. "Dumplings? I don't think so. I think this is probably more about the waitress who put the dumplings aside for him. Peggy told me an old pro was working the counter at Mama's. I'm guessing that old pro must be Foxer's age, single or widowed, and foxy in orthopedic, rubber-soled shoes."

"O-oh. I see."

"So does Foxer. Quite well. I doubt he's going to pass up a silver fox. There's a certain symmetry to that, don't you think?"

"What I think is that we're stuck here until his real reinforcements get here, and we need to get inside. My tip said the cellar was accessed from inside."

"Right. We've got business."

Unfinished business. I smiled and held the door. Poor Ida waltzed right into the empty, secluded building and never saw the danger coming. I closed my eyes for a few seconds before walking in behind her and shut the door.

"Hey! It's dark in here."

"Not a problem. I can see." I leaned over to drop a kiss on her neck.

"Stop that!"

"Why?"

"Because I want you to."

"No you don't." I proved it by turning her around and giving her the kiss I'd wanted to give her since locking the door in her office.

Ida stopped protesting.

The lip-lock would have been perfect

393

except for the moan. Normally I like a woman to moan. Unfortunately the moan wasn't coming from Ida. The scream came from Ida as a skeletal arm reached out and stroked her cheek and dragged fake cobwebs across it. She screamed, started batting at her head and then abruptly cut off the scream when she realized she'd been had by the haunted house and a mechanized skeleton. She closed her eyes. I assume she was counting to ten.

When she opened them, she said, "Seriously? You think that's funny?"

I did. I'm just not stupid enough or brave enough to actually say so. I couldn't do anything about the grin.

"Come on." She grabbed my arm and dragged me farther into the barn.

Each of the stalls held a tableau of horror which we could finally see now that our eyes had adjusted and got some help from the many stabs of light leaking through the joints and joins of the barn. The main attractions were two scenes with Rams dismembering various Mossy Creek opponents' mascots. It also featured Dracula, werewolves, an axe murderer and his unfortunate bride (she had a hatchet buried in her side and blood does not look good on a wedding dress), Frankenstein and the

394

mummy were all lined up neatly on both sides of the aisle. Sweeney Todd's innocent looking barber's chair had pride of place in the center of the barn. Cobwebs with dangling spiders and spooky witches looked ready to dive bomb the unsuspecting below. I'm pretty sure the caldron in the corner had eyeballs floating in some kind of liquid. Straw was scattered everywhere.

Ida surveyed it all, hands on her hips as she spun slowly around. "Where do we start?"

"The kiss was a good start." I dragged her back to me. "Let's start again."

"Let's not and say we did." But she half-smiled when she said it. Ida has an excellent poker face except when it comes to wanting me.

I was happy about that. I was happy about a lot lately. Which is probably why I agreed. "You're right." I settled her against me. Every curve. I tucked some hair behind her ear. "Let's not start again. Let's just say, 'I do,' and be done with all of this."

Tension, thy name is Ida.

I dropped a kiss on her mouth. "Two little words. No more thinking. No more strategy. You catch me. I catch you. Let's just do it." I kissed her in earnest then.

■ ■ ■ ■

Ida Hamilton Walker, Saturday

When Amos kisses me, I forget things. A lot of things. I forget how to think. I forget I'm older than he is. I forget that the Mayor has no business kissing her Chief of Police.

He broke the kiss and waited. I hated that about him. He was more comfortable in his skin than anyone I knew. More sure of what he wanted than most. Lord knows, I couldn't shake him or make him go away. He saw right through me and it scared the hell out of me. No secrets with this one. He wouldn't allow it. No holding back.

I knew that about him. I knew he was an all or nothing guy, I just didn't think he'd leap so quickly to "I do." I thought I had time. I thought wrong.

One look at his face erased all hope that we'd could ignore his question and get back to looking for the time capsule. So I answered him as honestly as I could. "We've only been on two real dates. You haven't seen all my crazy yet. You're going in blind."

"Too late to do anything about that now. I'm all in. So are you. Stop letting some idea of what your life was supposed to be without Jeb get in the way of us."

"I've dealt with my Jeb issues."

He let go of me. "I know. You just haven't dealt with *your* issues. It's time to redefine yourself, Ida. And it's not just me. It's your whole life. You didn't plan for me to be here in the middle of your is-this-all-there-is crisis. But I am. As much as it pains me to admit it, I didn't start this particular fire. I'm just the fuel for your flames." He stopped himself, looked away and then looked back. "Mayor Ida, there is a motion on the table. I'd like to hear your thoughts."

"No, you wouldn't," I snapped. "You'd like me to say yes to a question that really hasn't been asked."

If I could have called those testy words back, I would have. I didn't even know I was mad until the words came out. They revealed far too much I didn't want him to know. I'd just made it sound like I wanted skywriting or a proposal on the electronic score board at Yankee Stadium. Or a diamond ring in a glass of champagne. Somehow I wanted the kind of romance that was tied up in big goofy gestures. I thought I was better than that. But I wasn't.

Amos had tossed a proposal out there like an afterthought. I didn't like it. And now he knew I didn't like it. That was my mistake. Amos looked like I'd hit him in the head with a two-by-four. If he'd had a caption, it would say, *Amos gets a clue.*

He said, "I'm an idiot."

No argument from me.

He batted one of the spiders hanging from the ceiling in a frustrated gesture. "Wrong time. Wrong place. Except it's the right time and the right place because it's now and it's here. Come on." He dragged me over to small raised platform with Sweeney Todd's barber chair. "Sit." He scrounged a stool and sat down in front of me, elbows on his knees, hands clasped loosely as he studied me.

"I'm an idiot," he repeated.

"You said that."

"It bears repeating. Just listen. Ida, I am never going to be that guy. The one that says the right things at the right time. You need to be okay with that. I'm building a fence."

I'm sure I blinked. I wasn't sure what else to do other than call him an idiot. Instead I said, "Excuse me?"

"Rabbits ate every bit of your cabbage this year."

And then the penny dropped. The ridiculous wonderful idiot in front of me just told me he loved me enough to build a fence to save my next year's cabbage. He hated cabbage. Wouldn't touch coleslaw. But cabbage was important to me. So he'd protect my cabbage. He'd protect me. Instead of telling me he loved me, he'd just love me. Building a fence was an excellent big goofy gesture. One I could understand and hug tight to myself.

I smiled. "You are *not* an idiot."

"I am *not* an idiot." He stood up, and asked the right question as he pulled me up, "Ida Hamilton Walker, will you marry me?"

Things would have gone a whole lot smoother if I'd known I was pushing on a lever instead of the arm of the chair. I heard a thunk and the ground disappeared beneath us as a trap door dropped away.

Amos grabbed for me, and missed. I shut my eyes and prepared for the worst. I screamed again. Amos swore. We probably didn't drop more than eight feet. It felt like twice that.

When we hit bottom, I hoped mud was making the sound I heard. I didn't want to think about what else would sound more "splat" than "thud." Amos tried to steady us, but he fell a little faster than me and just about the time he got his feet under him, I kneed him in the groin. That rocked him back. He took me with him, and we both tumbled into something that smelled like dead things that got up and walked around in the night.

Squish was added to the symphony of sounds I really didn't want to think about. I refused to open my eyes. That was Amos's job. If he wanted to marry me, he could darn well kill the bugs and survey nasty trap door surprises. "Where are we?"

He shifted, lifting off me and pressing me a little deeper into the muck on his way up. "I'd say we found the root cellar. They rigged the door and moved the ladder to make the Sweeny set up look more real. I bet it scares the crap out of most people when that trap door gives way."

"Is that why it smells down here?"

I'm not sure which one of us lost it first, but it took a while to stop laughing. By then I'd opened my eyes. The root cellar was spectacularly empty. Just us. Some really nasty mud and a box in the corner. "Do you see what I see?"

"I'm on it." Amos had to bend over to get that far in the corner. The floor above apparently sloped. He dragged the box over to right under the trap door. "You want to do the honors?"

"No. You do it. The quicker the better."

The box was more a foot locker than time

capsule. Empty except for an old trumpet, one shoe and a pillbox hat. Not our capsule.

Amos flipped the lid shut a little harder than he had to. "Let's hope Louise and Peggy have better luck."

I motioned to the stink-mud plastered to him and the mud pie I'd become. "How could their luck be any worse?"

"Good point. Let's get out of here." He stood on the box, grabbed the edge of the opening and hauled himself out of the root cellar in one easy motion. Three seconds later he was hanging through the opening. Arm extended. "Your turn. Let's go."

When I hesitated, he added, "You are not fat. I can lift you and I promise not to make groaning noises while I do it."

"Yes."

He didn't say anything for a long time. "You sure?"

I stepped up on the box. "Yes. You had me at the fence, but not groaning cinched the deal."

Ida looked like three kinds of hell. Some of the mud was drying on her cheek where she must have swiped her hand. Her hair had miraculously escaped the mud for the most part but it was . . . interesting. The part was screwed up, but I didn't blame her for not running a hand through it. She'd managed to stick her hands in the mud to brace for impact.

There ought to be a law. You can't marry a woman unless you can slather her in sticky mud and still want to kiss her.

"Well, come on, woman. I have some plans for you. The first of which . . ." I paused long enough to snatch her out of the cellar and deposit her on the edge of the opening. ". . . is getting you out of those clothes."

The look on her face was priceless. At least for a few seconds until she realized I meant for hygenic and not nefarious reasons. She rolled her eyes. "Let's head back. We're already going to be late for the dance because we have to change. Capsule or no capsule, we still have to go."

I rolled up and stood. "You are not getting in my jeep like that. It's city property. If I ruin it, it's coming out of my paycheck."

"Put the upholstery cleaning bill on your expense report. I'll approve it."

My cell phone rang. When I got off, I looked at Ida. She wasn't going to like this. "That was Peggy. They found it. They're closer than we are. If we don't hurry, they'll open that thing without us there. That can't happen."

"I'm open for suggestions, but we can't go like this."

"You really aren't going to like my solution." I took her by the shoulders and turned her around to face the axe murdering groom in a tux and the unfortunate bride.

"No."

"Where's your sense of adventure? It'll be fine. It'll be good practice."

"I'm not wearing white at our wedding."

"That isn't white. It's red and white."

"I'm not wearing a hatchet at our wedding."

"Maybe the hatchet will come off."

"I hate you."

"I'm building you a fence."

We washed up in the caldron of eyeballs. Turns out they were floating in water. Ida made me turn my back. Technically, I still hadn't gotten my hands on Ida. But now, it was only a matter of time.

PART ELEVEN:
THE GREAT
TIME CAPSULE CAPER

Louise & Peggy, Saturday evening

Peggy wrenched the time capsule open in one twist. I made a mental note to call her the next time I needed a tire changed. As she raised the lid, the air filled with dust particles from the outside. I'd been expecting nothing but dry rot, but the contents looked pristine.

"They said it would be air and water tight," John said.

We peered inside. "Okay, here goes," Peggy said.

The first two or three items seemed innocuous enough — a Mod headband and a pair of leg warmers in iridescent stripes. I doubted they had come from Janey's stash.

Mac Campbell at the back of the crowd laughed. "Y'all remember when coach made us all take ballet so we'd stop falling over our feet running down field?"

"Yeah," John said. "But I don't remember

those crazy things."

"Silly," LuLynn slapped her husband's arm. "They're Bitzie's. The headband's mine, though. I can't believe we wore those awful things."

Behind us, the doors swung open. Everyone turned to see Amos and Ida rushing down the hall. Amos was dressed in an ill-fitting tux about fifty years out-of date, and Ida wore a wedding gown with what looked like a blood-soaked gash in the side. They were covered in dust and cobwebs and didn't look much better than Peggy and me.

"Where the Sam Hill have you been?" I snapped.

"And what in the Sam Hill are you wearing?" Peggy asked.

"Hey!" Foxer yelled from a side table. "You were supposed to look after the Haunted House, not steal from it."

Amos sent a snarl around the room. "Don't ask." Then he reached for the box. "I'll take that."

"Oh no, you don't," Peggy said. "First off, you'll drop it and break your foot. Second, it's a darned sight too late for damage control."

"Yeah, Amos. Might as well get it over with," Mac said. "How bad can it be?"

"You're pushing your luck," Ida said. "But

on your heads be it."

Peggy lifted out the first thing, a beat-up leather wallet. The three aged condoms inside had left circles in the cracked leather. She opened it and pulled out the student ID card. Three small photographs fell out along with the card.

"Hey, give me that." John McClure made a grab for it, but LuLynn was faster. "Oh, shoot," he whispered and edged away from her.

"John McClure, you're carrying pictures of half the Homecoming court," LuLynn snapped. "And three condoms? Huh."

He hung his head. "Shoot, that dudn't mean anything."

"If I'd seen these at the time, you wouldn't have been able to walk, much less play football."

"Nothin' ever happened, hon. You know you're the only woman I've ever loved."

"Humph." LuLynn stalked off, holding the wallet at arm's length as though it were a dead rat. John slunk after her, but turned back when Peggy held up a plastic sandwich bag with a lump of pink rubber inside.

"What's that?" Amos asked.

"That, Amos dear, is a falsie," Ida said. "One might call it 'boob in a bag.'"

Peggy said. "It's labeled." She looked up

at LuLynn, who had stopped halfway down the hall. Even at that distance I could see the blush start on the back of her neck.

"LuLynn," snarled Eugenia Townsend, that year's runner up for Homecoming Queen. She pointed at LuLynn's bosoms. "You swore those were both yours. If you hadn't cheated, I would have been Queen!"

"They were both mine. Bought and paid for," LuLynn said. "I didn't win because of those. I won because people liked me better."

"Ladies, ladies," Amos said. "That was a long time ago, and nobody was Homecoming Queen, remember? The fire?"

Peggy reached across Amos, pulled out a photo and burst out laughing. Amos snatched at it. "Give me that!"

She danced away from him. "No way. I knew you were a hellion back then, Amos, but I now know more about your rear end than I ever expected to." She held up the photo or a naked male rear end with its pants down. The crowd hooted.

"You don't know that's me," Amos said. His ears were scarlet.

I peered over Peggy's shoulder. "Who else is going to moon the world out the window of your daddy's squad car? Amos, he'd have killed you if he'd ever seen this."

"He's not the only one. Peggy, hand it over," Amos demanded. "No way. This is my get-out-of-jail card for speeding tickets the rest of my life." She pointedly tucked the photo down the front of her shirt.

Amos rolled his eyes and sighed as I pulled out the final photo — this one a professionally enlarged black and white. It was grainy and had obviously been taken at night, but both cars and drivers were recognizable. So were some of the spectators as well as the girl holding the starting flag. "My word, Amos, isn't that Loralee Atwater holding the starting flag?"

"I guess," he said.

"Drag racing?" I said. "Amos, you are absolutely death on drag racers, and here you are revving up your old Trans Am."

"That's why I come down so hard on drag racers. One time we nearly killed ourselves and a bunch of innocent bystanders. Give me that." I handed it over. "I'll hang onto this. Good teaching device the next time I bust one of your grandsons, Louise."

"Huh, Loralee's two thugs are more into drag racing than my grandsons."

"Who's that in the other car? I can't tell," Peggy said.

"I'm sorry to say it's me," Mac Campbell said sheepishly. "Not too good for my image as a upstanding family lawyer."

"We were kids, Mac," Amos said. "And damned good drivers if I do say so myself." He glared at the crowd. "That's not to say I won't bust y'all for doing the same thing."

"What's this?" Peggy asked. "Looks like some kind of report or theme. Whatever it was, it got an 'A-plus.' "

"There's an article from a newspaper clipped to it," Amos said. "With a note that says 'plagiarized' on it." He looked up.

"Ha! Miss Know-it-all!" Tammy Jo Bigelow turned on Francine Quinlan. "Can't even write your own essays."

Francine rounded on her. "That's not true. I was just quoting."

"Extensively and without attribution," Peggy said. As a college professor, she hated plagiarized work.

"That's the only time I ever did it, I swear," Francine said. She was on the verge of tears.

"Riiiiigght," Tammy Jo whispered.

Janey went to a great deal of trouble over her secrets, and I'd say they had the desired effect. We remembered her, all right. The Homecoming dance would be a tad less cheerful because of her. Once we started unearthing them, it was simple to see her little packets stuffed down the side of the box. In the low lights at the first dance, nobody would have noticed anything amiss before they closed the box.

There seemed to be only a couple of items left. One was a small steel flask.

Amos unscrewed the top, took a whiff, then wet his finger and tasted the contents.

"Bourbon?" I asked.

He shook his head. "North Georgia moonshine would be my guess. Tastes like a good grade of Kerosene."

"After all these years?"

"It's a good flask. See, he's etched his name on it. Walter Hickman."

Everyone looked at the minister of the Mossy Creek Mt. Gilead Methodist Church.

He scowled. "I was named after my Daddy, you know."

"I can't believe it," I said. "You preach about the evils of alcohol at least once a month."

"And for our final exhibit, ladies and gentlemen," Peggy said. She held up a baggie filled with desiccated bits of greenery. Inside were a couple of yellowed and brittle hand-rolled cigarettes and a grainy photo of a young man smoking. A very good-looking young man.

Beau Belmont. Mossy Creek's own hellraiser-turned-Hollywood.

Everyone looked over at Beau, who merely shrugged.

"Why am I not surprised?" Ida said.

"So what do we do with all this stuff?" Peggy asked.

"Burn it," John McClure said. He had his arm around LuLynn, but I saw she still carried his wallet and stood stiff as a board. I suspected John might sleep on the sofa tonight.

Peggy nodded. "All except for the photo of Amos's tusch I intend to keep in my safety deposit box."

"Now, Peggy," Amos said.

She grinned and lifted her eyebrows. "I could be persuaded to make a print for our esteemed Mayoress."

"You wouldn't!"

"I'll leave it to you in my will."

"Why bother burning it?" I asked. "We all know the worst. Everybody can keep or toss the stuff that pertains to them. How about that?"

"Hey, we still haven't looked at the stuff we put in," Pruitt Cecil said.

"Except for the legwarmers and headband," Francine said. Now that the secrets were out in the open, the rest of the box could have been anti-climactic, but instead,

411

it was a great success. I don't remember last week. I certainly can't remember what went on the year I graduated from high school. From the howls of laughter as each item in the box was pulled out, I don't think anyone else could either.

Here's what they buried the night of the fire:

- A small reproduction of the space shuttle Columbia, which made its maiden voyage that year.
- A coffee mug with a wedding photo of Diana and Charles on the side.
- A folded and creased poster from *Raiders of the Lost Ark*. In pristine condition, it was probably worth some real money.
- A flier from the Simon and Garfunkel free concert in Central Park, also valuable to a collector.
- A small packet of Post-It Notes. How did we live without them?
- An adoption certificate for a Cabbage Patch doll.
- A photo of the back of somebody playing PacMan, out that year.
- A .45 record of *Sailing* by Christopher Cross. I'd never heard of it, but somebody said it was the top-selling record

that year.

- The first album by Anthrax, and an album of *Slow Rollers* by the Rolling Stones. They looked like children.
- A Rubik's cube. I never could finish one of the things, but I remember them.
- A bootleg copy of the first MTV production called *Video killed the Radio Star.*
- A five dollar pre-paid telephone card — no cell phones in those days.
- A pink My Little Pony. My daughter Margaret had a stable full.
- A folded-up poster for *Cannonball Run,* also probably of some value.
- Somebody's old white Pixie boots, the knee-high pull-up ones that all the cheerleaders wore. And a pair of 'jellies,' the inexpensive plastic sandal the girls wore that summer.
- Lulynn's neon orange headband.
- An extra large (and extra ugly) man's Hawaiian shirt straight out of Magnum P.I.
- One pair of men's polka dot bikini jockey shorts. No one would admit to owning them.
- A pair of huge Rambo style sunglasses
- Finally, a bottle of black Goth nail pol-

ish. I'm sure whoever added that felt it was a passing fad.

Except for the items of clothing, there wasn't much actually about Mossy Creek itself. I suppose the teenagers thought there wasn't much of interest inside their own city limits.

But then, we'd already removed the really interesting Mossy Creek items.

Peggy and I watched until the last item was laid on the nametag table, and then backed away.

"Tonto, our work here is done," I whispered.

"Hi-yo Silver," she whispered back.

I took her arm. "Hey, that's my line."

Once we were back in the car, Peggy leaned back and closed her eyes. "Louise, I cannot believe we worked that hard for those little bitty secrets."

"That's what passes for scandal in Mossy Creek."

"No way. Those were high school secrets. The real scandal is buried a whole lot deeper than that box ever was."

Mossy Creek Gazette
106 Main Street • Mossy Creek, GA 30000

From the desk of Katie Bell

Lady Victoria Salter Stanhope
The Clifts
Seaward Road
St. Ives, Cornwall, TR3 7PJ
United Kingdom

Hey, Vick!
Well! What a Homecoming this
has been. I tell ya--it don't
get any better than this, en-
tertainmentwise. The whole
town turned out for the Homecoming Dance, just to see what
kind of trouble folks were in
who attended the Mossy Creek
High School just before it
burned.

Everyone was talking about it,
too. Nobody knew if it had
been found, or who found it,
or what was in it. But they
all *wanted* to know! About an

hour into the festivities, Louise Sawyer and Peggy Caldwell wheeled the sucker into the room. What a buzz! I put the list of incriminating evidence in the next issue of the *Gazette,* so I'll let you stew awhile yourself so you can see what we went through all week. It'll all be in my next *Bellringer* column, though. The whole town got a real hoot out of the entire evening!

Oh, I almost forgot to tell you the most interesting part of the evening. Amos and Ida-- yep, the Police Chief and the Mayor--came prancing in just after the time capsule arrived. And they weren't in their own clothes! They were in the tux and wedding dress off of murdered dummies in the Masonic Haunted House. Ida had "blood" all over her. It was downright ghastly. What's even more interesting is that I received several reports of various Creekites trying to get ahold of both of them all Saturday afternoon, but neither one was answering their cell phones. Don't that just grab your fancy and run away with it? They weren't saying nothing about what went on, neither, but I'll get to the bottom of it or I ain't a professional snoop!

I'll keep you posted! Never you fear!

Until next time--
    Your friend and confidante,
                    Katie

■ ■ ■ ■

RECIPES FROM BUBBA RICE

■ ■ ■ ■

ASIAN SLOPPY JOES

Here's an Eastern version of an old American tailgating favorite. Simple, quick and just as sloppy as the American version.

Ingredients:

1/2 cup hoisin sauce
1/3 cup soy sauce
1/3 cup honey
2 tbsp rice vinegar
2 tsp minced ginger
4 cloves garlic, minced
1 shallot, diced
1 pound ground chuck

Preparation:

In a large skillet, brown the ground chuck, then drain and set aside. In a medium saucepan, combine the remaining ingredients and bring to a boil, then reduce heat and simmer covered for 10 minutes or until the minced shallots are translucent. Combine all the ingredients in the skillet over medium heat until boiling, and then reduce the heat to a slow simmer for 20 minutes.

Preparation time: 10 minutes
Cooking time: 30 minutes
Serve on sesame seed buns.
Makes 6 sandwiches.

HAWAIIAN SLIDERS

This one should be done at home before leaving for the game. You can warm them up on the grill before serving.

Ingredients:
1 dozen Hawaiian rolls
1 dozen slices of ham
1 dozen slices Swiss cheese

Sauce ingredients:

1 stick of butter
2 tbsp brown sugar
2 tbsp yellow mustard
1/2 cup sweet yellow onion (Vidalia, if they're in season), finely diced
1 tbsp poppy seeds

Sauce:
Combine all sauce ingredients in a saucepan and bring to a rolling boil, then lower heat and simmer covered for 5 minutes.

Sliders:
Assemble sandwiches, 1 slice of ham and 1 slice of Swiss cheese per sandwich. Place the sandwiches in a 9 × 13 baking dish and pour the sauce over the sandwiches. Bake at 350 degrees for 15 minutes or until the cheese melts.

GAME DAY APPLE CIDER

A great drink for the cooler weather of football season.

Ingredients:

2 tbsp butter
2 tbsp brown sugar
2 cinnamon sticks
2 × 2 inch strips of orange peel
6 cups of apple cider
1 cup brandy

Instructions:

Melt the butter in a large sauce pan over low/medium heat. Add the sugar, cinnamon sticks and orange peel and cook for 1 minute. Add the apple cider and bring to a boil, then reduce heat to a low simmer for 15 minutes. Remove from heat and add the brandy. Remove the cinnamon sticks and orange peel and pour the cider into your favorite Thermos and head to the game.

GRILLED POTATO SKINS

Requires a little prep work at home prior to the game.

Ingredients:

4 large red potatoes (or russet if you prefer)
6 strips of thick sliced bacon, diced

1 cup Vidalia onion, diced
1/2 cup banana pepper, chopped
1 tsp ancho chili powder
1 cup shredded gruyere cheese

At home:

Bake potatoes at 400° for 45 minutes. Remove from oven and let rest until warm to the touch. Slice lengthwise and scoop out the center of each half. In a large cast iron skillet, render the bacon until crisp, remove and drain on paper towel, retaining a little of the bacon grease in the skillet. In 2 Tbsp of the bacon grease, sauté the onion and banana pepper until translucent. Stir in the ancho chili powder.

At the game:

Place potatoes on the grill, skin side up, for 10 minutes, then turn. Spoon in some of the bacon/onion/pepper/ancho chili mixture into each and cook another 10 minutes. Remove from grill and top with shredded gruyere cheese.

Mrs. Henderson's
Red Hot Apple Rings

Ingredients:

8 firm, tart apples - peeled, cored, sliced
2 cups granulated sugar
1 cup water
1/2 cup red hot cinnamon candies
2 Tbls. lemon juice
1 Tbls. whole cloves

Instructions:

Slice apples into 1/2″ rings.

In a Dutch oven, put the water, sugar, lemon juice & red cinnamon candies.

Bring the mixture to a boil and then reduce heat to medium, stirring occasionally.

When the cinnamon candies have dissolved, add apple rings.

Simmer for 15 minutes on low heat until the apples are tender, stirring occasionally and spooning candy mixture over apples.

When the apples are tender, turn off heat and allow apples to cool in the syrup.

They will continue to darken in color as they sit in the syrup.

Serve either chilled or at room temperature.

Can be canned using your favorite canning recipe.

ROSE'S CHOCOLATE MERINGUE PIE

Chocolate Filling:

2 cups half-n-half

1 cup granulated sugar

1/4 cup cornstarch

1/8 teaspoon salt

1-1/2 tablespoons Hershey's Unsweetened Cocoa

3 egg yolks (beaten) [save the whites for meringue]

2 teaspoons vanilla

2 tablespoons butter

1 deep dish pie crust, baked according to directions

Instructions:

Heat 1-1/2 cups of the half-n-half, but don't let it boil. While heating half-n-half to a near simmer, mix together dry ingredients: cocoa, cornstarch and salt in a separate bowl. Separate yolks from whites. Set aside whites in large metal or glass bowl to get to room temperature for making the meringue later.

Whisk the remaining 1/2 cup of half-n-half with the egg yolks. Whisk the mixed dry ingredients into the egg yolk and half-n-half mixture until smooth. Remove half-n-half from heat and gradually whisk into chocolate/yolk mixture. Once everything is incorporated, place back on heat on medium-high and continue to whisk (so as not to burn the bottom) until the mixture boils. Remove from heat, add butter and vanilla and whisk. Cover with plastic wrap while cooling and make meringue.

Meringue:
3 egg whites
1/2 teaspoon cream of tartar
4 tablespoons powdered sugar
1/2 teaspoon vanilla

Beat egg whites until frothy. Add cream of tartar and continue beating until soft peaks form. Beat in powdered sugar until stiff peaks form. Add vanilla.

Pour chocolate mixture into cool pie crust. Spread meringue over chocolate filling, covering crust edge. Use spoon to create peaks. Bake at 325° in preheated oven for 10–15 minutes, until peaks are browned. Cool for one hour, then refrigerate until serving.

THE MOSSY CREEK
STORYTELLING CLUB

(in order of appearance)

Peggy & Louise. . . . . Carolyn McSparren
The Great Time Capsule Caper

Clementine & Hayday . . . Darcy Crowder
'Shine On, Harvest Moon

Argie . . . . Berta Platas
Pas de Gridiron

Fred . . . . Nancy Knight
New Guy in Town

Jayne . . . . Martha Crockett
Everybody Knows

Inez & Lucy Belle . . . . . Susan Goggins
Bake Sale Blitz

Hermia . . . . Brenna Crowder
Mossy Creek by Any Other Name . . .

The employees of Thorndike Press hope you have enjoyed this Large Print book. All our Thorndike, Wheeler, and Kennebec Large Print titles are designed for easy reading, and all our books are made to last. Other Thorndike Press Large Print books are available at your library, through selected bookstores, or directly from us.

For information about titles, please call:
(800) 223-1244

or visit our Web site at:
http://gale.cengage.com/thorndike

To share your comments, please write:
Publisher
Thorndike Press
10 Water St., Suite 310
Waterville, ME 04901